CONFLICTED
Lies

Warning

This book contains sexually explicit scenes and adult language and may be considered offensive to some readers. This book is intended for adults ONLY. Please store your books wisely, where they cannot be accessed by under-aged readers.

Blurb

Detective Braxton Hero should keep his distance from me. Even though I can't seem to stay away from him.

Letting him get too close is a mistake. One I can't stop making.

He sees me. The woman I pretend to be, and the one behind the mask. And for the first time, I don't know which version is real.

Even though I've spent my life in the shadows, I've never been conflicted about who I am...until he blurred the lines. The thought of him seeing my darkness does something to me.

He makes me want things. Things I can't have.

A life that isn't mine to take.

A love built on lies.

*I heard you like your books dirty. Well, I like my women
wet. So let's get dirty and wet together.
Sincerely, your book husband.*

CHAPTER 1
Hope

I know it's wrong. I shouldn't be here. But I got sucked into it anyway. Charlotte runs off, laughing with a concoction of too much alcohol and adrenaline pumping through her veins. I try to catch up to her, but I'm tired, and there's also way too much alcohol in my system.

I want to sleep.

"Hope, you better run, girl," she yells from too far ahead of me.

I wave her off and decide *fuck it I don't care.* It's not that I'm unfit, but I don't care for running even if we're being chased. Charlotte looks back once but doesn't stop as she runs through Central Park in the dark. I huff, defeated as I drop to the wet grass and lie back, soaking my jeans.

Trying to catch my breath, I don't even hear their

footsteps approach until they come to a stop and bark a command.

"On your feet, miss," one of the two men says.

Oh, fuck me. Let me catch my breath first.

"Can't a girl rest?" I whine, not even opening my eyes.

"Now," the second voice says, far more lethal than the first.

I huff and open my eyes. *Yep, definitely the same two police officers*—the ones Charlotte stole from—are looming over me. While I lie here like a fool. Honestly, I didn't realize what she was doing until she grabbed something and yelled for me to run.

"You can't tell me what to do." I scrunch my nose at them. The first officer, whose wallet Charlotte stole, is shaking his head, clearly pissed. The second one, who is tall and built like a military man, is wearing a hat that covers his eyes.

"Of course we can," he says and then shoves his hand into his pocket and pulls out a badge, flashing it at me. I narrow my eyes at it. To be honest, it's a little bit blurry, and I know it has nothing to do with my wet glasses and everything to do with the too many margaritas, which is not a problem, in my opinion.

"That's fake," I say, being ignorant.

"No, it's not," he argues.

"It totally is. "Would you believe me if I pulled one out right now? I doubt it." I argue back.

"Fucking hell, woman, where is the wallet?" He huffs, putting his badge back in his pocket. I lie back down and look up at the dark sky, pushing my glasses up my nose so they don't fall off.

"I have no idea what you're talking about," I say, too tired for this. My legs are heavy, and I have a stitch in my side. Okay, maybe I'm not as fit as I thought.

"Cuff her," he tells the second officer.

"Don't you dare touch me," I seethe, my eyes flying open.

The one with the cap has a slight smirk as he leans down to grab me. He pulls me up by my wrist, but I shove back, immediately landing back on my ass. Fuck, those margaritas went straight to my head.

"Jesus, how drunk are you?" the first cop scoffs.

I look away, indignant, despite my current messy state. "That's none of your business. And if you don't step back, I'll scream."

"Good, scream," he says as the officer in the cap attempts to cuff me again. When he reaches for my hands, I move quickly, trying to get back to my feet. Apparently, it was too quickly because my head spins, and I fall again.

Fuck me. Was it the margaritas or extra tequila shots we had? How many did I have?

They both start laughing, and that makes me even more mad. "Put your hands behind your back," Mr. Authority with the hat says.

"Fuck off," I snap back.

"I don't remember you having this much attitude. You seemed far tamer back then," cap cop notes.

What?

I'm suddenly lifted up, and before I can ask what he means, my hands are cuffed behind my back. I try to fight it, break them apart, but my shoulders scream. To say I'm not fit is an understatement, but this is sobering. If only I ran a little longer. Then again, looking at the heights and builds of the two men, and me only coming in at five foot three, they have the advantage.

"You don't know me. I don't associate with police," I spit. He seems to find that hilarious, laughing as he half drags me through Central Park because my legs keep crossing over one another.

I try a few times to fall backward to avoid the inevitable. He grabs the cuffs and lifts me again. It hurts. "I can throw you over my shoulder and carry you instead if your legs are suddenly broken," Mr. Authority taunts. His partner is walking slightly ahead of us now.

"Be my guest. But don't bitch when I bite at your throat," I growl as I stand on my feet again.

"I might like it, Shortcake, so be careful what threats you're making."

My mouth drops open. "You can't say that to me. Aren't you supposed to uphold the law?"

He shoves me forward, encouraging me to walk again. "I thought you said my badge is fake."

I try to eye him, to really get a good look at him, but through the dark and with the hat shadowing half his face, I can't see very clearly. That and my glasses are slightly wet from the rain.

"Better be careful with these handcuffs; I might be into them," I tease, trying to make him uncomfortable so he lets go. Aren't they under some sort of fucked-up code?

"And I'm into gags. Should we try the two together, Shortcake?" he offers.

Heat rushes through me because, although I can't see his face clearly, I like the tight muscles beneath his damp shirt that's stuck to his upper body. He looks as tall as my cousins, around six foot two, and I know he could throw me around like a fucking rag doll.

Jesus, has it been that long for you that you're actually fantasizing about a cop because he cuffed you?

"Got no response to that one, huh?" he asks as we approach the street, where I see a sleek black car. They might not be in uniform or drive a police car, but Charlotte knew they were cops when they were flashing around those ego-ass badges when we were stumbling out of the nightclub trying to ask people questions.

I go to speak, but our attention is taken by the police officer walking ahead of us. He's talking into a radio, describing how I look.

"Hope Ivanov is her name." My head swings around

to look at Mr. Authority at the mention of my name. *How the fuck does this guy know who I am?*

But I still can't see him clearly.

I tug on my restraints again, but it's useless with his tight grip as he leads me to the car.

My father is going to be pissed.

He hates the police.

I may be twenty-two, but make no mistake, I'm still scared of my father when he gets angry. He may never hurt me, but that man is terrifying when someone hurts his family or even looks at him wrong.

He's tried all his life to shelter me from his murderous tendencies; however, there have been a few times he's accidentally lost control. Not to mention how many times my auntie, Anya Ivanov, has unapologetically killed people in front of me and then argued with my mother, telling her it's a good lesson for every woman to learn.

Ahhh. This isn't going to end well. They might actually ransack the entire police station just to get me out.

"Okay, I can pay you. Just remove the cuffs."

This is going to get messy. If this guy knows who I am, he should know better than to bring me in.

"Are you trying to bribe a police officer?" the one holding me asks.

"No," I say while nodding my head yes.

"No?" he repeats.

"No," I reply flatly. What the fuck? How did that not work?

"Didn't think so, Shortcake." He grins, then says to the other officer, "Let's take her into holding." Officer number one opens the back door so Mr. Authority can not-so-gently shove me into the back seat. I'd be lying if I said it didn't create an immediate fire in my gut because I fucking *like* it.

Before the door is closed, I look up, furiously scowling at the man who shoved me in. He's dressed in all black. He rests his hand on the roof of the car as he leans in, and his sleeve tugs up, exposing a few tattoos. Then I see his face as he pulls his hat off.

"Nice to see you again, Hope." He winks, and I recognize that cocky smile as he leans over me to buckle my seat belt.

"You're fucking kidding me." I sigh and let my head hit the back of the seat.

Braxton Hero.

The very man I lost my virginity to when I was eighteen.

Fuck.

He looks good.

"I heard that," he says just before he slams the door shut, locking me in the back of the cop car with my hands still cuffed behind my back.

Fuck, I'm in so much trouble.

CHAPTER 2

Braxton

I can't fight the smirk on my lips as I walk over to my partner.

He doesn't seem too impressed, though. He jerks his head in the direction of where she's restrained in the car. "You know her?"

Lucas and I were forced into a partnership. I consider it a love-hate relationship, depending on what type of day he's having. But he's a good fucking detective and has my back.

"Who doesn't know her family?" I ask, not at all appreciating his tone. It's not a lie; we all know her family and how none of us can touch them. *Under normal circumstances.* Hope just made it far too easy this evening. She hadn't even run a quarter of a mile before giving up and throwing herself to the ground in exhaustion like a sacrificial lamb, one I was happy to slaughter tonight.

"That's not what I am asking," he says. I shake my head as he slides into the driver's seat, and I take the passenger seat.

I glance at her over my shoulder. Her head is tilted back awkwardly, and she appears to be asleep. Shit, she passed out quickly, clearly unfazed by her predicament.

And why would she be? At twenty-two years old, the woman has more power and wealth than she knows what to do with. But I didn't know that when I first met her.

Until tonight, I haven't seen her for four years, and I'd be lying if I said I hadn't thought about her. Though, I don't remember her being so feisty. She was quiet and reserved as if she carefully chose who she gave her time to. It's what drew me to her. I wanted to break something so sickly sweet and innocent, but there were little glimmers of her feisty side here. One I'm certain very few see and more prone to come out with the assistance of alcohol. I didn't know she was a virgin the first night we met until she bled all over my cock. She'd reassured me she wanted it and told me not to change my pace.

So we fucked. Three times.

By the time I went for a shower and came back to the room, she was gone. And I haven't seen her since.

I was going to reach out to her again. Finding people is my specialty as a detective, after all, but that changed when I discovered who she was. Not the alias she gave me, but the truth of who she actually was. I wonder if she knew who I was that night. Or did it just so happen we were on opposite sides of a fence that neither of us should've crossed. She's not just any criminal's daughter; she's Alek Ivanov's fucking daughter. The name alone runs so deeply in the underbelly of black-market auctions and has heavily tied connections with Manhattan's Italian mafia, the Monti's.

So I left it alone and haven't seen her since.

Until now.

Drunk in a park, defeated by one minute of running after stealing my partner's wallet. Though I'm pretty sure it was her friend and not her who actually did the pick-pocketing. Had they targeted me, they wouldn't have gotten any farther than down the block. Unfortunately, my partner likes donuts, which is why he's the driver—so I can jump out of the car at any given moment and run.

"So, do you know her or not?" he presses. I side-eye him, having thought he'd dropped it.

"No. In family reputation alone." I finally answer him, unsure of what else to say. Do I know her? Not really. Could I tell him about the way her body moves when she's under me? Yes. Yes, I could. In very graphic detail, actually. I grind my teeth, thinking back on that night. I've not been able to forget it.

"I don't think she has the wallet," he says, looking at her through the rearview mirror. Her mouth is wide open, so she's definitely fucking snoozing.

"No, it was her friend," I agree.

I tap my fingers against the door. Ordinarily, we

shouldn't touch her. In fact, we might get reprimanded for doing so. But this is different. I let her escape once. Why couldn't I have a different type of fun with it the second time? Even if it rains down hell at the police station and creates more paperwork for me.

I'm just doing my job, I convince myself, trying to hide a smirk.

It's not long until we arrive at the station, and when we park, she's still out cold. *You've got to be kidding me.*

I pull her across the back seat and lift her, bridal style. She's so fucking small in my arms, and her head bobbles around as she murmurs something. I'm walking her into the station as she mumbles again, and this time, I press my ear close to her lips so I can hear her...

"I'll kill you," she slurs.

Of course.

I sit her at the desk of the officer who will question her. He seems nervous as he looks over her file. "Are you sure? This is Ivanov's kid, isn't it?" he whisper-shouts.

I grab a bottle of water, open it, and tip it over her head. She gasps, bolting upright, flailing like a fish. "I'm sure," I say with an evil grin.

"What the fuck?!" Her eyes snap in my direction, but I make a point to leave without so much as a word to her. I know the police officer will only ask a few questions, hardly daring to touch her. Protocol bullshit, but I can't help enjoying watching her intimidate him with her gaze alone.

He's floundering as he tries to handle her. I wonder how many see this side of Hope Ivanov. I'd done my research on her after our night together. To the world she looks divinely sweet and innocent, but when she needs it, this side of her slips through, where she has a little more bite. It's like two sides of the same coin. She mostly takes after her mother, Lena Love, who is a famous singer. But when she gets like this, she's more like her father, who is feared in the underworld, and for good reason.

Her vibrant red hair is stuck to her skin, and she restlessly shakes her cuffs. She keeps glancing my way, and I smirk. That seems to piss her off even more.

Lucas is busily typing up our report of the incident, more pissed than usual because it's his wallet that's been taken. "We won't be able to keep her for long, but we have to get her for something. My wallet has my fucking baseball game tickets for next weekend in it."

"Don't you use digital ones like everyone else?" I ask, raising an eyebrow.

"It's not the point. I was going to ask Heidi if she'd come with me. It doesn't look as cool if I'm just showing her a screen."

I say nothing. He's had a crush on Heidi, the receptionist, since he started working here six years ago. I've never had the heart to tell him I fucked her within the first week of her being here. Every time he goes to ask her out, he suddenly has a reason why he can't. This time, it was taken out of his hands by a certain little redheaded vixen.

Hope sighs, frustrated, as the police officer stands and comes over to me. "I don't know how long we can keep her here."

"For as long as it takes until we know where the wallet is," I tell him.

"She said her friend has it." I already know this.

"So find out what her friend's name is and where she lives," Lucas growls. I refrain from smirking at his anger. I cross my arms expectantly.

The officer licks his lips as he glances at the door as if waiting for hell to rain over us. I can't fucking wait because I doubt even Alek Ivanov is that much of a savage to burst into a police station, especially if it might reflect badly on his wife's career.

The officer gulps. "She said snitches get stitches."

I can't hold back the laughter at how terrified he is of one tiny woman.

"You want to question her?" he asks me, almost begging me to take over.

She's slouched in the chair now as if trying to go back to sleep.

"Sure." I'd fucking love to. My partner looks up at me and raises a brow. "Do you want your wallet back or not? Can't have you missing out on a hot date."

Red stains his cheeks, and I find it amusing at how

straight and narrow this guy is and the mention of a date has him blushing.

I wait for them to take her into the interrogation room, and then I watch her from the other side of the one-way glass as she impatiently blows at her messy, damp hair. Hope Ivanov has definitely had better days. But even with mascara streaking down her face, she still looks like a goddess. I like this sight of her best. It's like unmasking the little she-devil that so very few see.

Except for me. I did that night.

Explicitly.

She starts questioning if the cuffs are necessary as an officer hooks her wrists to the ring bolted to the table. The officer doesn't engage as he walks away, and she screams, telling him he's going bald at the back.

So very drunk and opposite to her usual self.

"Do you want me in there?" Lucas asks.

"No. Let me handle this one."

"I don't care if you have to use your charm on this one. Just get my wallet back, please," he demands, then slams the door behind him.

I fold my arms over my chest, smirking.

I guess now it's time to talk to her.

CHAPTER 3

Hope

My foot bounces, and I know I'm sobering up.

Shit, how did I let her get me into this? Charlotte is a friend from school, and while I don't see her all that often since we graduated, when I do, she always has some crazy scheme planned.

The door creaks open, and my gaze shoots to it. My hands are cuffed to the table, but if they were free, I'd fucking strangle this asshole's neck.

They're treating me like a common criminal.

And I wasn't even the one who took the fucking wallet.

"Miss Ivanov." There he is again, dressed in all black, his sleeves still pushed up, but this time, he doesn't have the hat on. His dark hair is messy, with loose, short curls on top, and a distant memory returns of a time I once ran my fingers through it.

"Mr. Hero," I sneer, now wishing I'd actually looked at the badge he flashed me in the park before taunting him that it's fake. If I had, maybe I wouldn't have been so surprised by my captor. He doesn't smile as he approaches, then leans over and unlocks the cuffs.

"You can behave?" he asks. I nod and rub my wrists where I've hidden them in my lap. "I just have a few questions."

"I didn't do anything." Those are the words that leave my mouth when I'd really like to tell him to fuck right off.

Those crystal-blue eyes pin me in place. "Did you not try to bribe me?"

"I..." Words fail to leave my mouth now, and all I can do is shake my head.

"If you want me to take this further, the next step will be a strip search."

My jaw drops just as a loud knock comes on the door. We both turn as his partner enters the room. Braxton gets up and joins him. And after exchanging a few quiet words, both turn to look at me before his partner leaves and Braxton moves to stand next to my chair. He leans down, and I smell him, my nostrils flaring at his fucking intoxicating scent. I avert my gaze because I should not be attracted to a cop. That's a disaster waiting to happen. I didn't know he was a cop that night we spent together, and I wish I didn't know now.

"I'll be seeing you real soon, Shortcake." He pulls away then and goes back to the door, holding it open. "Your father is waiting for you."

My stomach drops.

"Oh fuck. Maybe you should arrest me," I say, not getting up. It's not that I'm scared of my father. It's more that I hate to disappoint the man.

"You want me to arrest you?" Braxton raises a brow.

"If I hit you right now, would you arrest me?" I ask.

I notice the smirk he tries to hide as he leans against the doorjamb, expecting me to leave.

"Good night, Hope." He nods to the door, and I manage to stand and force my feet to move in that direction. I contemplate hitting him. I really do. But I keep walking, and he follows right behind me. I pause as I reach the door that leads back into the main room of the precinct, and in a deadly serious tone, he says, "I'll be seeing you real soon."

I bite my lip. *Shit*. Did I just get in the bad graces of a detective? I think I did. His gaze flicks to my lips, and I remember how he bit them all those years ago.

Braxton is five years older than me, and he looks even better than when I last saw him.

I push through the door and find my father waiting with Rya Monti, one of the best criminal lawyers in Manhattan. They both turn to me, and my father nods toward the exit, not saying a word. Not that I expected him to. I don't bother looking back as we leave, and when we reach the car, he thanks Rya.

I see her husband, Crue Monti, standing beside his car. I don't even know what fucking time it is, but my father wasn't messing around when he called the ex-head of the Italian mafia and his wife in.

"Thank you for your time. The money's been transferred," my father tells Rya.

She kicks up a smile, her silvery eyes twinkling as she turns to me. "Our children are growing up faster than we're ready for, it would appear."

My father's jaw tics and I internally wince. He's so disappointed. Most likely because I got caught. Crue and my father exchange a brief nod, and then my father turns on me.

"I didn't mean to," I start.

"It's fine, Hope," he says, and his Russian accent is thicker than usual, which means he's angry.

When I sit in the passenger seat, he closes the door behind me, and I watch him prowl around to the driver's seat. He looks like he's considering whether to burn down the building or not.

I gather the courage to speak again ten minutes into the drive. His gloved hands grip the steering wheel tightly, and I know he's thinking about contingency plans. Most parents would be disappointed at having to bail their child out of temporary lockup, and I hope he doesn't force me to have some type of security after this.

"You're angry," I finally say.

He shakes his head, and when we stop at a red light, his green gaze meets mine for the first time since picking me up. I know he's seeing eyes that remind him so much of my mother's ocean blue ones and vibrant red hair similar to my Aunt Anya's. I've been told I look a lot like she did when she was younger, just shorter and plumper with my mother's figure.

"I'm mad that they would have left anyone else alone, except they knew who you were."

Ohhhh. He's mad that they picked on me for my name.

"If you want to go back and take your revenge, I'll cover you. If you want me to kill any of them, let me know, and it'll be done by dawn." He pauses before he says, "Do you understand?"

I try to hide my smile. "Mom would hit you over the head if she heard you talking like that. But I understand, and it's fine. I was drunk and got caught."

"We don't have to tell your mother if we kill someone; it can be our little secret. But speaking of your mother, she's not going to be happy. She only flew in tonight, and you had her worried."

The guilt immediately floods me. My mother embraces the dark within my father, but she's far more the worrying type, and I know she's probably pacing the house, waiting for my return. It's moments like this that I feel like a child again.

I explain everything that happened in detail, leaving out one fact—that I know Braxton.

When we arrive at my parents' house, my mother is waiting at the front of their three-story home. She immediately runs down the stairs and pulls my door open.

"You're okay?" she asks, a tenor in her tone..

"Yes," I tell her before she pulls me in for a hug. She smothers me, but I hug her back since it's been about a month since I last saw her in person. With both of us traveling so much for our respective art, it feels like it's been forever, even though we FaceTime almost daily.

"Let her get into the house," my father says, chuckling as he embraces us both and then leads us to the door.

I silently thank him, and my mother laughs, bumping against my hip as if I betrayed her by taking his side. She catches me before I stumble over.

"Oh my, you're drunk," she chides.

"We should get her a bodyguard for when—"

"No!" I yell, interrupting him. "We discussed this. When I turned twenty-one, there would be no more security."

My mother bites her bottom lip but tries not to laugh as my father practically sulks as we walk back into the house.

"I was worried," she continues as she pulls me in for another hug.

"I'm fine. Just need a shower and some sleep."

"You do reek of alcohol." She chuckles. They seem to find it so hilarious because I don't go out all that often. But when I do, I always end up like this. Like an alter ego of my usual quiet self comes out.

"I was drinking with Charlotte."

"That explains it. Let me guess. She left you behind while the police cuffed you up." When I don't reply, she shakes her head. "I had a friend like that once. You'll one day learn they aren't the best type of people to have in your life. Why didn't you ask Billie or Ivy if they were free?"

My father heads toward their bedroom, most likely going to prepare for sleep or a business meeting. Three in the morning seems like prime time for criminals to get on calls.

"Ivy's not in the country, and Billie said she was busy this weekend, but I'll meet with them soon." Ivy Walker and Billie Taylor are my two closest friends. Much like me, they were raised with fathers who were on the shadier side of business. Ironically, our fathers, who all have lethal reputations, raised us like little princesses.

"Were there any boys?" she asks.

"Mo-om," I groan. "I am not having this discussion with you. I need to sleep."

She presses a kiss to my forehead. "Fine, but we're going to have a serious discussion about this tomorrow."

I roll my eyes because that isn't going to happen. I've

never been the bad girl type. I keep to myself and was a good student. This is the most mischief I've gotten up to, and it's almost as if they're relieved I'm living a "semi-normal" life.

I head to my room, which hasn't changed much since I was a teenager, and fall onto my bed.

I've considered getting my own place, but I travel so much that I'm rarely in one place for any length of time.

"I knew I left this here," I say to myself as I reach for my phone on my bedside table.

After having a shower and getting into bed, I check my Instagram page. It's become a habit. I have over one million followers, and I'm always curious as to what they're saying about my new collections. Not that I care so much what they think, but I'm always intrigued as to how many people truly understand the message I'm trying to send through my sculptures.

I have a new message, which isn't uncommon. Most of the time, I ignore them. But the name of the account is what has me opening it.

Hello, Shortcake...

I stare at it, thinking this night couldn't have gone any

more astray. Why the fuck is Braxton Hero messaging me? Is he seriously trying to get himself killed?

I don't reply. Instead, curiosity gets the better of me, and I stalk his profile.

"Boring," I say on a yawn. He barely has any photos, and those he does have are of him and his workmates when he's receiving awards. A real A+ plus type of guy— the furthest thing from the man I met four years ago, who strangled me in pleasure.

Closing the app, I fall asleep almost immediately.

And dream of him.

CHAPTER 4
Braxton

I stand over a body, admiring the killer's handiwork. This is the sixth body in just as many months. Don't get me wrong, in Manhattan, there are always murders, but we've got a serial killer on the loose. One who doesn't seem to have a method of killing. It makes them dangerous because it seems like they're experimenting. The only indication we have that all six murders were committed by the same person is the type of target, all being male, and the openness the body was left to be found. The killer wants to be noticed.

"Any cameras around here?" I ask the bouncer who found the body in the club's alley and called it in two hours ago. It was right after Hope Ivanov was escorted out of the station by the famed Aleksandr Ivanov and Rya Monti. I knew there were deep ties running through the families, but that is a combination of disaster for any law enforcement to try and come down on, which is exactly why they haven't.

"No cameras," he says.

I sigh. How the fuck does this person evade cameras every time?

Photos are being taken of the crime scene, and I stare at the man's bleeding eyes. Fucking hell. I'm guessing poison, maybe?

"Have we confirmed if he was in the club?"

The bouncer nods. "I had my boss look over the security footage, and he was one of the people registered for the night."

"I want to see that list. And have the videos sent to the station," I tell him. He nods again, swallowing as he stares down at the body. I imagine he doesn't often see dead people firsthand.

Lucas walks over, dark circles under his eyes. We don't usually work such long hours, but we're doing overtime this evening, trying to figure out if this murder is linked to the one from the same night. Two people in three nights. The other victim had their throat slit, however.

It makes it trickier to track a killer when the methods aren't consistent. Or it means we have more than one killer on the loose. Anything is fucking possible in this city.

"He's been dead for about twelve hours. Until we get an autopsy, we can't confirm how long before he died that he consumed the poison. Assuming that's what this is," Lucas says.

I look up at him. "What else do you think it could be?"

He shifts on his feet. "Well, that's some demonic shit."

My eyebrows raise in surprise. "You think we have a demon on our hands?" I turn back to the body. Now, wouldn't that be something. I've never caught a demon before.

The man's lying face down, most likely because he stumbled down the alley and then fell forward. I crouch next to him, then grab a nearby stick and use it to lift his hand.

Lucas looks away. We're not supposed to move the body until forensics and photos are taken, and he doesn't always agree with my methods of investigation, but if I see something that will be of use to the case, I'm not scared to skirt the rules. I study the body carefully and a muddied type of dirt on the victims' nails grabs my attention. I lift his hand slowly and assess them closely. Beneath them is what looks like dirt... or clay.

We're called for a murder on the very same night a renowned sculptor attends the same club with her friend. Now that is not a coincidence.

"Can I look at his profile again?" I demand of Lucas. He hands it to me, and I scan the page, spotting what I was looking for. He does sculpture as a hobby.

Immediately, I think of a little redheaded shortcake. I know it's probably a coincidence, but it doesn't make me any less intrigued. What if there's a link between this body and the renowned sculpture artist Hope Ivanov? In this line of work especially one thing I've always done is follow my intuition.

It's been a week since I've seen Hope, and to say she hasn't left my mind would be an understatement. She's become my obsession. More specifically, it's very unfortunate for the little redheaded vixen we've trailed back the most recent victim to attending a lecture and class she was a guest host at. Granted, hundreds of people would've passed through those doors on the day, and the asshole could've pissed anyone off. He already had a record against him from his ex-girlfriend, who he used to hit. A stand-up guy. But one who fits the bill for our little serial killer.

Unfortunately, it doesn't give me much evidence to pin against her since she was in custody close to the time of his death. Lucas has been backtracking his movements and anyone else he might've pissed off over the last few weeks, but my hunch says she's somehow involved.

Maybe I'm clutching at straws, looking for evidence to pursue her. Without a doubt, it's become my personal fixation to follow her since she's been haunting me ever since I found her lying on that wet grass in Central Park.

I search for her online. I look into everything I can find about her and her routine, which isn't very much. I even messaged her the first night I saw her again, but she never replied. Not that I expected her to. I wouldn't even know if she sees her messages.

If she wasn't going to come to me, I'd figure out how to go to her and find out what the little vixen is up to and how she might be connected with this crime.

Coincidence is not something I overlook, and I always follow my gut feelings. And my gut is telling me that Hope Ivanov is far from the sweet, shy, and critically acclaimed artist she's made out to be. Because surely, the apple doesn't fall far from the tree, especially when it's poisoned with sin.

CHAPTER 5

Hope

My first mistake is concentrating on balancing the sculpture in my hand and not looking where I'm going. I run into a hard body, knocking myself back a step. A hand grabs me, keeping me on my feet, but my heart stops as I watch in horror as the sculpture lands on the floor, shattering.

"Oh my God!" I drop to my knees in a panic, trying to scoop up all the pieces.

I stare in shock, my mind going momentarily blank.

Fuck. Fuck. Fuck.

I know I can't save it because it's in a million fucking pieces, but I will time to reverse.

Rage boils in my blood.

This is my space.

My sanctuary.

So who the fuck has the audacity to interrupt me?

I'm supposed to be alone, so who the fuck just ruined my piece? I look up then, pushing my glasses up my nose, and trail my gaze up from a pair of shiny black shoes, black pants, and a black t-shirt to the face I want to punch most.

Braxton Hero is standing in front of me, not seeming remorseful in the slightest that he caused to me break a piece of art that took me ages to complete.

"You should watch where you're going," he says. I bite my tongue and look away from his cocky grin as I start picking up the broken pieces at his feet. He makes no move to help me or even get out of my way. No, he stays exactly where he is, and I fucking hate the arrogance radiating off him.

When I don't say anything, he drops down to a crouch. At first, I think he is going to help after all, like a normal person would. Instead, I feel his gaze boring into me through his black sunglasses, as if studying me like some kind of animal.

Why the fuck is he even here?

"Hope, look at me." I don't. I just keep picking up the pieces of broken clay. My mind's in frantic overdrive. I'm too freaked out to even think about how mad he makes me because I need to remake this ASAP. This piece was paid for, and it wasn't cheap. All my pieces sell for high prices; it's one thing I love about what I do. I can earn money from something I love doing... and be left alone in my studio. Ordinarily.

"I don't have time for your antics," I hiss, cupping the broken pieces in my hand as I stand and then hurry back to the studio. I might've had liquid courage last time I saw Braxton, but then and now are entirely different situations, and I certainly don't do well with someone coming into my space uninvited.

I quickly realize that he's following me into my private space. His shoes squeak against the wooden floorboards, and I turn on him. I'm wearing a free-flowing dress and no shoes. I prefer to work barefoot; it makes me feel more grounded. But right now I'm wishing I was wearing heels, as he towers over me with that smug fucking smirk.

"This is private property," I'm quick to inform him as I push the door open with my hip.

Nope, Braxton takes that as an invitation to follow me.

My studio space is my domain. It's where I feel most safe and at peace. It's filled with plants that flourish under the bright sunshine coming in through the skylights. Classical music plays softly in the background and a small water fountain bubbles in the middle of the room. We're on the top floor of the building, and right now, I'm very tempted to push him out one of the windows when he starts touching my things.

I try not to let him distract me as I throw the pieces into the trash, but my eye twitches as his hands smooth over the face of one of my sculptures. And then he runs them over an eagle's wings. I drag out some clay so I can prepare to start the sculpture over again. I know the concept by heart, but it took me months to make it. There's no way I'm going to get it done in time.

Fuck.

I can't ignore his imposing presence any longer, and besides, I'm fucking furious. *He did this.* Having a man in my space, especially one that I don't like, is intolerable.

"What's wrong, Hope?" he asks, glancing at me as if susceptible to my inner rage.

"I'd like you to leave," I say, putting my hands on my hips. But my voice is weak, and he smirks.

"You seem to have lost your fire. I remember when you were far more demanding. Or perhaps that's only when you're asking to be choked." Heat floods my core, and I hate it so much that we ever spent any time together. Had I known he was a cop, I would've never gone there. Right?

He admires some of the half-finished sculptures on a side table. Some are paid for, and some are not. But most importantly, no one has seen them except for me. I don't like when people look at my unfinished work. They'll see the flaws or make suggestions, and it's infuriating. It's about my vision, not theirs.

"Is there something I can help you with? If not, I'll call security and have them show you out." His presence makes me nervous, and it has nothing to do with the fact that he's a police officer. It's just him; his undeniable presence, the way he stares at me like he's sizing me up as if I'm some sort of prey. That night we spent together thrilled me. But this is something wholly different. There is something darker here. I know because I'm surrounded by men who have that same palpable presence.

"There is. I have a few more questions about the other night I didn't get to ask before Daddy came and picked you up," he says with a cocky grin. I know he does it on purpose, to antagonize me. Little does he know, I've worked with the press and media for years. I know when someone is baiting me or trying to get an explosive reaction.

"Can we do this another time?" I ask, waving a hand around. "I have work to do."

"No. You'll answer my questions now."

"Why?" I snap, frustrated, a lock of my red hair falling into my face from my loose top bun.

"There she is," he says, his expression smug.

"What questions do you have?" I sigh and then notice the gun holstered at his hip. His gaze follows mine. The guy's probably so self-absorbed that he's thinking I'm staring at his cock. Not that there's anything wrong with his cock since I know what he's packing. I swallow hard.

Get your mind out of the gutter. I internally reprimand myself.

"You would be familiar with these, wouldn't you?"

He takes the gun out of the holster and holds it up. "Considering what your father does."

"I have no idea what you're talking about," I scoff, knowing exactly what my father does. He and his twin sister, Anya, deal in guns, among other things.

"Yes, of course you'd say that." He picks up a piece of clay and squeezes it in his hand. He moves around my work table until we're face-to-face. Only a foot separates us as he leans in and says, "Show me what you do."

"No." When I work, I can't do it with anyone watching me. I have to be alone. "And although I'm sure it makes you feel very strong, intimidating me for whatever reasons, I really have to work."

"Show me," he says again.

"No. You need to leave." I just barely refrain from shoving him out the door. But laying hands on this asshole is the last thing I can do. He'll cuff me for it, and I don't have time to play this game.

"Why? What are you going to do, call the police on me?" he asks as his lips thin. "I'll have you arrested again."

"Unless you have a warrant, you can kindly leave." My voice is low and steady, but my glare screams, *"You can kindly fuck off."*

He smirks. "A body was found the night you and your friend were at the nightclub. Remember the night you two mugged a police officer?"

I fold my arms over my chest. "So?"

"The man was poisoned. Clay was found under his nails. It was a rather gnarly scene, actually." He pauses, brow raised. "Turns out, earlier that day, he was at one of the classes you taught as a guest instructor. Small world, huh?"

I stare at him in disbelief. "Wait. Do you think because a person was at a class I taught, that I... killed him? Are you delusional?"

"You seemed to have forgotten to mention it that night when you were cuffed in the interrogation room. Besides, murder runs in the family, doesn't it?"

"Is this all because you're annoyed about me leaving your room without saying goodbye four years ago? It was a one-night stand. Surely, you're not that hurt over it. Or was I the only woman who didn't stick around to inflate your narcissistic ego?"

"Such a poisonous tongue from the perfect daughter." He smirks again.

"Stop that," I chastise. He's purposefully riling me up. He has no evidence, and he fucking knows it, so he's trying to what... have me lose my shit at him so he can arrest me again? I'm not falling for his provocation.

There's a knock on my door. It's Charlotte's voice on the other side, "Hope. Come on, girl, we're going to be late."

"Late for what?" he asks. "Do you plan to rob another victim?" I snort at the idea of him being a victim. "You find that funny?"

With my lack of response, Charlotte opens the door, looking down at her phone. "Your car is out front, Hope. I know you prefer to be left alone, but we have to go. I can't believe I'm the one dragging you to be on it—" She stops in her tracks as she looks up, and her eyes go wide when she spots Braxton.

"Another suspect, considering she was in the same class as you."

"There were over a hundred people in that class. Are you interrogating all of them as well?"

"I just start at where my gut tells me to," he says and heads for the door. Charlotte tenses as he approaches her.

"I expect you to give Miss Ivanov my partner's wallet, Charlotte. That little stunt cost him a date that he was very much looking forward to."

Charlotte's family is almost as influential as mine, which is most likely why she hasn't been called into the station yet. But I'm certain that Braxton is one of few daring enough to do it, damned the consequences.

"S-sure," she stutters, then looks at me, silently screaming for help. I'm not the one to look at since I've been trying to get rid of him myself. I look at my watch, having not realized the time. Fuck I really am behind schedule.

"I'll be seeing you real soon, Hope," Braxton says over his shoulder, then walks out.

Charlotte's mouth is hanging open, but I don't really have time to explain anything to her. I lost track of time, and now I have to hurry if I'm going to get the broken sculpture remade.

"I can't go with you today," I tell her busily. I need to start this piece immediately.

"What do you mean? It's a charity event for the arts. Everyone who is anyone will be there. We have to go." Like me, Charlotte is an artist, though she does mostly pottery.

Those types of events aren't important to me. I don't care for parties. I prefer to be by myself whenever I can. And especially in a heated moment when I have to prioritize starting this sculpture from the start.

When I don't reply, she looks back at the door. "Was that one of the detectives from last weekend?"

I sigh, frustrated because I just need to get to work.

"Yes. Apparently, there was a murder at the club on the same night you stole the other detective's wallet, and he's investigating." I look up distractedly and add, "Can you shut the door on your way out?"

I grab my apron and put it on.

"A murder?" She gasps. "He thinks we had something to do with it?"

"I never said that."

She seems uncomfortable. "Oh. I just assumed. Anyway, it's fine. I'll go to the event on my own. Also, he doesn't seriously expect me to return the wallet, does he? I threw it out on the same night."

"Go and see if you can find it," I say, exasperated.

Because I know what will happen if she doesn't—he'll come back. And I don't want him back here.

"Fuck." She stomps her foot. "It was supposed to be a fun night." I give her a warning glare. Charlotte is immature. She's used to getting everything she wants when she wants, and when consequences are being rolled out, she throws a tantrum. She exasperates a sigh when I don't agree with her. "Ugh, fine. I'm leaving," she grumbles, dismissing herself and closing the door behind her.

I close my eyes and take a deep breath, letting the rhythm of the classical music take over.

Everything is going to be okay. I'll deal with the investigation bullshit later. Hopefully, the questioning about the murder is a one-time thing, but I have a nagging suspicion it won't be the last time I see Braxton Hero.

I release a heavy sigh.

I'm going to have to call the buyer of the sculpture and tell her there's been a delay.

I hate that.

I'm never late.

I'm always on time.

I have a feeling this is only the start of my time being encroached upon as a certain detective sniffs too closely. If my family catches wind of this, he won't make it out alive. I'm trying to make the point to my parents I can stand on my own two feet, so I absolutely refuse to ask for help.

I can handle this asshole myself.

CHAPTER 6

Braxton

I'm sitting in my car when Charlotte exits the building a few minutes after me... alone. She pulls out her phone and starts quickly typing.

I get out of the car and approach her. She raises her head just as I reach her. Her brown eyes meet mine, and they're nothing compared to the magnetic blue of Hope's, which are so striking with her vibrant red hair and porcelain skin.

She clutches her phone tightly to her chest and blurts, "I'm going to try to find the wallet."

"I should hope so because I'd hate to bring you down to the station," I tell her, and she pales. The thing with these people is they always think they're above the law because they can pay to make any problem go away. And although that might be true, if I really wanted to, I'm sure I could find far more to pin them with.

"Charlotte, how long have you known Hope Ivanov?"

"About four years," she answers.

"How did you meet?"

"We went to high school together, and now we're attending the same college."

Interesting. I assumed she had been focusing on her career alone, and though I saw she'd enrolled in college, I thought with her busy schedule there was no way she could balance both. Unless, of course, she does mostly everything online.

I wonder why she felt the need to go to college. Not only are her parents wealthy, but she also earns enough from her sculptures to maintain any sort of lifestyle she wants.

"Would you like to explain to me what you were doing on the night we last met?"

She darts a glance to the car waiting for her. "Umm, we just went clubbing. It's not usually Hope's thing, so if there's too many people, she'll often drink a lot. I did, too. And then we left, and we, umm... Well, you know the rest."

I show her a photo of the victim who was murdered at the club. "Do you know this man?"

She studies it. "No? Maybe? I don't know."

"Really? Because this camera footage shows you making out with him on the same night." This makes her a prime suspect, although fortunately for her, he also made out with another two women from the same class, and she was too busy causing mischief, mugging my partner alongside Hope.

She pales as she stares at the photo of the two of them in a lip lock. "Honestly, I had so many drinks that night. I made out with a few guys. It's kind of my thing. But I swear to God, I didn't hurt him."

"Of course not," I say sarcastically. She goes even paler. I'm not about using intimidation tactics on women; if they'll crack even just the slightest bit to give me a new lead, I'll uncover it, no matter what. These two girls are trouble, but only one of them is related to a family of killers.

"There were other people there from the sculpting class that night," she quickly adds. "Like a bunch of us. They all wanted to hang out with Hope. You know, get pictures and stuff for their social media pages."

Shallow assholes.

If those are the type of people Hope hangs out with, no wonder she locks herself in a rooftop studio away from the world.

"Can you send me a list of the names of those who attended?" I already have a list of the majority who attended the class, but I can get the names of those who attended their little afterparty event.

"Like their last names and everything? Because I

don't know half of them that well. I can try, though," she replies. "But you don't seriously think we're involved in this, do you? That would be crazy!"

I wonder if Charlotte is aware of her friend's connections with the underworld.

"Was anyone from Hope's family there?"

She scrunches up her nose. "No, they're pretty private. She does have twin cousins we've bumped into from time to time. They're like super-hot and popular, but we don't hang with them too much. But they weren't there that night."

"The Ivanov twins?" I ask. The twins were adopted by Hope's aunt, Anya Ivanov, and they have strong connections to Eli Monti, the current Mafia boss. From what I've gathered, they are his second in command. They certainly wouldn't be against killing someone.

"Yeah. They're super-hot and have that bad-boy air about them, you know." As if realizing she's rambling, she's quick to add, "But I don't think they're capable of murdering someone. I mean, come on. They're rich. Why would they have to kill anyone?"

I can't figure out if she's playing dumb or if she truly has no idea who her friend is. But my bullshit radar isn't sounding, so maybe the poor girl really has no idea how close she is to a family full of killers.

"You can go now." I wave her along, and she hurries off to her waiting car without a backward glance.

I'm suddenly realizing I've followed a trail that leads

to a hornet's nest. I smirk as I look up at the tall building Hope works in, embracing the fact I'm not someone who is scared to be stung.

I'll uncover what Hope Ivanov is hiding.

Whether it be her or her family, I'll be unmasking something deadly. I know it.

CHAPTER 7

Hope

I spend all day and night reworking the sculpture. By the time I finally walk out of my workshop the sun is starting to rise on a new day, and hardly anyone is on the streets. It's true that New York is the city that never sleeps, but it's times like this that I like it the most.

I don't have to worry about my overbearing father trying to enforce security anymore, either. I always felt guilty staying here at ungodly hours and keeping bodyguards by my side because of it. But that all changed last year when I turned twenty-one, and I've adopted new habits that offer me a sense of freedom and normality from the bright shine of stardom and recognition I've been under since I was sixteen. It was bad enough that I'm Lena Love's daughter, not that I begrudge my mother for being incredible—if anything, she's inspiring

—but there was always an expectation as to how I should act in public. Not that she applied that personally. I just felt socially awkward by society's expectations. And then when I started getting recognized for my own work, everything blew up.

I went from a teenager to a woman overnight, being bombarded with compliments but being spoken about behind my back and, at times, not so discreetly in articles and critics' reviews. So it's nice to be at a place in my career now where I can be by myself and enjoy my own company—which is how I prefer it.

I walk five blocks down to a twenty-four-hour diner that I frequent often, especially in the early hours. I'm still wide awake, and as I walk, I think back to how Braxton intruded on my space. Hardly anyone visits me when I'm working, and it infuriates me that because of him, I'm behind on a project. He didn't even apologize. Not that I would expect someone like him to do such a thing, but the fact he has a bullshit badge makes him think he can do whatever the fuck he pleases.

It grates on my nerves that he touched everything in my studio, his hands all over my things that aren't his to touch. I have the distinct impression it won't be the last time I see him either, so I start pondering on ideas as to how I should best deal with the situation. Having a cop snoop around my business isn't ideal, and had it been anyone else, I might've actually let my father deal with them. But I want to manage this situation myself.

Braxton has made it personal and I don't like anyone sniffing around that might jeopardize me or my family. If it weren't for my last name I wonder if he would have such persistent interest in the first place.

When I arrive at the diner, I order a stack of pancakes, then I sit back and read my book. I've been quite consumed by the thriller series and find it the easiest way to wind down after an intense creative session.

I absentmindedly pick at my pancakes, and after an hour of sipping on a cup of coffee, someone pulls out the chair across from me.

At first, I think it's the waitress taking my plate away, but when I raise my head to check, I'm met with a crystal-blue gaze.

I swear my left fucking eye twitches.

Braxton.

"Are you lost?" I ask, pushing my glasses back up my nose and looking back to the book, which is far more interesting than the man who just intruded on my quiet time.

"Your friend returned the wallet this evening," he says, starting another conversation I have no interest in.

"Mmhmm." I'm not sure what else I'm supposed to say. Did he really have to come and track me down to tell me that he got the wallet back? I'm sure most detectives don't go to these lengths to provide updates, so I'm unsure why he's here.

"Charlotte admitted to it and explained that you just went along with her." Still, I say nothing. It's a week after the fact. Had they wanted to do something about it, they would've done it sooner, and frankly, I don't give a shit. I pick up my coffee and take a sip.

"She's being held at the station right now. Do you want to see her?"

My gaze snaps in his direction. "You arrested her after she returned it?"

"Yes. She committed a crime and then admitted to it. Charges will be brought against her."

A cool, calculating calm spreads through my veins. Fuck this guy. Is he really trying to make an enemy of me? What is this? Him having some fun at our expense?

"But you got it back," I say, doing everything I can not to be baited by his purposeful antagonizing. For all I know, he's lying, and he's just trying to get a rise out of me because... Because why?

"Yes," he answers. "Any crimes you want to admit to?" Ah, because he's clearly trying to pin me with something. So he's investigating a crime that I was unlucky enough to be standing in the same room with the victim for, but he can't pin me for anything, and he knows it, so why is he even wasting his resources? Why is he suddenly fixated on me when there were literally hundreds in attendance? The death happened after arresting me. I was literally with him. Surely, he's not that hung up that I left him alone in his bed four years ago.

Then again, men can be petty once their fragile egos are broken.

I continue to ignore him as I flip to the next page in my book. I can feel his intensity as he watches me, and it fucking bothers me more than it should. He reaches out a hand, and I watch as he picks up the fork, begins digging into my leftover pancakes, and takes a giant bite.

I close my book, my calm facade finally snapping. "Are you lost? Do they not give you enough work at the station that you have to resort to harassing civilians?"

"Nope. Not lost," he says, taking another bite. "I have plenty of work to do, but I always make time for things I prioritize. These are good pancakes; I can see why you come here often."

My gaze narrows. How does he know I come here often? He smirks, and it's answer enough that he's clearly been following me. It makes my skin crawl. The waitress is looking over at us curiously. I usually don't come here with anyone, and now I'm forced to sit in uncomfortable silence as he finishes my breakfast.

I'm not going to ask why I'm a priority when I think that's what he's hoping I'll bite at. The more I jump into his provocations, the more he's winning.

He smiles once he's done. It's a blinding, arrogant smirk that I'm sure makes him a lady killer.

Unfortunately, his charm doesn't work on me. It might've once when I was looking for someone to lose my virginity to since I was absolutely forbidden by Aunt

Anya to auction my virginity to the highest bidder in one of Dutton Taylor's virginity auctions. And this guy was easy on the eyes and easy for the taking. Turns out it's come back to haunt me four years later.

"I'll be seeing you around, Hope. Thanks for the date," he says, throwing a twenty on the table and then striding out without another word. My gaze practically bores a hole in his back as he leaves.

Fuck this. And fuck him.

What does he think he's doing, tormenting me? It's definitely making me uneasy, having him show up all the time. The fact that he's very good-looking is beside the point.

Grabbing my bag with clear determination, I call my driver to take me to my cousin's house. I know I'll find at least one of them at this time of day, and if fate smiles down on me, they'll both be there. Because I have a problem I think only they can assist me with—without my father finding out, of course.

Braxton Hero sniffing closely is a liability around my family. There are literally a million things they could pin on any of my family members, except my mother, of course, and I refuse to be the reason why my family name is receiving unwanted attention. I can handle this myself. I don't want my father to think I need to run to him for help on something I've managed to get myself into, especially after pleading my independence for so many years.

I knock on the door several times. As I'm waiting, I

notice a letter on the front porch, and I pick it up. It's my cousin, Ford, who answers the door. I hand him the envelope as I push past him. The moment I get a whiff of bacon, I know Hawke is here too. It's Ford's house, but Hawke can't often go even a few days without his twin.

The two of them work for the Italian mafia boss, Eli Monti, and were personally trained by my Aunt Anya, who is as ruthless as they come. If anyone can help me with this request, it's them.

Technically, they aren't my blood cousins. My auntie adopted them when they were teenagers. I know not to trust many men in this world, but I do trust both of my cousins. Because I know they'd do anything for me.

Ford seems surprised to see me but rolls with it. I follow the smell of bacon, noticing a black cat sleeping in the hallway. That's definitely new, but I'm not going to ask questions about the peculiarities of what they get up to in their spare time or how they've started adopting strays.

Hawke smiles as I enter the kitchen, and he starts plating up food. I want to tell him that I've already eaten, but Hawke will serve it anyway. He always tells me if I eat more protein, I might get taller. The guy's an asshole.

I politely accept the offered food, then just push it around on my plate.

"Is everything okay?" Ford asks.

I finally gather the courage to voice the reason I came

here. "I want you to teach me how to kill someone," I state.

They both look at me in the same predatory way. They're both demons in their own right, feared for their bloodlust and gory ways of executing people.

"Sorry, what did you say?" Ford blurts.

"Oh, yes, little red, we totally can. As long as Uncle Alek won't remove our balls because of it," Hawke gushes, and it's exactly the response I expected from him. He's always up to no good, which is exactly why I came to them.

"I don't want my father to not find out," I tell him with a smile.

"Not find out?" Ford asks me. "You know who your father is, right?"

I push my glasses up my nose and nod my head. "If we can keep it between us, that would be great," I say.

"Okay, so who are we helping you kill?" Hawke asks. I swear he's going to start bouncing excitedly.

"*I* want to be the one to kill him. Just teach me how." I need to do this myself.

"Who knew there was a little bit of devil in there," Hawke jokes as Ford opens the envelope I give him. "Who pissed you off? And why do you want to kill him?"

"He's a detective. And he lied to me about who he is." That is somewhat true. I mean, he didn't exactly announce who he was the first time we met years ago, neither did I but that's not the point. But I don't want my cousins asking further about my association with him so if I say I didn't know who he was, it's the truth. Now that I do, I realize he's problematic.

They both stare at me.

"You want to kill a police officer?" Ford asks.

"Yep." I nod. "Dead."

Hawke whistles, seemingly impressed. He looks at his arms. "I actually have goosebumps because of how proud I am."

We both look at Ford expectantly. He's usually the one of calm guidance, but when I face him, he's paled, his face stricken.

I go to ask if he's okay, but he closes the envelope and is already leaving the room.

"Hey!" Hawke yells out after him. "We're not done here. What the fuck was in that note?"

A cold dread fills my stomach, and I don't know what's happened, Ford leaving abruptly isn't entirely new, but it just feels off...

"Nothing. Don't follow me," he yells back, a quiet calm, but that's when he's the deadliest.

"What the fuck?" Hawke curses at the entrance of the kitchen, looking out after him. I can tell he's unsettled.

"Do you think everything's okay?" I ask Hawke quietly.

His eyebrows furrow, and I can tell he's concerned. He pulls out his phone, and I see the name *Lover* appear as he rapidly messages. He sends a message, and I only catch a glimpse of the words tracking Ford as he says. "So, how do you want to kill him? Because if it's a crowbar you want to use, you'll have to wait for the rude asshole who just abandoned us to get back since that's his specialty," Hawke says.

"Crowbar?" I'd heard stories about my cousins. I've never seen them in action, but rumors circulate very quickly. Especially when they come with a warning. Ford prefers to fight with two crowbars, while Hawke, the brute who eats way too many carbs and spends the majority of his time either lifting weights or fucking women, uses spiked gloves.

"How about guns?"

Hawke's eyebrows perk up and he looks at me now after the text is sent. I can tell he's unsettled by Ford leaving.

"You're serious about wanting to kill this guy? Why? I know it's in the family business, but you're not a killer, Hope." He says, but I can tell he's only half listening.

I bite my bottom lip because although I'm surrounded by killers for family members, I've never come for help to anyone for something like this. Me asking this is as abnormal as me enjoying being in a roomful of people. But if Braxton has made it his fixation to sniff too closely to me for a murder he's trying to pin on me, I know it'll put my family in jeopardy. I know they can look after themselves, but I don't want to bring this trouble to my doorstep. Or my mother, for that matter. I don't want to lose my independence because if I can't protect myself and my family. If that happens, then my father will no doubt revoke all the freedom I've acquired in the last year.

It's just one detective, right? It can't be that hard, and if I do fuck up, which I won't, then at least I know I can depend on my cousins to help me.

Hawke receives a message, and his eyebrows furrow. Whatever business Ford has himself involved with it's not good. Even if I did have an answer for Hawke, I don't think he'd hear me right now.

"Go Hawke. Something's wrong, right?" I say. My cousins are always involved in shenanigans. Not the good kind and often leaving a trail of bodies behind them, but one thing is for certain—they're always together.

"We're not done with this, little red. I'll teach you how to shoot, okay?" he says, pulling his keys out of his pocket and racing down the hallway. I hear him call out from the door. "Close up when you leave!"

I pick at my plate of food. Looking down at the small cat, who stares up at me as if knowing.

I wonder if this was a mistake. Sure, I'm pissed at Braxton, but is killing a police officer the answer?

My gut tells me yes.

Always yes to protect myself and family.

But maybe I'm in over my head on this one.

CHAPTER 8

Braxton

I'm exhausted. The cases keep piling up with this serial killer. Two nights ago it was a man on the outskirts of town: no cameras or witnesses. The guy's phone and wallet were missing, and even when we tracked his digital prints, there was no indication as to who he might have been meeting out near the bridge where he was drowned or why.

Had the killer left his body in the river, it would have floated downstream and not been found for days, if at all. But they'd had the balls to pull him back out and leave him on the riverbank.

It doesn't make sense. Whoever this person is, it's like they're almost screaming to be caught. Or they've become so arrogant that they don't even care about gloating to the police. Worse, it's creating too much paperwork.

The only reason we assume it's the same killer is because of the victim. He was reported two days ago to authorities for harassing a woman in her mid-twenties. The man got off on the charges with the right lawyers involved.

Someone certainly thinks of themselves as a hero, which makes them the deadliest kind of vigilante.

I look down at my phone, at the photos taken from today by the man I hired to trail Hope Ivanov. I haven't had a chance to see her all day, but that doesn't mean I haven't been tracking her every move. Photos come through of her at the airport, coming off her family's private plane. She was in Rome for less than forty-eight hours, and now she's back in town. Keeping tabs on how often she's here is the tricky part. I've downloaded her schedule of international shows, but it's not a bullet-proof schedule to track.

I haven't yet expressed to my partner, Lucas, my interest in the Ivanov daughter until I know what I want to do with her. For now all I can do is watch.

Walking into my studio apartment, I throw my car keys on the counter and then remove my gun and store it safely. I start to undress, pulling my shirt over my head first. Then, I pause in the middle of the room.

Something feels off. And it's glaringly obvious. A black box sits at the end of my bed. I silently search the apartment. Intuitively, I know no one else is in my home, but I have a top-of-the-line security system, so how the fuck did someone break in without setting off the alarms?

I pull out my phone and bring up the security cameras to find they were all down for precisely twenty-four minutes. Who the fuck was in my apartment, and how did they know how to disable my security cameras?

I eye the box. I know I should call it in. It could be a bomb, for fuck's sake, yet unfortunately, curiosity has always been a weakness of mine.

I lift the lid to reveal something reflective. Glass? I pull out the sculpture, appreciating its exquisite detail. *What the fuck?* It's a replica of a crime scene image from the club where the man was poisoned weeks ago. The detail is uncanny. There's no message or further tidbit in the box.

My jaw clenches as a set of innocent blue eyes come to mind. Is it hyper fixation, or is my gut telling me something? I know Hope does sculptures in clay and not glass, but for some reason, I just feel like this is somehow connected with her. Everything keeps coming back to her, but I'm certain it's more to do with personal intrigue than anything. Her family is woven through the underworld, and I'm hellbent on making her confess her sins. Catching someone like Hope Ivanov is like drawing out the rest of the hornets' nest. This goes beyond simply a serial killer, and that's my lead in.

What makes this matter worse is this sculpture is identical to a photo taken by our forensic team, which means our data has been compromised. Who the fuck is hacking our system for morbid inspiration? And why leave this in *my* apartment?

This is personal. The killer knows I'm on their tail. But what's the meaning behind the sculpture?

Deep down in my gut, I fucking know this has something to do with Hope. She may appear innocent, but I know she has something darker lurking beneath those pretty blue eyes. And I really want to find out what it is.

You're letting your fixation with her impair your judgment, a more logical part of me says, but I push it away because receiving a glass sculpture as a gift is new. And the only thing I've changed in my routine over the last few weeks is following Hope Ivanov.

CHAPTER 9

Hope

He's back again. It's been almost two weeks since our last run-in, and I honestly thought he'd gained some common sense about snooping around a killer's daughter. Alas, here we are. Braxton takes the exact same seat he took the last time he invited himself to join me at the café.

This time, I have an entire pancake left over, and he immediately picks up the fork and starts eating it. I don't bother telling him to stop because I don't think he'd listen. I simply purse my lips and stick to the tactic I've been using since he re-entered my life—I try my best to ignore him. Even though he's quiet while scarfing back the last of my breakfast, his presence is loud, screaming at me for attention. I fucking refuse to engage with him.

I scan over to the next page. "Hey!" I yell as he snatches my book from my hands. I'm too slow as he angles himself across from me and begins to read. One of his eyebrows raises curiously, and he glances up at me.

"Thought it would be about glass sculptures," he says as he lowers the book.

"What?" I quickly snatch it from his grasp.

"Are we playing dumb?" He tsks at me. "Didn't take you for a dumb person."

"Thank you?" I roll my eyes. "I can see why you're so popular with the ladies now." He smirks and clasps his hands together on top of the table, studying me in a way that pisses me off.

"Did you miss me?" he asks.

"No." Not to say that I didn't expect him to show up at any moment. A part of me was relieved when he never did, while the other part was wondering when he would. Because one thing I'm coming to learn about Braxton Hero is that he's equally as beautiful and persistent as he is stupid and arrogant.

"I would really like to know how you got into my apartment," he says.

I sigh, frustrated. "Whatever are you talking about?"

"I think you know exactly what I'm talking about."

We sit here in a stare-off, and I shake my head in disbelief.

"Whether you want to believe it or not, Detective Hero, you're the only one of the two of us who is fixated on the other. I don't have the time or mental space to devote to you. It comes with the territory of running a successful career," I jab. "I'm certain there are plenty of criminals out there who want to break into your apartment. You aren't exactly the type to make friends."

"I seemed friendly enough to entice you into my bed once upon a time," he says. Heat flushes my cheeks, but I don't look away, holding my ground.

"To be frank, it was more your appearance that enticed me. And you didn't talk much that night. You speaking is what ruins it all for me now."

He smirks, leaning in to study me closer. "You think you're untouchable, don't you?"

"Excuse me?"

"I'm sure you're Daddy's little girl, and you think no one can touch you."

I scoff. "Are you done? You're really grasping at straws if all you can do is antagonize a woman minding her own business, reading a book in a diner, wouldn't you say?"

"Where were you before this?" he questions.

"Is this an interrogation?" I bite back.

"Just a simple question."

I don't want to answer the asshole. And, technically, I don't have to. But it's not hard for anyone to piece together my whereabouts at these hours. "I was in my studio, working on that sculpture you broke. Should I be sending a bill to your supervisor and mentioning how you invaded my space unwarranted?"

He should know better than to underestimate someone, especially in his profession.

I'm more than happy to play his game. In fact, I hope when I actually kill him, the experience will be humbling for him. *Killing him.* It's not as unsettling as I thought it might be, especially even when sitting across from him. If anything, it makes me feel powerful, almost superior, as if I'm in it for the long game, stalking my prey. Is this how my father and cousins feel when they choose a victim? Or do they just do without a care for who the person even is?

"Does everyone see this side of you?" he asks. "Or am I the only lucky one?"

I sigh, realizing any type of enjoyment is long forgotten, as I stand and grab my book, tucking it into my bag.

"I have places to be," I tell him, throwing a twenty on the table.

He stands and blocks my path. I release a furious sigh.

"Where are you going?" he asks.

I glare up at him. Why is this fucker so tall? I seriously need to start wearing heels more often. But unless it's for an event, I just couldn't be bothered.

"Is that a police question?" I ask, resting my hand on my hip.

"No, just a general one," he replies casually but makes no move to clear out of my path.

Fine. If he wants to play, we'll play.

"I have a meeting with my cousin, actually. He's

teaching me how to shoot a gun," I inform him with a sweet smile, letting my eyes scream how much I can't wait to fucking kill him. He's like a pesky bug that won't go away. I can't help but grin at the idea of it and how offended he might be if he could see the same visual.

He seems to pick up on some of the tension. "I'm surprised your father hasn't already taught you. Since he's a murderer and all."

"Those are some very damning accusations." I tsk.

"Why don't I show you how to shoot? You know, as I'm an upstanding citizen and all, wouldn't your parents approve of someone as skilled as me to teach their daughter how to handle a weapon?"

"Often, when a man guarantees me about their skills, I later discover they're *lying.* So, no, thank you."

I go to step past him, but he blocks my path.

"Come on, it could be fun. I can teach you."

How funny it is that the person I want to kill is offering to train me to take him out?

If only he knew I had every intention of killing him. And I was right to assume I will have to take him out because I was certain Braxton will only escalate his appearances, and he's doing exactly that. It'll only get worse over time, of that much I'm certain. The longer I let him sniff around, the more likely my father will find out, which I absolutely cannot let happen—not before I've dealt with the situation myself. My freedom hangs on the line here.

I offer another sickly-sweet smile. "No, thank you."

I can't wait to turn the tables on him.

"Why not?" he asks. I don't have to answer, so this time, I manage to step around him and head toward the door.

"Oh, I just thought I should make a point that it's not only my father who's protective of me. So if I were you, I'd leave me alone."

"Is that a threat?" he all but growls.

With a wink, I simply say, "Goodnight, detective," before calling my driver.

I'm still not entirely sure what Braxton wants with me, but the more time I spend with him, the more I want to fuck him as much as I want to kill him. Because, damn, he has no right looking like that when he's a fucking cop.

CHAPTER 10

Hope

"Fuck, little red. I hate to tell you this, but you suck." Hawke takes the gun from my hand as if it's contaminated by my efforts of shooting. We've been practicing aiming and shooting at an old car for close to an hour. Hawke's enthusiasm went from "no one gets it right on their first shot" to "not everyone is a natural" to "how the fuck do the bullets keep curving? Do you have a repellent aim?"

I sigh.

We're both defeated today, not that Hawke will talk about his situation but I found out from Ivy. Only a few weeks ago, Ford almost died from being poisoned. Apparently, he and Billie, who is one of my best friends, have been hooking up for over a year behind everyone's backs, and they got into a sticky situation. He drank the poison to save her, survived, and now they're "official" or whatever. It's strange to see them together. Not that it looks wrong in any way.

They're complete opposites, but I think someone as calm as Ford would be good for my best friend Billie, with a short fuse. I hadn't seen her until after missing her brother, Dutton Taylors wedding due to having an international engagement myself.

Whatever happened that day, Hawke seems off since. Most likely sulking because his brother, his ride or die, is now paired up, and he can't spend all of his waking time with him. But I suspect it's something past that. He's still carefree, but at times, it almost feels forced. Or maybe I'm reading into it too much, considering how intense the situation is. Billie didn't want to talk about it too much, either. We had a girls' movie night after the wedding with Ivy as well and she was satisfied to simply cuddle up together. If she doesn't want to talk, I'm not going to force her. Besides I'm not the best when it comes to those kinds of conversations.

I'm not too good with a gun either, apparently.

"Maybe you should try something else that doesn't involve aiming?" he suggests.

I glance back to the car, where he drew a huge bullseye on the side, and bite my lip. I missed it every time. In fact, I think I hit the car itself only a handful of times.

"I'm sure I'm a late bloomer," I say, rubbing my sweaty palms on my pants. I hate not being good at something. It's been so long since I've failed at something that it leaves a bitter taste in my mouth. "Show me again."

Hawke raises a brow. "I don't want to shit on your hopes and dreams, little red, but some people just don't have a killer instinct." He lifts the gun with one hand, maintaining eye contact as the arrogance oozes off him in waves. "I'm gifted." He winks as he pulls the trigger without looking. When I turn to check the target I've been missing miserably this whole time, I see he's hit the dead center of the bullseye.

"Why can't I do that!" I exclaim, throwing my hands in the air. It really shouldn't be this hard to try to kill someone with a gun.

"Talent," he says cockily, with a shrug that's anything but humble. He's self-assured, upfront, and, for the most part, easy to get along with. It makes it difficult to see him as a killer when he's always been like an older brother to me, especially in situations like now.

I grab a bottle of water and sip from it. How many times am I going to have to do this? Sure, there are other ways to kill Braxton, but I'm not going to resort to brute strength since I'm self-aware enough to know I'm tiny compared to him, and it also seems like a lot of effort. My mind starts whirring.

"You know who has the best aim out of all of us?" Hawke says, and I'm surprised he's willing to give anyone else credit. "Jewel. That woman..." He whistles. "She could shoot you from a mile away."

"That doesn't help me," I seethe. And while it might be great to spend some time with Jewel, I doubt her husband, the mafia head, Eli, is willing to loan her to anyone. Besides, I think this is good for Hawke. Not that he'll ever admit it.

But everyone is slowly starting relationships. They're maturing in ways I don't think Hawke and I ever will.

I'm certain neither of us has ever seriously considered being in a relationship. I eye my cousin from the side. He's texting someone, most likely a woman. I definitely don't have to ask him because I already know the answer.

He pockets the phone and then starts to pack up the guns. "I think that's enough for today. I don't want you to feel discouraged. It was your first day."

"You're not a good liar."

He smirks. "You were fucking awful, and I think you should give up now. But I'm willing to entertain it for a few more practice sessions until you come to that conclusion yourself."

I sigh. "Thanks for trying to lie to make me feel better."

"Why don't you ask your father to train you at home? He's a great shot."

"No."

Hawke doesn't look in my direction, but I can hear

the teasing in his voice as he says, "Little miss independent now, I see."

No way am I asking my father to teach me to shoot. He would be curious why I have interest in it all of a sudden, and he would do everything in his power to delve behind the reason as to why.

The burner phone in my bag buzzes. I take it out, making sure Hawke can't see the message from the unverified number. I smile when a crime scene photo appears, showing a man who was drowned to death. He's pale, and I study the complexities of his lifeless body, immediately inspired as to what I'll be creating next.

I have a hobby that I've never told a single soul about. Something I know is morbid, twisted, and fucked up. I create sculptures of the dead.

It excites me.

It challenges me.

My curiosity started after I saw my first corpse. The body was being removed from my aunt's house by a couple of her men. He had a stiletto heel puncturing his throat, his eyes wide open. My father belatedly ushered me into another room, most likely terrified of my mother finding out. It became our little secret. I was ten years old at the time, but instead of being frightened, I was curious.

It's not hard to find a dead body when you live in the world I do. I would take sneaky photos here or there when my family wasn't so quick to cover my eyes.

I see the world in shapes and forms, and the dead weight of a lifeless body has a beauty about it. It's nothing but a vacant shell. The remains of where a soul once resided. And each death has a story.

I can't have anyone discovering this guilty pleasure. Not only is it incriminating, but people would see a part of me that's best left in the dark. They would look at me weird and it'd most likely ruin my career. So I stick to my socially acceptable sculptures for the public eye, and in my spare time, when no one knows where I am or what I'm doing, I capture the beauty of the dead.

When I was fifteen, I started learning glass sculpting but never pursued it seriously. Not for my sellable pieces, anyway. But that skillset is mostly a secret. My parents know I had a tutor for three months, but I let her go and taught myself thereafter. I've kept this little part of me to myself. Until last night.

Granted, I didn't expect the homicide detective to assume I was the one who left the gift in his apartment. Maybe I was too confident in having my friend Ivy hack his surveillance, and something went wrong.

But I wanted to toy with him, just as he's been toying with me. I was hoping it might even spook him a little. That's why I hired someone specifically to hack into the police's systems and send me photos of bodies.

I just wasn't expecting Braxton to clue in so quickly, especially when he clearly has no hard evidence. But it intrigues me how his mind works. Denying my talents and not taking credit for my work can sometimes be hard, and he's the first person I've ever shared my secret art with.

I'd thought, *why not dance with him a little before I put a bullet in his brain?*

Or not, maybe. Considering how shocking it would be that I actually hit my target.

"Little red, you know you can always hire someone. Hell, tell me who the detective is, and I'll do it for free as an early birthday present," he suggests as we walk back to his car.

"No, this one, I need to deal with myself. It's personal," I tell him. He opens the trunk and loads the cases inside. The sound of sirens reaches our ears, and I freeze as Hawke draws one of the guns. I'm quick to hold down his hand as he tries to point it in the direction of the sleek black sedan coming toward us with its siren blaring.

"Don't," I hiss.

My blood boils. Fuck, Braxton is persistent.

"You do realize my car is full of illegal guns right now," he comments. "But you're in charge, little red." He places the gun back in the trunk and then slams the lid down. He's most likely got another two guns on his person, which is why he seems so calm, leaning against the car with his legs crossed at the ankles as Braxton pulls over and steps out of the sedan.

"Stalking is a crime, isn't it?" I say to Braxton, who simply smirks as he approaches. This asshole actually thinks he's God's gift. It's insufferable, and I'd be tempted to grab a gun and shoot him right now if I didn't already know how fucking bad my aim is.

Braxton and Hawke size one another up, both sporting cocky expressions, as if this is the most normal interaction in the world. But they're both beasts parading around as men. Fuck, this is bad. If Hawke reacts, he will end up murdering Braxton, and that thought infuriates me because *I* want to kill the asshole.

"Thought I'd take in the scenery," Braxton says with a smile.

Hawke looks around the barren land, then says, "I think it'll look better with a touch of red."

"I couldn't agree more," Braxton says.

I huff at the amount of testosterone filling the air.

"Are you following me?" I demand of Braxton as I stand in front of Hawke, making a clear message that neither of them is to start shooting or exchanging blows. The last thing I want is to give Braxton more of a reason to trail me.

"Yes," he says matter-of-factly. Of course, he is. I can't see his crystal-blue eyes behind the black sunglasses, but I know when he's staring at me intently. "I'm making sure I don't get any more unexpected items delivered to my home. This seemed like the most practical approach."

"Does someone want to explain to me what the fuck is happening?" Hawke snaps. "I don't know how to tell you this, buttercup, but Hope is a very dear cousin of mine. Our family is extremely protective. We wouldn't want you to suddenly disappear because of a misunderstanding, would we?"

"No misunderstanding here," Braxton says with a lethal smile, and I know he's purposely antagonizing Hawke. He's so fucking good at pushing my buttons, and Hawke is someone who can go from zero to one hundred flat. I put my hand against his chest as he changes his stance.

"What's in the car?" Braxton asks, nodding to it.

"Do you have a search warrant?" Hawke bites back. When Braxton doesn't answer, Hawke smiles, shakes his head, and gets in the car. "Little red, get in."

"Little red?" Braxton asks curiously, and I can feel his intimate gaze tracing over me again. I ignore him and get in the car. It's nice to see that Hawke sometimes has a brain or cares to listen. Though I'm sure, this has more to do with not wanting to show me what he really is beneath the mask.

Hawke doesn't waste any time as he revs the engine and slowly backs up. A little tingle of curiosity makes me question what Braxton might look like if he got hit by the car and died. I haven't seen that type of death yet.

I push the morbid inspiration down.

When Hawke drives past Braxton, he says out the window, "I wouldn't show your face near her again."

Braxton raises a brow, his deadly energy radiating off him. "I'm certain she's as curious about me as I am her," he says to Hawke, then he focuses his gaze on me. "I'll be seeing you real soon, Shortcake."

I flip him off and watch his reaction in the rearview mirror.

Hawke's jaw is grinding as he growls, "That's the detective, isn't it?"

"Yes," I reply, still eyeing Braxton as he slides back into his car.

"Oh damn. You got yourself into some hot shit, little red." He laughs.

I'm actually shocked at his reaction, but a small part of me feels almost gleeful. Like I've been accepted into some secretive little murderous group. Instead of him telling me to run to my father or ask for help, he's accepting my terms to deal with it myself. And I'm grateful for it.

"It's going to be fun watching you get out of this," he says, checking the rearview mirror as he skids out onto the main road. "Though I really did want to hit him with my car."

I try to hide the humor I find in the fact that we both had the same thought. Maybe I'm not so different from the killers in my family. And it's a thrilling notion, not that I would ever admit it out loud.

"Just take me home," I tell him.

CHAPTER 11

Braxton

I watch as the car drives off. There's no point in hiding the fact that I was tracking her. After all, she basically handed me the information about her wanting to learn to shoot as if I wouldn't be curious about it. Because why would someone who pretends to be so pure and innocent need to use a gun? I know she provoked me on purpose, trying to be lethal in her own way, but it only inflames my curiosity.

I wonder how deep a blood bond goes. I want to know how deadly the daughter of a killer might be. I can feel the gentle caress of her inner darkness every time I look into her blue eyes, and it calls to me like sin and destruction. I'm a fool for being charmed and drawn to her temptation, but what makes it so deliciously sweet is I don't even think she knows she's doing it.

She's changed a lot since I first met her. Although

Hope is still reserved and quiet, there's a fire behind those eyes. That's what drew me to her in the first place. There's a part of her she wants to hide from the rest of the world, and for some reason, I can't rest until I understand everything about her brilliant mind.

I should know better than to continue pursuing her. It could impact my job. I'm hiding behind the excuse of investigating her, which I am actually doing, but it goes beyond that. *I want her.*

I want to be so deeply embedded in her thoughts that the beautiful little monster unravels for me.

It's sick and twisted, and I don't entirely understand it, but I can't stop. It's the same curiosity one has when they see a fire and have to decide whether to let it burn out in its own time or add more fuel and find out how much it's able to consume and destroy in its path.

Unfortunately, I've never been great at dousing flames. I'm fascinated by human behavior, and I find it the most delicious when it borders on the edge of losing humanity completely. I hope she burns the whole fucking house down.

Trouble. That's what she is to me.

My partner is calling, but I ignore him. Technically, I'm supposed to have today off, but that means shit to us when there's an ongoing case. He's also picked up on my keen interest in Hope Ivanov. But for now, I have every intention of keeping that investigation private.

I get back into my car, smirking at my exchange with

Hawke Ivanov. He's fucking massive, built like a giant, and yet I can't help but want to provoke him. The second he hits me, I'll imprison him, and I can't wait to see how Hope might react, how she'll beg and plead for me to set him free. The idea of that power and control over her excites me.

It's the first time I've taken pleasure in a personal pursuit in a long time. I open my phone and look through her Instagram page. I'm certain she has someone running it for her, but I don't care. I look at the candid shots. Then the upcoming events she's attending, curious about her day-to-day life.

The minute I was old enough to know what I wanted to do, no one was stopping me from becoming who I am today. With my home life completely fucked up because of my mother being a drug addict and prostitute, I learned very quickly the value of the lifestyle I wanted. It was easy for me to identify patterns in people, and I was intrigued by corrupt minds. It makes them a mystery until they're not.

It wasn't a surprise when my sister turned into a drunk at sixteen, and I was surrounded by their disastrous nature with men who were bigger than me. The bastards often hit them and me when I tried to defend them. But they'd both always went crawling right back to their abusers, reprimanding me for intervening.

I was fourteen when I first decided to punish men like that and hold them accountable for their actions. I'd told my mother I wanted to join law enforcement, and she kicked me out of the house the same day and told me never to come back, that she would never have a cop living under her roof.

I start the engine of the car, surprised at my trip down memory lane. It'd been a long time since I revisited any of this, which meant Hope was shifting something within me. That gave her too much power already.

It's funny how someone like me is considered an enemy to her and her family, yet I'd done plenty of good saving people in the line of duty. But perhaps they looked down their noses at those who needed protection instead of protecting themselves.

The only reason I survived is because a friend's family took me in for two years, letting me live in their attic. I picked up multiple jobs to save up money and create the life I have now. I will never ask anything of anyone again. And I certainly am not here for her to abuse all over again.

I wonder if it might've been different for me if I'd had some kind of protection when I was younger. I doubt it. It was only when my mother threw me out that I discovered my father was thrown in jail because of a corrupt cop. I later delved into his crimes, which he deserved to be behind bars for, but my mother was in the habit of pardoning men who treated her and other women like shit.

Truth be told, I don't even know if he was my real

father. His name wasn't on my birth certificate, and my mother informed me she did it out of spite because she found him fucking some other woman when she was pregnant with me.

Not that it matters. I'm glad he wasn't on my birth certificate because it might've impeded my ease of transitioning into my current position; being connected to criminals is definitely not a great start for a cop.

The fewer people who know where I come from, the better. And so I've purposely gone out of my way to excel and surpass all expectations. Brilliant, they call me, blowing smoke up my ass. Very few of my peers tried to associate with me when that brilliance didn't equate to friendliness. I'm not here to make friends. I'm here to bring powerful people to their knees, to see how many enemies I can collect by outsmarting them at their own game.

Sure, a therapist may have mentioned I might have an authority complex, but I could suggest the same thing for her if I psychoanalyzed her in return. I didn't disagree with her, but I also never went back to her.

As if the devil himself has a sick sense of humor, my mother's name appears on my phone screen. I ignore it as I pull out onto the road, Hope and her cousin long gone. My mother only calls when she wants something. I've only seen her once in the last four years because she was arrested for trying to prostitute herself to an undercover cop.

It wasn't surprising that she used my name to get herself out of trouble. I ended up having to pay off the police officer who arrested her, which I fucking hate. I don't like owing anyone favors or getting mixed up in things that might ruin my job. It turns out that having a cop in the family is useful to her after all. Not that she ever said thanks.

I haven't spoken to my sister since I was kicked out of the house. I'm pretty sure she's married to a man who is probably also a drunk and cheats on her constantly. I don't know why people commit to one another with no desire to remain faithful. Marriage and relationships are complete bullshit.

I never really understood that concept. If you want to fuck someone else, leave the person you're with first. It's pretty fucking simple. Or better yet, just don't enter into a relationship.

My partner calls again, and I sigh, finally answering it. "Hey, you're not at your desk this morning. Where are you?" he asks.

"Shouldn't you be enjoying your day off?" I ask, avoiding his question. It's not like we aren't usually out on the field.

"Yeah, well, I'm just going over these details of the most recent murder. It's a fucking mess, and the chief is breathing down our necks for answers."

"Isn't he always?" I droll. Admittedly, this one's been stretching out for longer than it should, and we still can't confirm that it's only one killer, even though my gut says it is.

"Come on, man, you're busting my balls. Do you have any more hunches? Your instincts are usually on point. I propose we try to get some spies out there among the main underworld families. It might not be one of them, but surely, if there's a serial killer on the loose, they'll know about it. We need a lead, and where better to start than the criminals themselves."

My eyebrows shoot up. That's fucking bold of Lucas. I still haven't told him that I'm looking into Hope Ivanov personally, but this line of thinking is risky. It's why I didn't want to get him involved. "What? You know these families are tough to break into. The last time someone attempted that was a year ago. We never found the body of the officer after disappearing not even a week later."

That's the fucking truth. We don't know who to trust, and there are always things that slide under the radar or go missing. Once, Lucas and I went directly to the chief about the Monti family, and suddenly, the evidence went *poof!* Instead of pursuing it, we read the message loud and clear.

"I have two friends. They're ex-military. I trust them," he says.

If I weren't already known by the Monti's, Taylor's, and Ivanov's, I'd go undercover myself. But it's risky.

"Why now?" I ask. "There's so many hoops we have to jump through to do this above board."

"We don't tell the chief." He says, and this shocks me and I can't help but smile.

"Lucas I dare say I've rubbed off on you for the better."

"Shut the fuck up. This is going too far. I can't figure it out, and I'm sick of losing sleep over this case. I need my life back, and this killer needs to be behind bars."

I can hear how tired he is and understand how frustrating it is not to figure it out. He's getting desperate, which sometimes can become messy.

"And who's paying them for this?" I question.

Lucas goes quiet. "I don't know yet. I have a little bit of savings..."

I laugh. "Lucas, we're detectives. We don't earn even close to enough to buy their loyalty when the families can buy them out so easily."

"I-I trust them," he splutters. This is bold for Lucas, showing he's at his wits' end. I don't exactly think it will work, but we've been going in circles.

"Fine. But I can't offer much money. It's risky, so I hope your men are as competent as you think because they might end up in a body bag."

"They know the risks. And they both owe me a favor."

"Who are you targeting first?" I ask.

"The Taylor's mostly focus on the sex industry, so I

figured I might as well begin with the bloodthirsty ones: the Monti's and Ivanov's."

I shake my head because I'm certain his men are going to end up dead in a matter of days. He can't send in two men to try and cut off the head of the snake that owns an entire den of vipers. *But I have to trust in my partner,* I remind myself.

I don't like the idea of them snooping around Hope when I've already decided she's my case, but they have no reason to target her when they'll go for the bigger fish instead. Either Alek or Anya.

"Good luck to them is all I'm going to say."

I hang up the phone. I'm after a serial killer, not a mysterious artist. Yet, I can't curb my curiosity about Hope Ivanov.

I laugh, remembering her shitty shots with the gun. Am I turning into a crazy man ensnared by a little she-devil?

One thing's for certain—she really does suck with a gun.

CHAPTER 12

Hope

I've flown out for a show in Paris, but not before I scheduled an elegant black box to be delivered to Braxton's address and left at his door. My stomach flutters, just imagining his reaction. Will he be mortified at the drowned man I took inspiration from? Can he appreciate the work that went into the piece? I know it's risky sending them to him, but I've never felt more alive, finally being able to show someone my secret art.

It doesn't make sense to me, but maybe I decided to take the risk because if anyone might appreciate a dead body in the same light I do, it's surely a homicide detective. It's a thrill to fuck with him in retaliation for him constantly popping up uninvited in my everyday life. We might move our pieces on the board differently, but we're both here to play a game, and I'm curious about the outcome.

Me killing him is the ultimate goal, but it excites me to think he might be the first person ever to corner me. Ford and I often play chess, but I'm understanding there's a very different thrill when playing with your life and reputation on the line.

"Angle yourself like this," the photographer instructs, and I'm brought back to my reality at the art exhibition. I've donated two pieces for charity, and although I specifically told my agent I didn't want to attend the event, I was told, as always, that it's a must if I want to keep my name out there and continue building my career. I wonder when enough is enough. When are people satisfied by their level of fame? If it were up to me, I wouldn't be in the spotlight at all. It's the shadows I prefer.

But I mimic her movement, running my hands down the very expensive gown I'm wearing. "Perfect. Now, lightly brush your fingers against the pearls on your neck. Oh, and let's remove the glasses. Do you mind? You have such beautiful blue eyes."

"It's a rarity to have red hair and blue eyes," my agent, Candice, interjects, peering over the photographer's shoulder at the photos that have already been taken. The photographer's assistant holds out her hand, and I hesitantly take off my glasses and pass them to her. Candice has suggested for years now I switch to contact lenses, but the glasses are like a security blanket for me. Another layer I can hide behind.

"Fantastic. Now, the pearls," the photographer

instructs again. I fake a smile, wishing I was in my pajamas, hanging with Billie and Ivy in their apartment for a movie night.

After a few more minutes, Candice and the photographer seem confident they have enough photos to choose from. The first thing I do is grab my glasses before I head into the showroom, Candice beside me, briefly going over the details of pieces and other artists I might be interested in connecting with. I'm not. Although I can admire others' work in all forms, it always seems lacking in creative genius to me, or maybe it's because what truly excites me is taboo.

I'm always on the go, traveling the world and appearing at events such as these, even though they exhaust me mentally and physically. I'm not a people person. While my mother can captivate any room she steps into, I'd rather be home alone, reading a good book.

There are times when I'm jealous of my mother's ability to be so comfortable in social situations. Then again, my auntie and my father never cared about wooing anyone, and I think I took a little bit—or a lot—of that from them.

I walk through the masses as hands reach for me, squeezing and congratulating me on my pieces. Their faces blur, their energies mingling and yapping at my own. I smile like I'm supposed to. But, for some reason, tonight is more exhausting, maybe because I really wish I were hanging out with the girls, or even the twins for that matter.

The moment I see a waitress walking around with a tray of champagne, I grab a glass, just to have something in my hand to try to deter people from grabbing at me. I prefer to come alone to events, instead of inviting any family or friends. I don't want them to be bored when I don't have it in me to keep them entertained. Also, I want to keep my worlds separate. With my family, I'm just Hope. Here, I'm treated like some kind of icon. These people don't know the real me. I'm seen but not really.

"Gosh, Hope, you outdid yourself," the lady who runs the gallery gushes as she places a hand on my shoulder and starts guiding me around. She goes on to tell me how this is the most successful exhibition she's had all year, and that we need to book again soon for the next one. Sometimes making the pieces can take up to a whole year, while others I can do in just a week. It just depends how complicated the piece is. That's something I learned early on, but I can't rush something if I love it.

I spend the next hour mingling with people as I hold the same glass of champagne, never even taking a sip. It's not that I don't like to drink. I obviously do. But not when I'm at a work function like this. I want to make sure I'm on my best behavior. And I have to fly home in a matter of six hours and tell my parents that I've decided

I'm going to quit college because I'm not really sure what I'm doing there when I know for a fact it's being an artist that truly makes me happy. Why am I even studying art when I'm already in the field? My mother thought it'd be great for me to build a network of like-minded people, but my lack of social skills hasn't changed. I have my core people, and that's all I need or want. I have made a few acquaintances while going to college, but I now feel like I've learned all I can, and it's starting to eat into the few hours I have free to myself.

My mother also mentioned how unique of an experience it could be. And although she wasn't wrong, I feel like it's outlasted its season. I don't think they'll be disappointed, per se, but I'm still nervous about having the discussion.

I don't manage to get any sleep in the hotel after the event, so I give up and pack my bag. I do, however, get a few hours of sleep on the private jet returning home. Candice is busily scanning posts and articles that have already begun filtering out. Notifications have already started blowing up my phone because of the photo they posted of me in my elegant dress. I couldn't feel more like day or night as I now wear jeans that accentuate my curves, a midriff-baring top, and a pair of heels. If Candice weren't there to remind me of my 'appearance,' I would've worn my sweats on the flight. But we'd learned photos like that can appear quickly in gossip articles. When I was a teenager, I used to be followed often as

Lena Love's daughter, but that form of invasiveness slowly receded as my artwork began to be highlighted. I also think my father blackmailed and terrified certain newspapers to not encroach on my personal space.

The flight feels long but gives me time to also daydream with ideas of what I'll create next.

When we land, I perk up in my seat when I spot my cousin waiting for me on the tarmac beside his car, which is very unusual.

It's never a good thing when you arrive, and evil is already waiting for you. Hawke smiles as I exit the plane.

"You miss me that much?" I ask curiously. He walks up to me and takes the bag from my shoulder.

I notice the way Candice scans him up and down. It's always the same with Hawke; women are cautious of him but often led by their libido. He gives her a slow once-over with a cocky grin, and I roll my eyes.

"Off-limits," I growl. His grin grows wider as he carries my bag to the car.

"Nothing's off-limits to me," he says arrogantly as he opens the passenger door for me. "Does your friend want a lift?"

She blushes and glances at the car waiting for her. "No, I have work to do. But thank you for the offer."

"That's a shame. Sometimes play is important," he drawls, and I glare daggers at the side of his head as I lower into the car.

When I twist around to look at her, she's blushing

and tucking a piece of her hair behind her ear. When she notices my attention, she averts her gaze and clears her throat. "Thank you for the offer, but I'll be going home."

"Your loss." Hawke shrugs.

"You need to stop," I hiss.

Hawke laughs as he rounds the hood and then drops into the driver's seat. We wait patiently as Candice's car slowly pulls away.

"Want to tell me what's happening? You don't have anyone in the trunk, do you?" I ask as Hawke begins driving. That devilish smirk lights up his face.

My stomach drops. Oh fuck. Does he? Does he have Braxton in there?

"No. But I'm here so we can have a little fun. You have me lying to Uncle Alek, little red, and you know that man puts the fear of God in me." He shivers.

Hawke is... unpredictable, so I'm a little concerned at what his idea of fun might entail.

"Where are you going with this, Hawke? And where's your brother?" They're almost always together.

He groans and looks out the window. "Off fucking Billie, probably." I try not to smirk. Hawke hates it that he doesn't have his brother to himself all the time now, but he secretly loves Billie—in a brotherly way. But he loves his brother the most. So, I find the whole dynamic quite interesting.

"And how does that involve me?" I quip.

"Isn't it obvious? I need someone to party with, and I figured you owe me a favor." I stare at him in disbelief.

"You're desperate if you're inviting me to go out with you." I'm the least inclined out of all of us to want to party. Surely, there was someone else he could take. It's the middle of the night, and I want to go to bed.

"I don't think you've exactly been lying to my father, so what reason is there for me to go anywhere with you? Especially somewhere with people."

"Ah, but that's where you're wrong. He asked if I'd seen you, and I told him yes. But I didn't tell him about the guns, so that means I lied to him." I can't help but laugh. He idolizes my father, so I know not telling him the full truth would kill him.

"That doesn't mean you were lying, Hawke," I say flatly.

"Whatever. It made me feel icky, okay?" His shoulders bunch.

I shake my head. "I'm not going out with you. Take me home."

"Damn, you really are ruining all the fun," he grumbles, turning in the direction of my house.

I wonder if this is Hawke's way of checking up on me. I appreciate the fact that he hasn't told my father that I have a detective following me and that Hawke also hasn't moved against my wishes. I can't help but smile. The big oaf might be unorthodox, but he's certainly protective.

"What if I agree to go out with you tomorrow as a thank you?"

He perks up in the same way I imagine a dog might. I've just locked myself into God knows what.

When we reach my home, he gets out, grabs my bag, and follows me inside. It might be midnight, but he doesn't care. He basically grew up here. Hawke struggles to be alone, so he often stayed at our house or Eli's place. He makes haste to the kitchen, dumping my bag at the entrance and then finding himself a snack.

My father walks out with a glass of whiskey in his hand, clearly uncomfortable at the fact that Hawke's here without him knowing. His discomfort is probably because he's not wearing his gloves; he's never around people without them on.

It's not that he has scarring or anything, but physically touching people causes an adverse reaction in him.

"I see you brought company," my father says, taking a sip of his drink.

"Figured you'd appreciate her getting home safe," Hawke says with a mouthful of food. This guy's always eating.

"Yes, thank you," my father grits as he comes over to me and presses a kiss to my forehead.

Hawke smiles at him like he won a prize.

"How was the event?" my father asks.

"Good."

I want to tell him about my decision regarding

college, but with my mother out of town, it's best to wait for her to return in a few days.

Hawke looks between us expectantly, never quite able to read a room. "You sure are lonely without your sidekick," my father observes. "Go to bed, Hawke." He turns and walks off, leaving me alone with Hawke.

"See, he loves me. He noticed how lonely I was." He shovels more food into his face and then pulls me in for a side hug. "I'm holding you to your word. I'll see you later, little red. I'll be here when the sun goes down tomorrow."

I expel a sigh. *What have I signed up for?* "Oh, and for future reference. My agent is off-limits, as is anyone else I work with, for that matter."

He smirks, devouring what looks like a plain white roll. "How presumptuous of you to think we don't already have history."

Hawke's laughing when he leaves, and I glare serious daggers at his back.

I don't know why he needs a sidekick to go out with, considering he ends up with women all over him. I've been out with him before, and while he might walk in with everyone else, he never leaves with us, so that means tomorrow night, I'll be on my own. Not if I invite someone, of course. He never said I couldn't. And I know one particular party girl who might be able to keep up with him. I pull out my phone and message Ivy. And then Billie. It depends, though, if Billie's willing to step away from Ford for a night; they've been tied at the hip ever since they became official.

Ivy, however, is free as a bird. She loves to party, and as a bonus, she draws most of the attention, which immediately puts me at ease.

CHAPTER 13

Braxton

I can't prove that it was her who left the "special gift" at my door. Not yet, anyway. She was in another country, so that makes it a little bit harder to point blame when she has that kind of alibi. But I just know it was her. I take the small statue from its box. Hues of blues mix with the glass as I turn it over in my hand, fascinated by the detail of the drowned man.

I still have no idea how she's getting the images from the forensic team. I plan on investigating the team members personally just in case any of them are leaking photos. But a woman like Hope Ivanov has enough money to afford any bribe or service, so it might be an outside source entirely.

The statue is impressive.

And grotesque.

The perfect display of the darkness pumping through her veins.

I know it's her. I just do.

I slide it under my bed with the other one. The detail in the art is quite intricate but also fucked up. How she keeps on getting hold of these cases that I'm working on is interesting to me. I always knew her family had deep connections, but that also means the connections run very deep in the police force.

I did plan to give Hope another surprise visit today at the diner, but I drive out to see my mother instead. I basically want to see if she was still alive.

She's been calling me non-stop, and she only ever does that when she needs something. I never entertain her, but I don't delete her number either. Maybe I have a morbid curiosity myself. I wouldn't go as far as to say I care about her, but there will always be an attachment between us, whether I like it or not.

I don't stop to talk to her. I just drive past the trailer she's lived in for almost fifteen years, and there she is, sitting out front on a ratty lawn chair, a bottle of beer in one hand and a cigarette in the other. It's like time hasn't changed at all except that her leathery skin drapes off her bones worse than ever. I don't remember a time when my mother ever had life in her, but as the years go by, it only worsens. I know one day she'll prove me right, continuing the same patterns I warned her about that will most likely put her in an early grave. But that's not today.

I don't know why I put myself through this shit to check up on her. Perhaps I've been feeling sentimental lately. I forsake Hope because of her family name, but at least she can stand proudly. I, however, have done everything I can to clean my hands of any association with my family.

I'm sure my therapist would love to talk about it, but I just don't care. Some things can't be changed, and some things are better left behind.

When I'm driving back into the city, my partner calls.

"It's ten in the evening. Shouldn't you be asleep?" I tease Lucas.

"I have an interesting update I thought might interest you."

"In the case?" I demand.

"Maybe. One of my friends is following two of the Ivanov's. You might be shocked to discover who's with them."

My grip tightens on the steering wheel because I don't like the idea of Lucas being perceptive to my interest in Hope. Then again, he probably has a personal grudge since her friend stole his wallet. He doesn't even have to say it's her because I know it is. "Where?"

"I'll send you the coordinates."

The location pops up on my screen. "You stay put. I'll investigate it myself. Send me a photo of your guy."

He does as I request, and a photo of a bald man with brown eyes comes up on the screen.

It looks like everything is in full swing already.

It takes me forty minutes to get there, and when I do, I don't give a flying fuck as I flash my badge and waltz in like I own the place. This club is one of the few establishments the Mafia families don't own. Which means this is neutral turf.

People call out and grumble complaints as I skip the line and walk inside.

The minute I enter, the music hits me hard, and I realize it's been a long time since I've had a night out. I don't even know the fucking music that's playing. The last time I had some fun on a night out was when I first crossed paths with Hope. I find it ironic how similar that night is to this one. I've fucked plenty of women since her, but I haven't taken interest in one like I did with her that night. The one woman that I should avoid.

The one woman who thinks she's out of my reach and circle of influence.

That night seems to be repeating itself because here I am, on my night off, in a fucking club, searching for a little redhead with glasses and a sinister smile.

I'm on the hunt for the little monster that rarely leaves her cage. And I'm hoping to catch her in the act of something damning.

CHAPTER 14

Hope

I couldn't get out of going to the club with Hawke, and believe me when I say I definitely tried.

So I enlisted the best sidekick one could ask for—Ivy. She's wearing a sparkly dress with knee-high boots. I've never understood Ivy and Hawke's relationship. They seem to get along like the rest of us but have a strange reverence for one another being... well, whores. They love it. They live for the chase and indulge in the catch.

Ivy's a party girl through and through, and when you mix that with Hawke, who likes to party just as hard, I know it's going to be a crazy night, and my batteries are already drained. Billie couldn't make it because of a work trip but, honestly, I'm happy for her and Ford. They're definitely in the honeymoon stage, so even if she was staying with him for the evening, I wouldn't be opposed to it. Hell, I'd much rather that for myself as well.

Ivy dressed me in a yellow fitted dress, which surprisingly works with my porcelain complexion, red hair, and blue eyes, but I can't help noticing she's dressed me up like a sunflower when I'm anything but. I usually stick to darker tones, but she was so excited and can sometimes step into dress-up doll mode, which I'm not entirely against. It takes the work out of it for me. I also put contacts in tonight.

It's not like anyone here will know who I am, and I'm not entirely against having a night out. I just somehow end up making stupid decisions when I've had a few drinks—case in point: running through Central Park with detectives chasing me down.

Hawke picks me and Ivy up from her and Billie's apartment, and the moment we walk into the club, Hawke guides us to the VIP area as if he has it booked out every single night. I don't really know the logistics behind him and these clubs' he frequents, but he always has an area waiting for him. We've only just sat down when a waitress appears with a bottle of tequila and shot glasses. And from out of nowhere, women flock to our booth to come sit on Hawke's lap.

"Wow, they're fast," I say to Ivy. But when I turn to her, she's looking over her shoulder at the dance floor below us. I can tell she's on the prowl. Damn, I might still end up on my own even though I brought her as my backup.

Ivy lives in the moment. It's the thing I like about her the most. She isn't afraid of who she is or how she presents herself to the world, and she unapologetically goes for what she wants.

"They're catering to his poor, broken heart now that Ford's practically married off." She bites her bottom lip, trying to hide the smile. "But who cares. We're not here for him. Let's drink." She pours numerous shots, and Hawke raises his eyebrows, impressed. We all lean in, clink our glasses in cheers, then throw back the tequila.

It fucking burns, but I embrace it.

Okay, this is going to be a fun night. I try to amp myself up, even though in the back of my mind, I'm thinking about the new book I started reading this morning. I take another shot.

Hawke entertains two beautiful women, and I can tell he's extra needy lately. He's so used to going everywhere and doing everything with Ford. I wonder if he feels the same way I do. I mean, he, Ivy, and I are basically the last three who aren't in any kind of relationship, and I'm pretty sure we're all overtly against it.

A group of four guys approach our table, and Hawke immediately stands to intimidate them away. Ivy, however, smiles at him with a look that promises imminent death if he doesn't stand down. "Boys, how's your evening? Care for a shot?" She dangles the tequila bottle.

We have another shot, and a round of cocktails is handed out. Hawke seems torn between keeping an eye on us and the women currently perching on his knees.

Ivy giggles at two of the men, and I can't help but notice she and Hawke are practically mirroring one another. It's almost as if it's a contest at this point. I'm not at all opposed to it, though, and I'm enjoying the subtle buzz of the alcohol feeding my system.

I stand and move to the balcony, watching everyone on the dance floor. I wonder what it would look like if someone came in and gunned them all down. I imagine the red spray of blood splattering the room. I hear the screams. I see the twisted expressions.

I quickly push down the invasive thoughts.

If anyone knew I had these thoughts, they'd lock me up, and I'd be shunned. Certainly not by my family, but I think my mother might be surprised, even disappointed.

The urge to pee comes on strong, so I collect my purse from the couch and tell Ivy I'm just going to the bathroom. She tries to follow me but I insist I'll only be a few minutes. She lets me go, turning her attention back to the man on her right. And that's something I've always appreciated about Ivy and Billie; they may only be a couple of years older than me, but they've never treated me as a child who couldn't look after myself.

Shooting a glance over my shoulder, I notice Hawke making out with one woman while his hand is down the shirt of the other. A king in his domain, most certainly. I look back to Ivy, who's sitting on one guy's lap while entertaining the other three. She looks like a goddess in a reverse harem. It's rather impressive.

I take two steps down the stairs, and when I look up, I freeze.

Braxton is staring up at me from the bottom of the staircase, those crystal-blue eyes darker than usual in the dimly lit club.

He's here, tracking me again. I wish I could say I'm surprised, but I'm not. The man's tenacious, especially coming here when I'm with my cousin. It brings me flashbacks of the night we first met, and I'm quick to shove those down because I am not going down memory lane with this asshole.

I hold my head high, descending the stairs and pretending like I don't know him. I can tell in my peripheral he's smirking, but I pay him no attention.

The moment I reach the bottom of the stairs, he clasps my wrist.

"You weren't attempting to walk by without saying hello, were you?"

My gaze snakes over to his, and I'm forced to look up through thick eyelashes, even when wearing heels. I try to pull my hand back, but he doesn't let it go. Even though I'm still one step up, he's still taller than me. His scent of sandalwood drifts over to me, and I hate how it impairs my judgment. Or maybe that's the tequila. "Hello, Shortcake."

I want to say it's the alcohol that forces me to suck in a sharp breath, trying to counter the heavy impact his smell has on me. And it couldn't have anything to do with his beautiful fucking face with those plump lips. Said lips quirk up, but he quickly hides it as he leans in and drops his mouth beside my ear. "Did you miss me?"

"No. What's there to miss? A middle-class man skipping out on his duties to harass a woman who's not interested? I'm quite all right, thanks."

His smirk grows, and it causes butterflies in my lower stomach because only this man has ever reveled in my scathing words. But he lives for the challenge.

"'No' seems to be your favorite word. But I once remember you screaming another once upon a time. If memory serves correctly, it was my name."

I scoff, and his other hand cups my jaw. And tiny prickles erupt like a kicked hornet nest all over my skin. It brings me to life, startlingly and painfully, and I meet his gaze. "I got your present. I liked the colors." The compliment washes over my skin like he's the very thing that both antagonizes and soothes me.

"I really don't know what you're talking about," I lie. *Does he really like it?* I won't be baited by such an easy question, but I wonder what he really thought. I consider what his criticism might've been.

"You're lying," he says.

"Surely, you're a better detective than this," I tease, purposely hovering my lips near his. He inhales my breath, and the warmth of his flushes over my own lips, creating a tingling sensation. I remember what he tastes like. Memories flood my mind of heated, painful, and destructive sex.

My first time.

I pull away with a conniving smirk, but he doesn't remove his hand from my jaw as his gaze lingers on my lips.

"You think this cute little innocent act fools everyone, but I know how dangerous these hands of yours can be."

"You think I'm cute?" I ask breathlessly. "And the only thing I recall being small was... not my hands."

He laughs, and I'm so stunned by the break of character that I can't help but let loose a small smile. "It would appear your attitude still needs much work."

"I can't entirely say yours is favorable either."

"But *you* like it," he's quick to shoot back.

His hands are hot, feeling like brands against my skin.

"If that's what you tell yourself to get to sleep, then I think you're the only *cute* one here."

His gaze is locked on my mouth. And before I know it, he moves in closer, and his lips daringly brush against mine.

I'm so surprised by the action that I suck in a breath, and it's his air that I'm breathing. My tongue coaxes his, inviting more. His tongue slides against mine, and before I can think twice about it, I'm grabbing his shirt and pulling him into me so our chests are pressing together.

I don't think either of us is thinking of what we're doing. We're just being. This could turn into a colossal disaster, ripping at one another just like last time. It brings back all the reasons I liked him. The insults, the push and pull, the arrogance of this fucking man fuels every inch of my inexcusable hunger for him. Even when I know who he is, it just makes me want it more.

His hand grips my jaw even tighter, and his mouth assaults mine possessively. No other man's kiss has compared to his. No matter how I tried to find someone else who could replace those scorching memories, I never could. I may not have fully enjoyed our first time together that night, pushing through the pain of losing my virginity, but each time after that was a barbaric and carnal claiming I'd never known existed. But what I remember most are these fucking lips and hands, demanding and dominating every inch of me.

I'm jerked back suddenly. Braxton reaches for me, but a thick arm and hand keep him from touching me.

My heart races as I register what the fuck just happened. When I look over my shoulder, a cold, damning presence is smiling at us with death in his gaze.

Hawke is nothing but the killer right now, but Braxton holds his ground. The two square off, and I can feel the palpable tension. "It's best you leave," Hawke says in a low, gravelly tone.

Chills run down my body. Behind Hawke, I see Ivy staring, her mouth open wide, as she tries to assess the situation. Dread fills me because if Braxton does react, he's fucked. Hawke will literally beat him to death. But, somehow, my cousin, despite his killer edge, respects my wishes and my claim for my prey.

Braxton looks from Hawke to me, then dips his head and turns to walk away. I'm shocked because Braxton loves antagonizing people, especially if he can then pin them with a night or two behind bars. But it's as if that kiss was just as mind-melting for him as it was for me. What the fuck just happened?

He strides through the crowd, people moving out of his way as he makes for the exit.

"Little red, you're in trouble," Hawke says, looming behind me, and suddenly, it feels like my father just walked into the room. They might not be blood related, but Hawke is an Ivanov through and through.

Shit. I'm totally in trouble.

CHAPTER 15

Hope

"It's not what it looks like," I say sheepishly.

"It totally is!" Ivy pushes Hawke out of the way. "Who was that handsome, blue-eyed hottie? Damn, Hope, you've been keeping secrets!"

"Nothing's happening between them—us," Hawke and I snap at the same time, and we lock eyes.

Ivy's smile twists dangerously, and she pushes out her bottom lip. "Awww, is Hawke playing big brother? You never warn men away from me." She twirls a lock of her hair innocently.

"I need to warn the men *about* you," he corrects.

"High praise from the king of manwhores," she says with a smirk.

"That filthy mouth of yours is really going to get you into trouble someday," he bites back, still pissed.

"So many empty promises," she purrs.

Eww.

I blink once. Then twice. What the fuck is happening? "Stop!" I shout, coming between them with hands in both of their faces because I don't know if they're about to fight or fuck.

Ivy crosses her arms over her chest and looks at me expectantly. "Is everyone just pairing themselves off lately? Eli, Dutton, Billie, Ford. Like, what the fuck is happening? Have they polluted the water or something?"

"There's nothing happening between us. I just... might've hooked up with him once, and we fell into old habits."

Hawke's eyes narrow. "You've *fucked* him?"

"Oh, come on, Hawke, she's not an innocent angel. I knew there was a little she-devil in there." Ivy turns to me and encourages, "I think you should definitely do it again."

"No," Hawke adamantly says, and he's in his power pose—legs shoulder width apart, arms crossed, glaring down at me. It's rather intimidating to see him when he's like this. He may have respected my wishes so far, but this might change things.

Without going into detail, so Ivy doesn't become further interested, I simply say, "It's not something I intend to repeat." I want to add I didn't know who he was the first time, but those bits of information intrigue Ivy far too much. Her father, Will Walker, is well known for his tracking abilities. And the apple didn't fall far from the tree. However, she's never revealed to her parents how gifted she is. She pretended to lose interest in it in case she didn't want to pursue the career path. But she does it on the side for money, among other freelance IT things.

"Besides, weren't you two having fun? I think I might go home. Those tequila shots really went to my head," I say. It's true that the alcohol may be impairing my judgment, but really, these two don't need me here. And I'd much rather curl up in my bed and read. I also want to try and process what the fuck just happened.

"Noooo. The night's still young," Ivy whines, grabbing for my hand. She looks over her shoulder at her reverse harem, and I know she wants to stay. And I'd never stop her.

I laugh and pat her hand. "I can get home on my own. You know I prefer it that way."

"I'll call Ford to pick you up," Hawke offers, taking out his phone and calling his brother. I can't help but roll my eyes. He was so excited for me to come out tonight, but I know he's shifted into protector mode. And if that is the best way for me to get home, then I'm completely fine with it.

"You sure?" Ivy asks. "Don't think you're getting out of telling me all about Mr. Hottie, who left like a Cinderella story. I want all the gossip."

I avoid showing any interest in the matter in case Hawke's temple actually explodes.

Ford doesn't take long to arrive. He never does. If someone needs help, he's there the moment they call. Unless, of course, he's working for Eli. But if Hawke's out on the town for the night, it means they're both off duty. Basically, Eli wanted alone time with his wife, Jewel.

And one of the perks of Ford never drinking alcohol is he naturally turns into the designated driver. It's not common knowledge he doesn't drink. Only the people in his closest circle and those observant enough to notice he'll hold a drink but never consume it are aware of it.

When a bouncer helpfully escorts me outside safely because Lord forbid Hawke trust me to do it myself, I see Ford is waiting at the curb.

The bouncer opens the passenger door for me, and I slide into the car. Ford doesn't generally have a need for high-end luxury, even though he has the money to have such a lifestyle. His car, however, is something he splurged on.

"A detective?" he questions, clicking his tongue. I throw myself into the seat dramatically. Of course, that's the first thing out of his mouth.

"I'm so going to kill your brother." It didn't even take him ten minutes to spread the word.

"You should know better than to tell him anything," he chides. And I do know better. Hawke has the biggest mouth. Most of the time, he accidentally lets things slip out because he doesn't think before he speaks. But I know Ford is the only one he will tell about my predicament since I came to both of them for help.

"I know," I grumble.

"He hasn't told anyone else. Just me."

"For now." I bite my lip, then ask, "Do you think Dad and Auntie Anya will be mad?"

"Yes. So just don't tell them," he answers, and I turn my head to look at him. We're such a close family, and Ford is one of the most loyal people I know. But even he has his secrets. I mean, he snuck around with Billie for over a year. I had no idea. Granted, I was away for most of it, but apparently, they weren't exactly always discreet.

"I think you two are forgetting the fact that I asked you to train me with a gun so I can kill him."

"I don't know, Hope. I don't usually make out with the people I'm planning to kill."

I fold my arms over my chest. "Eli did."

He laughs, and I think it's the first time I've ever seen him freely do so. It lightens my heart to see the shift in him that definitely came as a result of being with Billie. He seems different. He's still intense but... happier. Is that what happens when people fall in love?

"Yeah, well, I wouldn't be creating any examples from the boss's love life. He's not entirely all there." He taps his temple as he says the words.

I arch my eyebrows. "Oh, so you're aware your boss is a methodical, cruel, and unhinged man?"

He shifts his gaze to me. "Aren't we all a little

unhinged? And need I remind you that my mother is the most cunning of them all, and your father is, respectfully, deranged?"

I want to defend my father, but it's not really even an insult, nor is it untrue. My father is the very best version of himself in our home. But outside that sanctuary, there's a reason why people fear him. The idea of him ever finding out about Braxton shoots fear through my veins.

Because he's my kill. That's the only reason. I immediately try to convince myself.

"Just don't tell them. Besides, you don't plan on anything else happening with him, right?" Ford's previous humor is long forgotten. His dark gaze drifts from the road to me again.

"Right," I say, and I can tell he's not convinced. Even I'm not convinced. Do I plan for something to happen? I don't know. But I do love the way he kisses me. And how would he be now that we're older and I'm not a virgin?

Would it be just as explosive and painful as that night?

A pounding in my core ignites, and I cross my legs uncomfortably.

Shit.

I should not be thinking about that.

At all.

Ford pulls into my driveway and parks in front of the house. "Are you going to come in?" I ask.

"No, I was sketching a new design when you called. I'm going to go back to that."

Another thing I like about Ford is that, much like me, he's a bit of a loner. Instead of partying, he'd much rather be at home with his sketches for new tattoo designs.

"Thank you for the lift," I say, getting out of the car.

"Be careful," he says, and his warning tone makes me stare at him over my shoulder. "I know it's exciting when you think you're in control of a situation. I know the game well. But sometimes, it can also catch us off guard and drown us. If the waters get too deep, let us know, and we'll deal with this for you."

A genuine smile spreads across my lips. I know I'm protected. Ford's projecting his own recent miscalculation that almost cost him and Billie their lives. I don't think I'm clever than him, and I'm slightly out of my comfort zone, but that's what makes messing with the detective so thrilling. But I won't ignore Ford's warning.

"Thank you, Ford. You and Hawke will be the first people I call. Please don't tell Billie about this."

"About what?" he asks with a grin.

I close the door and head to the house, a far deeper sense of dread filling my veins. I wasn't expecting to come home so early. So, as I've already faced down one demon tonight, I suppose I should manage another one.

My mother's home and I promised myself I'd tell my parents I want to drop out of college. I don't know how they'll react. I don't think they'll be too disappointed, but it doesn't make it any less nerve-racking.

I find my parents in the living room, my mother's head in my father's lap, him stroking her hair, his gloves removed, and on the arm of the sofa. They seem to be watching some singer on the TV. I know it's actually my mother who's watching; my father simply enjoys watching her.

It's fascinating that someone like him could find love, especially with someone as incredible as my mother. It reminds me that love happens in unpredictable ways. Their two worlds surely should've never crossed.

They both look up when I step into the living room.

"You're back," Mom says excitedly and waves me over. She sits up but doesn't leave my father's embrace.

"At a reasonable time, too," Dad adds.

My mother slaps his shoulder. "Please. Midnight is early," she says to him, then she turns back to me. "At least you went out. Was it fun?" she asks, making room for me on the couch. She embraces me, and it's nice when we can have moments like this. We're always so busy, our careers leaving us little time to be together. I was always inspired by my mother's work ethic, and so I cherish the moments when we can be a normal family like this, knowing it won't last forever.

When I'm overwhelmed or have too much going on, I know my safe place is right here with them. I want to tell them about Braxton, but I know if I do, my father wouldn't waste any time finding him and killing him without a second thought. And I do want Braxton dead, but I want to do it on my own terms. He's been toying with me for the last few weeks, so I feel it's only fair that I toy back.

I've kept my morbid curiosity about the dead from them, so surely, I can keep this a secret, too.

"What's wrong, sweetie?" Mom asks, angling her head.

"Did someone touch you tonight?" Dad grits.

"No, Dad. And if they did, you and I certainly wouldn't be having a discussion about it."

My mother laughs as he shoots me an unimpressed look. I cross my legs on the sofa as I turn to face them.

"I do, however, have news for you," I announce.

They seem worried, and I let out an exasperated breath.

"I think I want to drop out of college."

Silence fills the room. Then my father reaches for his phone, asking, "Should I make the arrangements now?"

"No, Dad. I can do that myself. Aren't you a little disappointed or something?"

My mother reaches out for my hand. "Sweetie, we would never be disappointed in you. You have excelled at so many things already at your young age. To be honest, we were hoping you might make some changes for yourself. We don't ever want you thinking you have to do anything to impress us. We love you. If anything, you can afford to loosen up a little."

I open my mouth to speak but snap it shut again.

"But not too loose," Dad is quick to add.

My mother rolls her eyes. "What he means to say is, you're only twenty-two, and we are so proud of you and you've exemplified to yourself already that if you put your mind to anything, you can achieve it. But sometimes having fun is part of the process, too."

I always find it ironic when my parents offer me a work-life balance discussion when they're the worst choices to ever give this speech to someone. But it does fill me with relief. I almost feel like I've gotten off too easily. But perhaps my studies really have become irrelevant. I went to college for the experience, but now it just feels like it's hindering my growth as an artist. And maybe I want to make time for other things.

Immediately, crystal-blue eyes gazing up at me from the bottom of a staircase come to mind, and I push Braxton out of my thoughts. I'm not making time for him, specifically, but maybe I can explore the dating thing. Maybe I can ask Ivy to organize a double date. Then again, I heard that a double date went tragically wrong with her and Billie.

I don't even know if I want these things. What I do know is I've lived in my routine for so long now, I need something more. Something that challenges me. Killing a detective seems like a very intense shift in direction, but I'm not at all discouraged by it.

"Thank you." I hug them both and press a kiss on both of their cheeks.

"You don't need a piece of paper to tell you how incredible you are," Mom says.

"We're proud of all of your accolades already," Dad is quick to say.

I roll my eyes. I really lucked out with the best parents in the world. But it's only a matter of time before I'll have to fly the nest, so to speak. And I feel a crackle of energy around me. I can tell something big is about to happen, and it excites me as much as it scares me.

"I'm going to go finish reading my book now," I tell them, then make my way to my bedroom. After I shower, snuggle into my bed, and light a candle, I quickly check my burner phone in my top drawer.

I have a new message. It's a photo of a bald man who appears to have had his neck broken. I think of the way I'll be able to shape the glass, highlighting the twisted neck. But my eyebrows furrow as something occurs to me. I think I saw this man at the club tonight. Didn't I? Or maybe it's my imagination.

I've specially requested the homicides that are put across Braxton's desk to be sent to me. So does this mean they think it's the same killer?

CHAPTER 16
Braxton

I'm back at the club I left only an hour ago, now staring at the body of the man my partner hired to tail the Ivanovs.

"You were here, too, weren't you? Did you see him? What the fuck happened?" Lucas spits. I clamp my hand on his shoulder, ushering him to the side of the building. A few officers are looking in our direction because it's very much unlike him to lose his cool. That's usually my job.

"You need to calm down; people are watching. Reel it in," I say firmly.

He looks over my shoulder and takes a heavy breath. "He was my friend."

"And you knew the risks they were taking."

"Yeah, but... literally on the first night?"

"I warned you these families move quickly. How's your other guy doing?"

"Not dead, as far as I know. Maybe I should pull him out."

I ignore whatever he says next as I scan the area. We're in the backyard of a small home only a block away from the nightclub. There are no surveillance cameras nearby, and the last thing caught on camera is four men following Ivy Walker, one of Hope's friends. He must've been following them and didn't even make it a block down.

"This throws off everything we know about the killer. It has to be two people," Lucas states. "We've always thought it could be a woman because they've never used brute strength, but he's had his neck broken, which takes strength. For him to have been overpowered like this, it has to be a man. On top of that, the fucker was careful enough not to leave any marks. Who goes in with that kind of cruel calculation?"

"Lower your voice," I growl, trying to think.

It's obvious the killer must've been wearing gloves or something of the sort. The first person who comes to mind is Hope's father, who is known for wearing gloves. I blanch at the idea of approaching them directly.

Surveillance shows it was only fifteen minutes after I took off that Hope left in a car identified as belonging to Ford Ivanov. Perhaps her father came back to the area?

Is it someone who is protective of Ivy Walker? It

could possibly have something to do with her father. There are so many different possibilities, and I can tell Lucas is thinking the same.

"Families like this are going to pick flies off within seconds. Maybe call your second guy off of following the Monti's?"

Lucas grinds his jaw. "I don't think he'll want to after he hears about this. There's something fishy going on."

I try not to laugh. Fishy is an understatement when it comes to this family.

I need to get closer to Hope. She needs to be cornered and confess all of her dark, twisted inner thoughts.

Another body on the pile and another layer to this already fucked-up tale.

I don't confide my thoughts to Lucas. Or that I intend to get closer to Alek Ivanov's daughter. I'm risking my fucking life doing everything I have been so far. But now we're going to throw more fuel onto that flame. Because, eventually, something will be smoked out.

CHAPTER 17

Hope

I haven't had a chance to deliver his special package yet because I had art shows I needed to attend. I was also working on officially dropping out of college, which oddly feels freeing.

When I told Billie and Ivy about me quitting school, neither of them was surprised. Charlotte seemed to be the only one who disagreed with my decision. But a small part of me, as petty as it seems, wonders if that's because she thinks we won't hang out as much. And honestly, that might be the case.

I don't expect her to understand, but I don't like the fact that she said it's easy for "someone like me." I think she was referring to the fact that I already have a booming career, and hers isn't where she wants to be. I don't have time for people like that in my inner circle.

The current exhibition has been a massive success. I

can tell by how exhausted I am, in desperate need of a recharge from how much peopling I've had to do.

"Don't forget, tomorrow our flight leaves at eight. In the car to the airport, we'll also be having an interview with a magazine that's been promoting your work for the last two years. I promised them an exclusive interview on the collection," Candice says.

When I turn my unimpressed expression her way, she levels me with a stare. "I said I'd cut back on the number of interviews. But 'exclusive' means only one for this collection and a fatter paycheck."

I sigh. It's exhausting, really.

"I'll call for the car to be brought around for you. I'm going to close out a few things here," she says, walking away.

I really envy Candice's gusto. She's ten years older than me. And, honestly, if I didn't have her, I wouldn't have a routine or half the success I do now. I just enjoy doing my art; the rest of it means very little to me. But if doing all of this now sets me up to be able to live independently and on my own schedule in later years, then that's what I'll strive for.

I want to remove my hair from its tight bun, but instead, I fidget with my glasses on my way out of the grandiose building. I lift the hem of my light-blue silk dress so I don't catch it as I descend the stairs. When the cool air of the evening hits me, I look up. And my heart flutters.

I immediately want to stomp on it.

Braxton is here, leaning against his car. One leg crossed casually over the other as he looks up and smirks. I'm not sure what it is about his smile that sends something off in my stomach. It's kind of like butterflies, but not exactly. I don't descend any farther as I stare at him, quite enjoying looking down my nose at him. He pulls his hat off, that arrogant smile not faltering.

"Shortcake." I raise a brow at the nickname.

"You back to tracking me?" I ask. "Should I call security? You wouldn't be the first raging fan I've had."

"I'm a detective. It's what I do. And a raging fan might be a bit of a stretch, don't you think? I only want you for your body. Not your work."

Heat floods to my core. Fuck this asshole.

"So, are you saying I should put a restraining order on you?" I quip.

"You could try, but it won't do much," he replies. "Why don't you come down here before I, in a chivalrous way, of course, throw you over my shoulder and into my car?"

"So you've resorted to kidnapping me?"

He looks around in mock shock. "Of course not. That's why I included the term 'chivalrous.' I'll make sure you don't hit your head when I gently place you into the trunk of the car. I might not even tie you up, even though I know how much you'll like it." He winks.

I bite the inside of my cheek, trying not to laugh. *Dickhead*.

A couple walks past me, leaving as the show comes to a close, and I wonder where my driver is. He should've come around by now.

"I had him arrested. Your driver." *Did he read my thoughts?* My jaw tightens as I glare at him again.

"You what?"

"He was drinking. We can't have him driving you while he's intoxicated, now can we? I'm not only chivalrous but also protective. Very sweet. Very mindful. Very heroic."

Again, I try not to laugh. This guy is such an asshole.

"You're lying." Larry, my driver has always been reliable.

"I guess you'll never know. Now, come on, Shortcake. Let's go for pancakes. We have much to discuss." He holds open the car door.

I shake my head. "I'm not getting into a police car."

"You are. Get in before I start the sirens." My dress bunches in my hands from how tightly I'm clutching it. This asshole is so insufferable.

"You have ten seconds." He starts counting. "Ten. Nine." His eyes pin mine. "Eight."

"Ugh. Shut up. I'm coming." Because I know he'll do it. And the last thing I need is for this to end up as a headlining story or even a minor article because my father will find out one way or another. And I don't want any of my family knowing I've been seen with a cop.

He watches my every step as I descend the stairs. It's like at the nightclub all over again, but this time, the tension is more palpable, and I can't blame it on the tequila. His gaze falls to my heels and remains there until I reach him. Then, ever so slowly, he drags his gaze up my body until it reaches my face.

He opens the passenger door and nods his head for me to get in. I look at him, contemplating whether or not I should get in. Someone could see me. But he doesn't care about that.

I don't even know why he's here. I haven't dropped off my little surprise to him yet, so other than that, I can't think of why he'd be here demanding I get into his car.

"I've been upgraded from the trunk?" I ask indignantly.

"That's reserved for the girls I like," he says with an arrogant smirk.

"Suddenly, I can see why you must be lonely, especially if you're so desperate for my attention."

I can tell he's trying to hide a laugh, which fills me with a flash of triumph of sorts. I slide into the car, not wanting him to see my tiny grin.

If my family discovered me *willingly* sliding into a detective's car, all the sentiments of how proud of me they are would be thrown out the window. And, yet, part of me wonders if that's why I'm doing it. It's the one thing I shouldn't be doing. The one thing my mother and father would entirely disapprove of. It makes it exciting.

No doubt they would kill him, though.

He knows this and is apparently willing to risk it.

And while he annoys me, I don't want him dead... yet. I like playing with him. It's been keeping me very entertained these last few weeks. Granted, I didn't think I would ever see him again, and now I can't get him to leave.

He shuts the car door and walks around to the driver's side. I make a point not to speak to him as he takes us to my favorite diner, He doesn't push for conversation, either. He just grins the entire fucking trip like he's already won.

When we park at the diner, he quickly comes around to open the door for me. I don't thank him. Because this is a kidnapping. Kidnappers do not get manners, even if they have a badge.

I stand out in my formal silk gown and expensive jewelry. And though the café isn't busy, the few diners scattered at the tables turn to look as we enter.

He leads us to my usual table, ordering two plates of pancakes with extra syrup and two mugs of black coffee as I take the seat opposite him.

It's eerie that he knows my regular order. A reminder that perhaps I'm too regimented. But if I were to compare myself to my father, then I'm not half as bad, but I don't know if that's a good comparison.

"Care to let me know why I'm here?" I ask.

"Because after this, you'll be coming back to my place, and we'll be fucking."

I sneer at him. "I'm not sleeping with a cop."

"You're really hung up on that, aren't you? Did Mommy and Daddy teach you that police are the enemy?"

My smile is cruel. "Yes. And they also taught me manners and that if I ever need them to make the scary monsters go away, they'll be there. But some monsters I prefer to slay myself."

"You seem to be shit at slaying anything. Maybe you'll have better luck with my cock."

"Well, it's significantly smaller, isn't it? Perhaps this time, I might use blades instead of my hands."

He's smirking as he says, "I much prefer it when you use your mouth."

My pussy throbs, and before I can reply, the waitress stops at our table and places our pancakes in front of us.

His eyes sparkle as he cuts the first bite and puts it into his mouth. "Are you saying you haven't thought about it? Your kiss the other night indicates otherwise."

"I..."

"You have. And you aren't a virgin anymore. So I don't plan to treat you like one this time." He takes another bite, and we both know he was the only one treating me like a virgin that night, and it certainly didn't end on that note. There was no sweet lovemaking. That's not why I was there. But next time... It could be disastrous.

I want to say I'm not interested, but I'm curious. I might not be able to kill him right now, but if I can strangle him through other means, I'd be crazy not to take that opportunity.

I'm conflicted. I can't stand this man, but my body is very interested in having another night with him.

"You hate me, so why would you want to have sex with me?" I ask. I don't understand why he started playing with me in the first place. It's most likely to get dirt on my family. But surely, he knows I'm not stupid enough to share information like that with him.

"No, I despise who you are. But hate? That's a strong word."

"Should you even be associating with me, knowing who my family is? You're lucky Hawke didn't break your legs last time," I say, keeping my gaze on my pancakes. And it goes without saying that if my father or aunt found out, he'd no longer be breathing.

"Eat. You'll need the carbs," he tells me.

I automatically get his reference—he plans to fuck me all night. And the thought of it doesn't disgust me. It excites me. That is so wrong on so many levels. I'm so conflicted, on the edge of wanting it so badly, but knowing better than to reach for it. I'm already lying to my family about him and our association, but this? This would be damning myself. Wouldn't it? Or can I gain my own fun from it?

I stab my fork into my pancakes and start to eat. Not because he told me to, but because I haven't eaten anything for at least six hours. I was too nervous to eat at the beginning of the event, and I chose not to eat during it.

I contemplate the high it'll give me to fuck him before I kill him. Won't that be a beautiful, poetic betrayal? The idea is so delicious it makes my pussy begin to pulse.

It's fucked up and twisted, but isn't that why he's here too? No matter our motives, aren't we both curious?

"Why do you pretend to be so shy?" he purrs.

I look up at him, pushing my glasses up my nose. "Excuse me?"

"I don't think I stuttered."

"I'm not pretending anything. I'm simply selective about who I give my time to. Don't be offended because it's not you," I say with fake calm because I'm anything but right now. Fucking him is one thing, but his judgment really pisses me off. Every time we meet, it's like he's studying me, purposely looking for... What? What does he expect to find? Am I scared of what he might find?

"Interesting." He finishes his pancakes and then sits

back to watch me slowly eat my own. We couldn't be more different. He demolishes his food like an animal, while I manage to only eat half before placing my fork down and folding my hands on the table.

"Are you done?" He glances down at my plate.

I'm not surprised by his appetite. After all, I grew up around the twins in their teens and watching teenage boys eat is like watching a documentary about hyenas on the Discovery Channel. Turns out, their appetites don't change much when they grow up.

When I nod, he pulls my plate over and starts eating the rest of my pancakes. What's peculiar is how much he doesn't care about eating from my plate. We don't really know one another. We're not friends. Yet he lacks so much in etiquette that it disgusts me as much as it fascinates me. He really doesn't give a shit who I am or who my family is.

It's unsettling.

The moment he's done, he stands and offers me his hand. I ignore it, getting up on my own. He throws a fifty-dollar bill down on the table and then leads me to the door.

My heart is racing. I know it's not just the fucking he's here for. He wants to uncover my weaknesses. But aren't I curious about his weaknesses as well?

"Are you really planning on taking me to your place?" I ask as we step out into the frigid cold of the night.

"Do you prefer we go back to yours? I'm sure your father would love waking up to his daughter screaming in pleasure," he says, opening the passenger door.

"You sound awfully cocky as if you know you can make me scream." I raise a brow at him.

"Oh, I do, Shortcake." He nods to the car. "Now, get in."

I want to stay exactly where I am, but I also want to get in that car because it's been a long time since I've been with a man. I've been so focused on my career. But I made a step this week to free myself ever so slightly. Perhaps this isn't what my parents would encourage, and my family might shame me for it, but it's thrilling. His blue eyes anchor me to him as if coaxing me to trust him. I don't.

I look around, just to make sure none of my family members have followed me. Then I slide into the car. And I wonder if it's like stepping into hell, because he smirks as he slams the door behind me. No kidnapping or restraints required.

I'm willingly playing with fire.

It could ruin me.

But I hope it ruins him tenfold in return.

If not tonight, then another when I kill him.

CHAPTER 18

Hope

The three-story apartment complex is on the outskirts of the city. It's small and quiet and exactly what I imagined—mediocre. It's nothing fancy, not compared to the homes and hotels past lovers have taken me to as if to try and impress me. Yet, it has a certain charm about it.

When he opens the door to his apartment, he turns on the light, revealing a studio room with wooden tones. The living area is simple, with a deep green couch and fireplace. There's a TV mounted on the wall. Beside it is a king-sized bed with black sheets and a black duvet.

The kitchen is done in black and white subway tile, with an island counter, and the dining table is the only thing that looks like it's regularly used. Mountains of paperwork cover the surface. A laptop sits in the center, and a half-filled jug of what looks like coffee and an empty mug take up the rest of the space.

He heads to the fridge as I further inspect his home. I quickly become curious about the string of photos on the brick wall beside his dining table. He opens a beer and then turns to me. "Want one?"

"No."

His lips quirk up, and he watches me with those bright blue eyes as if he were waiting for me to run. But I don't intend to run. He may have threatened to drag me here, but I came willingly.

Flashbacks from that night when we were together roll through my head, and I wonder how much we've both changed since then.

I push away the thoughts as I take in the images that cover the majority of the wall. It's a masterpiece, really. The red thread connects crime scene photos of different bodies. Bodies I know well. I've sculpted the majority of them. My fingers trail over the string, leading to the one that brings my face into the equation.

"Surely, you could've found a better picture?" I chide.

He comes up behind me, leaning against the table. It's common sense not to let me see this, especially because of my family. I don't know what game he's playing, but I very much like it. The photo he has is one taken from my Instagram account.

"The only image I'll replace it with is one of you on your knees, naked and sucking my cock."

A string of desire immediately tightens down my spine, and my skin feels taut over my muscles. "What would your colleagues think?"

"I don't see anyone else in this room."

I look over my shoulder suggestively. "Just photos of dead bodies?"

He points the mouth of the bottle at me. "I have a feeling you don't mind."

I try to hide the smirk as I turn back to study it. I'm in awe. The way it inspires me is a little worrisome. We both have our forms of art, but the thing that draws us together is our interest in bodies. Morbid as it may be, I think the detective and I are more similar than I first thought.

Maybe I'm deluding myself.

But doesn't that make it all a little bit more fun? Like at any moment, I might slip and fall to my death from this tightrope I'm balancing on.

I reach for the clip that's in my hair and remove it, shaking my head so the locks cascade down my back. I take in a long breath. We're really going to do this.

"Shortcake."

I look over my shoulder to find his intense gaze locked on me. I'm not sure why I don't find it intimidating. Instead, I find it alluring. I may be what he considers shy in many aspects of life. If I'm being frank, I'm just socially awkward. But when it comes to my body and sex, I've never felt shamed or timid. I guess part of that is due to the world I was brought up in. The men in my life treat their wives like queens.

Braxton was the only man who made me feel like that during sex, so it's no surprise I've returned. But having more experience now, I wonder if it'll be the same. What if it's not? What if it's disappointing?

I briefly look over my shoulder where he's removing his holster and gun, placing it on the table casually as if announcing the danger between us.

Well, you're going to kill him anyway, so why does it matter?

"Braxton. A little help with the dress?" I move my hair to the side and point to the clip that's near my neck. I hear him slide the bottle across the counter before his footsteps come to a stop behind me. He's so close that the heat of his body caresses me with invisible hands. I suck in a breath as his fingers brush the back of my neck before he undoes the dress.

The movement is slow, and the dress slides down my body like water until it catches on my hips. He grips my waist tightly. "How I've missed this fucking body," he breaths against my ear, molding his front to my back. I can feel his cock through his pants, pressing against the small of my back. "How I miss handling you and giving in to your every demand," he growls before brutally tugging at the dress so it falls to the floor, exposing my naked body, clad only in a pair of heels.

"Shortcake, turn around."

I look over my shoulder and up through thick eyelashes. Those crystal-blue eyes consume me as he exhales impatiently. He isn't happy because I'm not facing him.

"Turn around," he says again, and this time I do as he demands. Ever so slowly, I turn. His gaze takes all of me in from bottom to top as it drags over each part of me until his eyes meet mine. "So innocent." He whispers the words as his hand raises to my neck, and his fingers drag lightly down my skin.

"Is that what you get off on, innocent-looking girls?" I ask.

He smirks. "No, I usually like them a little dirtier, but you'll do." He leans in and adds, "And I prefer women now." I was only eighteen when we met.

I reach out and grab his cock, making a point that I'm not the sweet little girl he thinks I am. His eyes widen just a little, and that's the only hint of surprise I get from him.

"Shortcake, this is going to be fun."

"Let's see if you can make me come before you start throwing out promises," I purr, removing my hand from his cock and then stepping back to look at him the same way he did me. "Now, strip."

CHAPTER 19

Braxton

The fire I knew she always had in her is bright as the fucking sun right now. Her porcelain skin is smooth and blemish free—no bruises or bite marks to be seen. I have every intention of fixing that very soon. I want to pull her against me, but the big "fuck off" behind her gaze stops me. She nods at me. "Your turn."

I love the way this woman, without so much as knowing it yet, wields power like a queen. She might seem innocent, but in the bedroom, she's as demanding as any woman who won't have her time wasted. She looks down on me like she's superior, and it makes me want to break the little brat.

"Do you think it's your turn to make the rules?" I taunt.

Fuck, it turns me on, though.

"Yes."

My smile grows as I pull my shirt over my head. Her gaze roams over my arm, which is covered in tattoos, and then she swallows hard as it moves to my chest and abs. Even in her perfectly polished way, I can see the flutter of nerves and curiosity. I like throwing her off balance as much as she does me.

I begin to slowly undo my pants, enjoying her growing impatience. She clearly understands that I'm teasing her. She's the perfect example of how to deceive people with innocence. Because while she gives off good-girl vibes, we both know she's anything but. I drop my pants to the ground, and as I step toward her, she takes a step back, shaking her head no. My cock twitches at her dismissal as she stares at it longingly. She wants to play, but only by her rules. I supposed I could give in a little.

She's not smiling, but she doesn't look away either. I don't really know if she saw my cock last time. I know her fingers wrapped around it, but now she can see all of me.

"You like what you see, Shortcake?"

"I've seen bigger," she drawls.

"You'll be punished for that lie."

"I hope so. And let's just pray it's not all talk," she whispers, her blue eyes finally coming back to mine. My cock throbs at the challenge, and it takes everything in me not to reach for her, throw her over my shoulder, and take her to my bed to have my way with her. I want to savor my time with her.

It's like neither of us is willing to make the first move because the moment we do, all inhibitions will be lost. Who we are outside of this room will become irrelevant, and there will be nothing left in the aftermath but shattered pieces.

Her vanilla and strawberry scent wraps around me, and I'm suddenly craving something sweet. Something like a shortcake. Slowly, she skims her fingers over her hips, the dip in her waist, those curves a fucking magnet for any man she walks past. She caresses the skin of her stomach, then higher, until she grabs her huge, heavy tits.

Perfect tits.

Perfect pussy.

Perfect woman.

Teasing me like it was her goddamn purpose in this world.

And still not making a move to come any closer.

I let her touch herself, enjoy every fucking second of the show she's putting on for me. And she knows I'm enjoying it; my rock-hard dick is all the evidence she needs. She knows how much I want her. This isn't a game of lies anymore; we just need to get this frustration and conflict out of our bloodstreams.

I need her like my very last breath, and I hope to drown in her pussy.

And I plan to fuck her so brutally she'll barely be able to stumble out of this room and back into reality. Permanently marked and damaged by me.

CHAPTER 20

Hope

I fucking love it.

The way he watches me.

The palpable tension that threads around us like silken black tendrils. Knowing the moment we touch... we're damned.

We shouldn't be doing this.

But I've never wanted anything more.

He remains there, his cock giving me a standing ovation, as I trail my other hand over my stomach, pretending I'm rubbing his cum into my skin. The blue of his eyes darkens, and I see the moment the last of his control snaps.

He eliminates the distance between us, his arms wrapping around my waist possessively, feeling my curves until both hands grab my ass and he lifts me. He takes my breath away as he slams me against the board affixed to the wall, a few pins digging into my back. Photos and pins fall around us, pieces of string dangling from the board here and there as he lifts me higher, effortlessly hooking my legs around his shoulders.

"What are you—" And then his mouth is on me. Oh, fuck me. His tongue devours my pussy, kissing and nipping hungrily as if he's waited for this moment just as much as I have.

I have nothing to grab on to apart from his hair, and my head is almost touching the ceiling. I press one hand against the ceiling, trying to offer me some kind of support as he eats me out like a starved man. His tongue slides through my folds, and he tastes me like I'm his favorite dessert.

Fuck me, his tongue. It works fucking magic. I tighten my grip on his hair, pushing him deeper between my thighs. My legs squeeze his head and pull at his curls as he keeps me pinned to the wall.

Oh fuck. I'm stunned when my legs begin to shake, the buildup rising quickly. Am I seriously going to come this soon?

Surely, he's not that good?

I want to fight it, not at all wanting to give in to his ego, but the high overrides logic. My legs tremble from the onslaught of the orgasm that's hitting me. "Fuck!" I scream, shocked by how hard and fast it rips from me.

Shit, maybe I should've fucked someone sooner.

I don't want to give him credit—it might make his

ego inflate too big—but hell, he just made me come in a matter of minutes with his tongue alone.

That is some gift.

I grab under his chin and use force to pull him away from my pussy. An arrogant smirk graces his shiny lips as I tighten my grip on his throat, thinking about how good it might feel to choke him. So I do exactly that, and it only widens his smile as he suddenly drops me from his shoulders. Pins fall everywhere as my back drags over them. He catches me so I don't roll an ankle in my heels and wraps his own hand around my throat, restricting my airflow.

"We can play like this, Shortcake, but don't cry when I scare you."

"Why don't you actually do something to try and scare me," I manage to get out around the pressure on my throat.

His smile is devious as he releases me and licks his lips. "Now, get on your knees. Surely, you've learned something since I last saw you. Did you learn how to bite?"

"How did you know making men bleed was my favorite game?" I reply as I drop to my knees. I open my mouth, and he's already there, shoving his cock between my lips. I gag at its assault, wanting to shove back with just as much force. This might be a power imbalance, but even if I'm the one sucking him off, I'll fucking show him what kind of woman he's fucking with.

I bite down. Hard.

"Fuck!" he yells, then slowly drags his cock out of my mouth, gritting his teeth as a vein jumps in his neck.

"Are you scared?" I ask, pouting my lips.

His devilish smirk unravels. "We're just getting started, Shortcake. That can't be all you've learned."

Heat radiates in my core as I take him into the back of my throat again. Relaxing the muscles to take as much of him in as possible. My glasses keep hitting his lower abdomen as I swallow him, bite him, and drag curses from him that unfurl something dark and needy inside me.

I grab his balls and tug, and he jerks in my mouth, hissing at the pain but threading his fingers through my hair as he encourages me. I despise Braxton and everything he stands for. A do-gooder. An arrogant asshole. A temptation that I want to physically destroy. I tug hard again. I want to break him as much as he wants to break me.

He pulls out of my mouth and lowers himself to my level. "You're going to crawl to me, do you understand? Like a good girl."

He releases the tight grip on my hair, and I fall forward onto my hands and knees. Braxton steps back, leaning against the dining table.

"And what do I get for it?" I ask.

"Punishment."

My body is crawling to him of its own accord, drawn

to the promise of the type of sex I know only he can give me.

When I reach his feet, he offers me his hand. I take it and slide my body up his.

"You're too fucking beautiful," he seethes.

"And you're too sure of yourself," I bite back. "You're a fucking problem."

He smirks, grabbing my ass and lifting me up so I have to wrap my legs around his waist for support. He slams me onto the table, piles of papers scattered and drifting to the floor, and I move my leg so my stiletto is at his throat. His smile grows. "It'd be easy, wouldn't it?" he asks. He glances at a spot above my shoulder, and that's where I notice the gun in the holster placed on the table once again as if he's testing me or inviting me to take it.

I do, and his hand slides up my body to rest on my hand, which now has the gun. My stiletto is still at his throat, pressing in firmer as he leans over me. And then I feel him at my entrance, rubbing through my juices. Oh, fuck me. This man...

He edges closer, the tip nudging in and out as my hips automatically loosen to let him in deeper, but he doesn't move to do so. Instead, his hand wraps around the gun. My finger rests on the trigger, and a heated look passes between us.

"You want this cock, Shortcake?"

"You want to remain alive, asshole?"

"Why do I have a feeling you'd like fucking me if I'm dead?"

A very dangerous thing unfurls inside me. I don't want to fuck a dead person, but his innate understanding of this darkness within me calls to it and draws it out.

He takes the gun and points it at his head with a crazed smile.

"Is this what you want?" he asks, his voice like gravel.

"More than you know," I seethe.

"Oh, I know, Shortcake. I know," he says as he replaces his cock at my entrance with the barrel of the gun. I try to squeeze my thighs together, and a moment of dread runs through me. But a dark curiosity quickly overshadows it.

"What are you—?"

The cool muzzle of the barrel slides into my pussy, and the sense of danger riles something deranged within me. "You like that, don't you?" he questions.

"Yes," I breathe, shocked, broken, crazed. *Is this really me? Is this a part of me that I've tried so hard to keep at bay?* He thrusts the gun farther into me, and I take a sharp breath, not breaking eye contact as blood drips from his throat from where my heel has cut him.

"You're so fucking perfect," he whispers as his gaze skitters over me. "So fucking wild, waiting to be set free."

"I didn't ask for poetry. Fuck me," I demand, unsettled by the fact that he sees me. All of me. This part of me

I've tried to bury and conceal that he coaxes out with such ease.

His pumping of the gun continues as I roll back on my elbows, taking my pleasure. My hips rock back and forth, needy, and when I glance down, I see he's fisting his own cock, watching me like a crazy man.

He removes the gun, and I immediately feel its loss. "It was a trick, wasn't it?"

"What was?" he asks.

"The gun was a test."

"Was it?" He arches an eyebrow as he aims across the room and pulls the trigger. *Bang!* The light beside his bed explodes.

A jolt of adrenaline passes through me as I realize I could've shot him in the head. He could've shot me in the pussy. So many things could've gone wrong, and yet a wild, carnal feeling explodes within me and has me reaching for his neck and crushing his lips to mine.

We're hungry for each other, biting, clawing, sucking, viciously trying to take everything we can from one another. He picks me up again, my legs wrapping around his waist as I try my hardest to impale myself on his cock. Fuck me, this asshole is my wildest fantasy, and I didn't even fucking know it.

I'm led by something entirely animalistic that I've never tapped into before. His mouth leaves mine only momentarily as he bites along my neck. I hiss as he pinches my skin between my teeth, devouring me as he walks us over to his bed.

I get impatient, and as he places another bite on my neck, I nip at his cheek.

He hisses, grabbing my ass and squeezing hard. Braxton's gaze is lethal as he says, "This fucking mouth of yours is dangerous."

He sits on the edge of the bed, avoiding the broken porcelain on the floor. "Be a good girl and grab a condom from the top drawer and then impale yourself on my cock. Show me how needy you are."

When he releases my jaw, I'm almost salivating, my body alive and burning in pain, but I want more. *Need* more. I lean over to the top drawer, and he slaps my ass. Hard. I hiss, keeping the scream in, refusing to let him break me, even though I really fucking want him to.

I hastily tear open the condom and then slide it over his cock, trying not to show it's the first time I've put one on a guy; they usually do this part. But I so desperately need him inside of me. I need to feel his size destroying me from the inside, showing what damage he can cruelly deliver.

I put a knee on either side of him, straddling his hips, but I don't sit down. Instead, we lock eyes, and then he leans in and kisses me, stealing my words and everything else he can take. It's slower than before, the high at a lethal edge, and it's as if he's trying to coax it back ever so slightly. To make it feel more human.

Taking the lead as I melt into the abnormality that is Braxton Hero.

And I let him.

Oh boy, do I let him.

He lowers me until I can feel the tip of him at my entrance. He holds me there, not moving, his lips lightly brushing mine. I rock my hips, pressing down just a little bit with each movement until I feel more pressure at my opening. He doesn't stop the kiss and, slowly, I lower myself down, leaning back with my hands on either side of his knees as I take his entire length. His hands twist through my hair to keep me close, and he deepens our kiss.

I taste blood. I'm not sure if it's his or mine or both, but I lap it up.

It brings me to life, and who I am in this moment is far from the woman I present outside this room. This is my depravity and something I'll cling to if it's the only time it can see the light of day.

If there's one thing I know, I could never get sick of the way this man kisses me, and I'll think of him fondly even when I do have to put a bullet through his brain.

Once I'm fully seated on him, I almost take back the words about having seen a bigger cock than his, but fuck, he fills me so well. His hands glide down my body until they grip my hips. He starts rocking me back and forth, never breaking our kiss, and my breath becomes labored as I try to keep up with all the sensations running through my body right now.

I don't know how he can ignite every single piece of me that he touches, especially my lips. But he does. He pulls back, holding me still as he looks at me.

"Can you see without these?" He taps the arm of my glasses.

"Barely," I answer truthfully.

He takes them off, tosses them to the end of the bed, then quickly flips me onto my back so he's hovering above me. He doesn't waste any time as his hands find my wrists and pin them above my head. My legs wrap around his waist. And he fucks me. Into absolute oblivion.

He hits all the right fucking spots. He lowers his head and bites my breast, and I know he's marking it. Then he does the same with the other. All the while, his cock continues its punishing rhythm. I can feel the scream working its way up my throat, but before I can release it, he's kissing me again, taking it away.

He keeps tugging at that damning part of me that wants to be seen, stroked, pleased, and engulfed in danger and darkness, and he violates it, provoking it into the most toxic elixir I've ever consumed.

I never want this to stop. Ever.

For the first time, I feel fully alive and seen.

"Such a fucking bad girl," he growls as he grips my

throat and cuts off my air. I want to stop breathing. I want my heart to stop. I want to go to the extreme, to skirt the edge of no coming back. The build grows as I relinquish all control, riding the orgasm that he's about to rip out of me.

"I fu-fucking hate y-you," I scream, my body convulsing under his weight as a painful and electrifying buildup explodes within me.

"Fuck," he grits as he jerks inside me, breathing heavily into my ear as I curl my arms around his back, my nails dragging down his skin as if I'm petting him, but I also want to hurt him. But I'm too tired for the fight. I feel nothing but bliss.

The darkness within me recedes as if exhausted from being exposed and exploited.

He's heaving in breaths as he pulls out of me, rolls to the side, and then stands, looming over me. He brushes sweaty locks of hair from my face. I feel dead like he's sucked out my soul and left behind a barely functioning body. I can't see his expression because my eyesight isn't the best without my glasses, but I'm certain his gaze rakes over me. He bites his bottom lip and shakes his head, then turns and walks away.

I lie there, trying to catch my breath. I hear the fridge open and then close before the sound of his footsteps comes closer. That's when I see him again, holding out a bottle of water, but I don't want to move to take it. I'm not sure if my legs or arms will work right now. What the fuck just happened? It's so crazy that I want to laugh.

This is madness.

"I need to go," I tell him.

"But I haven't even shown you my gifts yet, Shortcake."

I manage enough energy to shake my head and sit up. Finding my glasses I put them on and look at the carnage of the room. All the photos, strings, and pins are scattered on the floor. The coffee mug from the dining table is shattered, and paperwork is strewn everywhere. A few droplets of blood dot the wooden floors. And when I look at Braxton's bare feet, I notice he must have cut himself on a shard of the coffee mug or lamp. He doesn't seem bothered by it, though. If he did, he'd care about the small bleeding hole at his throat from my stiletto. The gun rests on the table, and a guttural growl vibrates in my chest, recalling the smooth slide of it inside me.

Every part of me aches, and when I look down at myself, I see my skin is a map of bites and marks.

Oh my fucking God. What did we do?

I shouldn't be into this, right?

"I have your statues under my bed," he says, bringing my attention back to him. His hair is mussed, sweat glistening on his forehead.

"You bought some of my statues? I'm surprised you can afford them," I say, clicking my tongue and quickly falling back into indifference.

He smirks as if following suit, and we return to our usual selves.

"No, the special ones you have delivered here. The creepy ones of dead bodies."

My face twists in disgust. "Eww. I don't know what you're talking about, and of course, I don't want to see them."

His smirk widens. "Your best work, if you ask me."

Warmth settles in my heart, and I'm quick to conceal any kind of reaction. He's baiting me, waiting for my admission. But I'm not falling for it.

I scrunch my face and feign disgust. "This was a mistake. Maybe don't tell the next woman you bring over that you're into weird little dead figurines, okay? Tell them you play Xbox or something instead."

He laughs at that. "Look who's so quick to put herself back in her own cage."

I ignore his provocation, hating how much of me he sees and not knowing how he does it. He's the only one. Not even my family knows this part of me, so how can he so clearly see it?

Like calls to like.

I want to punch myself for that thought. I'm not romanticizing anything about Braxton Hero. *He's the asshole who I'm giddily waiting to kill.* I remind myself as I pick up my dress and slide it back on.

"Reclip this," I demand, turning my back and lifting my hair.

He chuckles but does as he's told.

"I have to go," I say.

"If you say so." He lies on the bed, completely naked, cock semi-hard, holding a bottle of water.

I lick my bottom lip, unable to stop staring at his cock. I mean, maybe one more round would be okay since I'm already here?

No!

What the fuck is wrong with me?

What have I done?

Did I really just sleep with the enemy? My family has many enemies, the police being one of the worst. And I've just climbed into bed with one of them.

I'm in so much trouble.

I grab the last of my things and hurry for the door.

"I'll be seeing you real soon, Shortcake."

I flip him off over my shoulder because kicking the hornet's nest is painful in a way I like.

And that's what makes it dangerous.

CHAPTER 21

Braxton

I watch her go, unable to wipe the smug smirk off my face. She hurries out the door like she's about to be caught at any moment, and I'm tempted to do exactly that. I knew having her again would be so much fucking better than the first time. And tasting her was literally the cherry on top. And that? That is something I'll relive for days, if not years, to come.

She's a redheaded little vixen, but at the same time, she oozes innocence. However, she and I both know that's just a mask she puts on for the rest of the world. I tempted that depraved side of her to crawl from the darkest part of her soul, and then I challenged and exposed it more than I ever thought she'd allow me to. She is my undoing as much as I am hers. Had she put that gun to my head, I might've actually let her pull the trigger. My cock twitches at the thought.

Oh no. Shortcake and I are far from done.

I thought she'd be out of my system once I had my fix.

But I haven't had enough.

My crime board is in a shambles, but perhaps it's what I need so I can come at it from a new perspective. I've looked at it so many times I've memorized it.

The room is destroyed, and it fills me with male pride.

She couldn't be more fucking perfect. Even if she is forbidden.

I'm not on call tonight, but my phone rings anyway. I'd considered just lying in my bed and doing sweet fuck all, but now that I notice her smell is everywhere, I know I should leave. Otherwise, I'll find a way to bring her back.

I'm sure whatever Lucas is calling me about is important, so I answer.

"He's dead," he announces. "My other guy."

"Where?"

He sends me the address, and I step on a broken piece of porcelain when I rise from the bed, making a note to clean that up when I return. I quickly throw on fresh clothes, grab my gun and badge, and briefly admire my gun, knowing it still has her juices on it. A masculine pride fuels me, and my cock twitches as I head for the door.

I'm not surprised both of his men have been taken

out so quickly. This time, the body was found in a dumpster. They're estimating the time of death to be about four to five hours ago, which means he was killed in the early evening.

When I arrive at the scene, it's the same fucking club where I kissed her. Lucas is barking orders, and other officers are keeping onlookers away from the scene.

This club is a fucking curse. Two bodies in a matter of weeks, and it's not even an establishment that any of the Mafia families own.

"I warned him that he should pull out," Lucas says as I come up beside him. He sweeps his hands through his hair, his gaze darting over the body with a slit throat. "He must've been in the dumpster for hours. The kitchen staff found him when they were taking out the trash. He didn't deserve this."

"The good ones often don't. It's why we do this," I say, scanning the area. Brute force was used in the last murder. This time it's a slit throat. No pattern to the methods used. "The culprit would've had to be strong enough to be able to throw him into the dumpster." Looking at the height of the bin, it'd have to be someone with significant enough strength.

"Cameras were tampered with for an hour," Lucas tells me. I peer down at the body.

I glance at the crowd, most of them drunks being ushered to move on, some of them not-so-discretely taking photos. That's when I see him. Hawke Ivanov. His dark eyes are penetrating as he stares at me with a woman under each arm. The guy has a fucking type.

What I don't like is how close he and Hope are, even if they are considered cousins. She trusts him, and somehow, he manages to always be around when someone is killed. He also clearly has the strength to push a fucking truck, so heaving a body into a dumpster would be nothing for him.

I approach him, and we smile insincerely at one another. It's like picking up where we left off. He's so fucking lucky I didn't break his hand for pulling Hope away from me. But it's a delicate dance with someone like Hawke. I consider whether I should bring him in as a suspect and weigh up the consequences if I do. I won't be able to pin anything on him. Not yet, anyway. But that smug fucking expression makes me want to.

They think they're fucking invincible, these men.

"Detective," he says. The women at his sides giggle, but I pay them no attention.

"Was this you?" I point a finger over my shoulder.

"Come on now, Detective, you couldn't possibly think I would reduce myself to something so simple as slitting a throat? If I were to ever seriously hurt someone, I think I'd just lose all control and it'd be a bloody fight to the death. I couldn't imagine anyone who might push me to that point, though."

My lips tilt up. Looks like he likes to dance on the outskirts.

"I'm just scared for everyone on the streets. How is our police force unable to do something about this? I mean, two bodies in two weeks. That serial killer is seriously invested," he says.

Oh, I definitely think he could do this and possibly even worse. I see straight through his feigned innocence. He's just as deadly as the rest of them, maybe even more so.

"Why are you here?" I ask.

Hawke looks at the two women as if that answers my question. "Are you saying it's illegal for me to be here?"

Just then, a black Ferrari pulls up, and a commotion erupts as the crowd parts to let an angry-looking five-foot-nothing shortcake through. She looks furious, and she's still wearing the dress I took off her only hours ago. Well, well, well, looks like I'm not the only one who has contacts, and I'm curious as to how she found out about the murder so quickly, or perhaps it has more to do with her cousin taunting a detective at the side of a crime scene.

Hawke seems wildly pissed to see her here, and my grin kicks up.

"Miss me that much you decided to track me down?" I ask her arrogantly.

"I think you need to research the definition of 'miss.' I've got my father on hold. If you're trying to press charges or something like that, we'll call in Rya Monti immediately," she threatens.

I can't help but be impressed by the little shortcake who will fight for her family. Maybe even kill for them. The very same family she betrayed by sleeping with me. And, oh, how that must irk her right now. I love having that leverage over her, dangling it like a piece of fruit, waiting for her to snatch it and throw it away. Waiting to see how she'll try to throw me away... because we are anything but done.

"I was simply asking a few questions," I say. "But, yes, one might say it's a coincidence that two bodies were found close to the same place, and he's been here both times."

She huffs out a breath, folding her arms over her chest. "Aren't you tired?"

"No. Want to go for round two?"

Hawke steps forward, abandoning his women, but Hope is quick to step in between us.

"What the fuck did you just say to her, pretty boy?" Hawke growls.

Fucking hit me. I dare you. Please fucking hit me.

"I was simply offering—"

"Enough!" Hope cuts me off and stares at me with the ferociousness of a lioness. My skin prickles with excitement. Such a small package for so much untapped violence. "Hawke, get in the car."

"But he—" The words die on his lips when he sees her expression. "Yes, little red." But then he turns back to me. "But if I see you again, motherfucker, you better run the other way."

"Are you threatening a detective?" I ask with a cocky smile.

"Enough!" Hope shoves at Hawke. "And, no, your women are not coming."

All the violence bleeds from Hawke as he whips his head in her direction, baffled. "Ugh, you're killing me, little red."

He heads for the car as she squares up with me. "Whatever game you're playing, you only play with me. Keep my family out of it."

I can tell my smirk is pissing her off. "I never took you for the jealous type."

"I never took you for the stupid type. They will kill you," she warns.

I place my hand to my heart. "Aww, that almost sounds like you care."

She scoffs and tosses her hair over her shoulder. "I don't. I just don't want anyone else interfering with my prey."

"Are *you* threatening a detective?"

Her blue eyes dance with mischief, but she says nothing as she turns and sways her hips seductively as she walks back to her car. My cock twitches, recalling that she's not wearing any panties.

Lucas comes up to my side, watching as they leave. "They're involved. They have to be."

"I told you they're quick on these types of things."

"You think it's her?" Lucas asks. I turn to face him, masking the lethal edge of my gaze. I don't like him sniffing after her. "I mean, she's an Ivanov. It's likely. And the expression on your face is the same one you get when you think you've found a lead. Should we investigate her further?"

"No. Leave her to me," I say, warning in my tone. His eyebrows dip slightly, understanding me well enough. But I refuse to let anyone else interfere or become consumed by Hope Ivanov. She's mine to explore and unravel.

Hawke sits in the passenger seat of her black Ferrari. It's a nice car, something she received as a gift from her parents for her twenty-first birthday, but it's very rare I see her drive herself. It's also amusing to see someone as large as Hawke squeeze into the front seat. The car is far too small for him.

Hope doesn't look back at me as she drives off, but Hawke does. He waves at me before flipping me off.

Fucking asshole.

CHAPTER 22

Hope

"Did you kill him?" I ask Hawke.

He huffs like a child, crossing his arms over his chest. "No. You wouldn't be finding a fucking body in the dumpster if I did it."

I expel a sigh. "Then who the fuck did it?"

"How the fuck should I know?" he exclaims. "I was just there for titty and ass, and since when do you care who I do and don't kill?"

I roll my eyes. "I don't care who you kill, Hawke. I just wanted to make sure you weren't becoming senile and messy. You know he's probably already suspicious of our family's involvement with this serial killer situation."

He clicks his tongue. "Well, I don't know who the fuck it is, but I tip my hat to them. They're running circles around everyone. However, I'm not getting pinned for their inability to clean up after themselves."

"That's rich, a killer criticizing another killer's process."

He stares at me wide-eyed. "What's gotten into you today? Are you fucking that detective? Because, I swear to God, if you are, the secret is out the window, and Daddy Gloves is finding out. That detective won't even last another twelve hours."

I snort. "Twelve hours is assuming my father decides to take a nap during that time. And, no, I'm not sleeping with him." I lie effortlessly. "But we just need to be careful; he's sniffing around our family. That's never a good thing, right?"

Hawke looks at me—really looks at me. "Since when did you get so involved with the family business or start caring about who's sniffing what? I thought your father kept you away from all of this."

The reality is he does. But it doesn't make me ignorant about it. And having Braxton's attention focused on us has made me more conscious about it than ever.

"He does, but I'm not a kid anymore."

Hawke doesn't seem convinced. "There's something you're not telling me about all of this. It feels off, and I think you're lying about something."

"Should we talk about how you've been off lately as well? You've been at clubs a lot more recently since the incident with Ford and Billie." I deflect. He opens and closes his mouth, then looks away, and I realize I hit home. I almost feel guilty for it.

I'm conflicted about telling him the truth. Yes, I'm lying. Only a marginal amount of guilt sits in my stomach about it, but not enough to tell him my secrets, especially when it'll only turn on me.

"I'm not lying. I just don't want anyone else touching him. I want to kill him myself. And I know if he keeps snooping, someone else is going to do it before me." I elaborate.

He snorts. "I give you credit, little red. I know it's your first time and all, but you're being very methodical about this. If you want someone dead, you just kill them. Fuck the gun. Slit his throat or something."

I know he's speaking the truth, but I've envisioned it so many times: how Braxton and I will come to an end with me pointing a gun at his head. I've lived it so many times in my head I can't pull away from it. I don't want to. It's the vision I hold, and once I see something so divinely, I have to express it. It's the same as with my work.

I pull up at Ford's house, and Hawke stares out the window, only just realizing I brought him here instead of his house. "You're miserable when you're by yourself. I figured you would want to come here instead."

"But if Billie's here, there's no point." He sulks.

I roll my eyes. Big baby. "I'm going to have a girls' night with Billie and Ivy. I was on my way to their place when I got the call from Ford that I was closest to the club and to get you out of there before you started any trouble." Before Hawke can ask, I add. "Your mother was tipped off by security about the murder."

His jaw snaps shut again because we know how quickly gossip spreads among our family, which is why my car was tracked to be the closest to get him out and my father was on the phone. My Aunt Anya has eyes and ears everywhere, just like every member of the family,

"Me? Trouble?" He smirks. "He does still care."

"Go and kiss and make up so I can have my girls' night."

Ford opens the front door, looming there with arms crossed over his chest, looking the part of a seriously pissed off dad as Felix, his cat, rubs against his legs. The two tolerate each other at best, and Ford is definitely not the cat's favorite person.

Hawke basically bounces out of the car but leans down before closing the door. "I'm serious, though, little red. If you're fucking that detective, you're in deep trouble. I just don't want to see you used or hurt."

I'm actually surprised. Hawke is the last person I thought capable of feelings, especially when they have anything to do with romance. "You think I would give someone that much power?" I ask with a smile that seems to fill him with confidence in the situation.

"I'm just saying, people start doing crazy shit when they're in love." He says it so loudly I know it's targeted at his brother. I'm laughing when he closes the door. I leave them to their sibling squabble as I pull away from the curb and head to Ivy and Billie's apartment.

When I left Braxton's place, I needed my girls. I can't explain it. I'm not often dependent on people, but the feeling of going home after being with Braxton felt wrong.

I'm not even through the door when Billie throws a cozy hoodie and some sweatpants in my direction.

"You're late. Strip. Mask on," Ivy says, shaking a cocktail mixer in their kitchen.

Billie laughs wearing, a pink sweatsuit and a face-mask. I do as they say, turning my back to them.

"Oh, gosh, why are you being so shy?" Billie asks.

"Shut up. I'm not wearing any underwear," I grit.

"I've seen worse," Ivy says, and I can hear the hint of a smile in her voice.

"Why were you late? You were supposed to be here an hour ago," Billie says, far more softly than Ivy.

I know they've been waiting for me so we can watch the new thriller that just came out. I'm grateful to these two because they'll often let me choose the movie, even if horror and thrillers aren't their usual scene. Sometimes, we'll soften the blow by watching a romantic comedy and end up more disgusted than with the blood and guts we'd see in my choices. Balance.

I readjust the clothes, which are slightly too big for me, at least in length. "There was a murder at a club, and I had to pick up Hawke from there. It's the same club we were at a few weeks ago." I make a pointed look at Ivy.

She gasps. "Oh shit! That doesn't look good for him. Did the cops try to take him in?" she asks, handing me a cocktail. I take a sip and am almost swept away by the amount of alcohol.

"Jesus. Are you trying to kill me with one drink?"

"It's girls' night." She shimmies her shoulders and takes a seat on the sofa. I follow suit. Billie is sitting with a bowl of popcorn in her lap, and an array of freshly baked sweets is spread out on the coffee table. Most likely cooked by Billie herself.

"And, no, I 'removed' Hawke from the situation before he could make it any worse."

Ivy smirks, and Billie tries not to laugh. Yes, that's classic Hawke. "He can't be trusted now that he's trying to go solo. He's miserable." I'm trying not to laugh as I say it.

Billie shrugs a shoulder. "I swear, I still give them plenty of brotherly bonding time."

"Oh God, please don't tell me they still shower together," Ivy says, and then her mind immediately wanders off. "Then again... I'm not against that scene at all."

Billie smacks her arm. "Hey, back off. No nasty thoughts of my man."

Ivy's laughing as she puts her hands up in surrender. "I'm joking. But not really. Speaking of men... Spill the beans, Hope."

"Oh yeah, about the detective!" Billie chirps as she grabs a pillow. *Fuck.* I was really hoping I could avoid this topic. "What does your father think of it?"

"Stop!" I'm quick to say. "It's not like that."

"It certainly looked like it at the club," Ivy murmurs as she takes a sip of her drink.

I sigh. "It was one kiss. I slept with him four years ago and didn't know he was a detective." I stop. "Wait, how do you know he's a detective?"

Ivy looks away, and I growl. "Did Hawke spill that info, or were your magic little fingers working a keyboard?"

"I'll have it known that my fingers are magical no matter what they touch. But, of course, I was curious as to who he was. I haven't seen you into anyone before, and you were *really* into eating his face."

Heat streaks my cheeks as I think not only of that kiss but the fact that I was with him not even two hours ago, being railed to within inches of my life. And allowing him to fuck me with a gun too. Fuck me, I'm so far gone.

"There's not much to tell. We had sex like four years ago. I didn't know at the time who he was. It was a one-night stand. The end. I had a few drinks that night, and it just happened. But that's it, and that's all that will happen." Billie and Ivy exchange a glance, biting their bottom lips. They want to argue. "I'm serious."

"Is that really all you're going to tell us? Is he at least packing a big cock?" Ivy asks.

Billie starts laughing, and I can't help but do the same. I'm used to hearing about Ivy's conquests and Billie's before Ford on the rare occasions her brother never found out and the poor guy didn't end up terrorized or dead. But it feels strange to be in this position, especially as I remind them nothing is going on between me and Braxton.

And it has to stay that way.

This can't get out. Even if I want to gossip with my best friends about it.

And besides, it was a one-off.

That delicious little creature in the depths of my soul wants to come to life all over again. But it's not a risk I can take. Having more sex like that will definitely ruin any other man for me. Braxton will ruin me and draw out that thing I've tried to suppress for so long.

It resides alongside my deepest darkest secrets, including my fixation with the dead.

Some lies are best buried, and so I'll take Braxton to the grave with me. But I'll be putting him in his own coffin first.

CHAPTER 23

Hope

I've been dreaming every fucking night about having his mouth on me, and I wake up with my hands between my legs. I hate that he can do this to me when all I want to do is strangle him—and his perfect cock.

Though, I think he'd actually like it if I strangled his cock.

Revisiting that night again and again like it's on a maddening, repetitive loop has been distracting me from my work in the studio.

I'm currently at the diner, half expecting him to appear. This morning, I had another statue delivered to his apartment. Just like the others, it was packaged in a black box.

This latest piece was of the victim at the nightclub who'd had his neck broken. I really enjoyed focusing on his throat, making those twists in the glass work. Despite not having proof that it's me sending the statues, Braxton's adamant that it is. It's flattering as much as it is annoying because there really is no connection between my normal art and the darker pieces. So I have no fucking idea how he knows. If he had proof, he would've called me down to the station already. Maybe I'm getting too daring and cocky. But I can't seem to stop.

If this asshole intends to continue showing up wherever my family is, of course, I'm going to bite back a little. Maybe a lot. And it has nothing to do with the fact that I can't stop imagining myself biting *him*.

Nothing's guaranteed with Braxton Hero, but one thing I can rely on is his ability to appear when he's not wanted. I just know he's going to show up to see me eventually.

I spent fourteen hours in the studio today. I'd become so immersed in my recent piece that I lost track of time, like I often do. And now I'm sitting in my usual booth, lost in my book. Reading helps me unwind; it takes me away from focusing on my creative flow and refills my well. And depending on the book, I get plenty of creative ideas from reading especially when I read thrillers.

It's the same when I'm creating art. I have the music up so loud that it's almost deafening, but it drowns out everything else and helps me concentrate. I like to keep the real world at a distance. I find it distracting, and interacting with people is draining. My father shares a similar sentiment, and it's my mother who always encourages us to get out of the house from time to time.

I bring the hot coffee to my lips as I flip to the next page. I'm at the part of the story where the main character finds her husband cheating on her. Suddenly, it's ripped from my hands.

"Excuse yo—" The words die on my lips as I meet Braxton's arrogant gaze.

"Hello, Shortcake."

It's not his dazzling beauty that has my breath hitching this time. It's what he's holding instead.

It's the most recent statue I had delivered to his home. I conceal any open appreciation for the piece. In fact, I try to act repulsed. "What is that?" I ask, pointing to it.

"It's a murder victim," he says, twisting the glass replica of the body back and forth. The detail in the throat really catches the light. It truly is a magnificent piece. Selfishly, I'm so glad I can share it with someone. For so long, they'd gone unseen. "You're still denying that you created these?"

I shake my head, still feigning ignorance. "I have no idea who made that. And I don't know why you're here, but maybe you're not as good at your job as everyone thinks you are if you keep insisting on harassing me without cause. Can I please have my book back now? I was just getting to the part where I'm certain the wife is about to murder the husband, and I simply can't wait," I say with a sickly sweet smile.

At first, I thought it would be easy to lie, but now it's grown into something far more sinister. I quite enjoy it.

It's not that I enjoy lying. In fact, I'm often conflicted by lies. But tormenting him is everything. If I'm honest with myself, I don't think I can stop any time soon. I'm not yet done with this detective. He might've been drawn to me first, but now I find myself circling and playing this dangerous game. One wrong move, and it's over for both of us.

It's riveting.

Delicious.

Forbidden.

I want it like my next breath.

"Do you like it?" he asks, raising a brow. "There's so much detail in it. A lot of love must've gone into creating this. I wonder who might have such a twisted mind to express something so... unique and macabre."

We're starting to draw attention. One person's lip actually pulls up in disgust, and I fucking hate the scorn my piece is receiving. There's a reason why I haven't shown this side of me to anyone. I know I'm an outcast, and although it doesn't bother me, facing the judgment of others terrifies me. *What if my parents look at me the same way?*

"Stop it. Just fucking stop," I grit out, not at all appreciating the attention. These people are nothing.

Insignificant. But I can't help feeling like the walls are closing in on me. This is my darkest secret. And I willingly chose to share it with *him*. It's not meant for others. I try to push away all of the negativity. "You're upsetting the customers."

He suddenly glances around at our surroundings as if he never even noticed anyone but me. He smirks unapologetically as he takes a seat across from me and puts the piece in the center of the table. I shoot a brief glance in its direction, again pretending to be horrified. His arrogant smile doesn't slip as he removes his jacket and sets it gently over the statue. A wave of relief washes over me at narrowly averting having this part of me exposed in the middle of what is one of my few safe spaces.

I'm furious by how quickly my play to toy with him backfired. I was enjoying taunting him, and yet he so easily flipped it on me.

Asshole.

"My partner and I stopped by my apartment this afternoon. And can you guess what was on my bed, wrapped up with a perfect little bow?"

"My underwear?" I reply with an eye roll.

"You didn't wear any that night," he points out, and I can't entirely hide my smile. Thoughts of that night immediately come back to mind. This man—this beast—who coaxes out the vilest of my fantasies is sitting across from me as if this is the most normal of conversations. "It was another black box with a glass statue inside to join the collection. I even upped my security after the last delivery, and yet low and behold, there was a glitch for twenty minutes this morning. I wonder who has the ability, or perhaps the connections, to do that."

I fix him with a bored look. "There are many mysteries to life. But if you don't mind, your work is very boring to me, especially considering how poor of a job you seem to be doing. Didn't I recently see the body count of this supposed serial killer is now up to nine? Do you really have time to be harassing me?"

His smile is anything but friendly. He sighs and removes his black glasses, and the dark circles under his eyes are obvious. He's exhausted. And I know for a fact he's been working these cases. He's done multiple interviews asking anyone to come forward with any information they might have about any of the murders. I've watched every single one. To be honest, I find his work life quite interesting, but I'll never admit it as much as I won't admit to having Ivy tap into his security system. I pay her for it, as well as paying her to keep quiet about it. Ivy hasn't asked any questions, but she most certainly knows there's more to the detective and me than I've told her and has most likely tracked it back to Braxton without further asking for answers I'm not willing to offer. Whatever. I'm certainly not asking her father to do it since he and my father are so close.

"My book, please?" I nod to it, and he hands it over. As I

grab it, my fingers brush his. It's like an electric shock. I take in a sharp breath, then snatch the book from him because I don't want him to see any signs of how he unsettles me. But, fuck me, do I want his hands all over my body again.

He's studying me, that smirk creeping up again as he begins to eat the cold remains of my pancakes. He's eating like a caveman, which most likely means he hasn't eaten all day. "Would you like me to order you more?" I offer.

He raises a brow at me but doesn't bother answering. He just continues to eat my leftovers. We sit in silence, and I can't help when my gaze flicks to where his jacket is covering the ominous statue. I can't believe he actually brought it with him. I never thought he'd do that. Perhaps I was too confident about my little secret.

He should be thankful that he gets to admire them, let alone hold them. Actually, I don't think he realizes how lucky he is. He could never afford any of my sculptures, but in my opinion, these are the most priceless pieces I've made.

I focus on my book again and read another two pages before he speaks because Lord forbid when a woman remains silent and ignores a man to where he has to entertain himself.

"This needs to stop," he warns, pointing the fork to his jacket.

"Okay..." I say, flicking to another page.

"I'm serious. I know it's you, Hope. I may not have the proof, but it's you. You're digging yourself deeper and deeper, past a point where Mommy and Daddy won't be able to get you out."

I still don't look up from my book. "If you say so. You're starting to sound a lot like you care, Detective. It's very unlike you."

He's watching me in that intense way that he does, setting my skin alight. It's like a caress that demands my attention, and I know the moment I give in, I'm a goner. So I refuse to be put under his fucking spell.

I saw Hawke briefly since our last altercation. Although he's promised to remain silent, anyone who knows him well enough knows he's a liability when it comes to keeping secrets. But if he thinks I'm in danger, he'll step in. He even questioned me as to how successful we might be at getting the detective to accept a bribe. That's very fucking unlikely. And if we try, we'll just be tipping our hand. And besides, I have no interest in playing that kind of game with him.

I don't want anyone else playing with my toy, so I shut Hawke and the conversation down.

My prey. My game.

Even if my family might chastise me for it later, I know they love me. We protect one another.

I look up at him when he grabs my cup of coffee and takes a sip. I know he does it to test me, but I just put down my book and bring my hands together on top of the table.

"Do you have family?" I ask.

He seems surprised by the question, but he masks it within seconds. "Yes."

"So why don't you spend time with them?"

He raises a perfect brow. His tattooed hand comes to rest on the table as he leans toward me. I don't like how little space he leaves between us, but I don't move from my position either.

"And how would you know if I spend time with them or not, Shortcake?"

"Because you're always trying to get into my pants when you aren't working." I bat my lashes at him.

Biting back a smile, he says, "Correction. I've tried getting in your dress once, and it worked." He winks. "I remember those sweet moans that left your lips and all the barbaric things your body demanded I give you."

Heat flushes my cheeks. I lift the book up again, trying to block him out so he doesn't see how flustered he makes me. I adjust my glasses. "Yes, I guess you do."

"When do you go back to London?" he asks, changing the subject. It's an obvious indication that he's following my schedule. He probably knows the answer before I give it to him, so I don't see any point in hiding it.

"Tonight."

He lifts his wrist and checks the time. "My car is outside. Do you need a lift?"

"No, I have a driver," I tell him distractedly, trying to reread the same line in my book. I just can't focus when this man is so fucking close. I can feel the heat of his breath. Suddenly, his foot nudges mine under the table, and I'm filled with a hot flush. Then his hand finds my knee.

"The drunk one?" he asks innocently.

I should shove his hand away. But I'm salivating at the idea of his callused hand running higher up my leg. My pussy throbs, begging for his touch.

"No," I answer tightly and try not to focus on his hand running circles over my inner thigh. It turns out that my previous driver actually was drinking every time he drove me to my events. When I mentioned it to my father, he killed him without a second thought. When my father asked me how I knew, I didn't dare tell him it was because of Braxton. I just mentioned that I could smell alcohol. I'm getting really good at this lying thing. So now I have one of my mother's drivers. And this one knows not to drink at all while he's driving me. He doesn't want to end up like my last driver, that's for sure.

"Good." He lifts his other hand, his bicep flexing with the movement. I try my hardest not to notice his muscles but, fuck me, it's impossible. And I know he's doing it on purpose.

I'm not sure why he's concerned if my driver is drinking or not, and I don't really care to ask him. Yes, he is amazing in bed, and his mouth knows exactly what it's doing, but that doesn't mean I want a relationship with him. I have enough common sense to know it would never work between us.

"Why don't you follow me to my car for a few minutes?" he says, his tone and the way his hand tightens on my thigh a lure. I look up into those provocative blue eyes. "So I can give you a proper send off."

I swallow hard, my body fully understanding his intention and demanding I go with him. But I notice a child looking in our direction, and I slide his hand off my leg. "We're not doing that again."

"Come on, Shortcake, you love how I work your body. Don't you miss my mouth?"

"Not while it's yapping," I grit, trying to override the heat rushing through my veins. Does this man have no shame? We're in the middle of a restaurant, and anyone could see or hear us.

"What if I'm sucking on your clit and making you whimper my name?"

My pussy is pounding now, and I couldn't dive back into my book even if I wanted to. My mind circles around all the things he can do to me. "I'm not fucking you" is all I can manage to say. It's not the best defense, but it's all I have.

That smile curves devilishly slow. "What if I make it about you? Worship you in the way I know you deserve?"

I scoff. "You think you know my body that well?"

"Yes," he says without hesitation. "Give me five minutes, and I'll prove it to you."

"Five minutes of my time is expensive," I reply, barely able to keep my voice steady.

"So are my fingers and mouth." He grins. "Orgasms don't come cheap. Especially when I know no other man has been able to make you come undone like I do."

This fucking arrogant prick. I glance toward the car in the parking lot where my driver waits. Farther back is Braxton's car.

I mean, if it's only five minutes... What's the harm, right?

I'm going to kill him soon, anyway, so I might as well make him useful before then.

Right?

CHAPTER 24

Braxton

I throw a fifty-dollar bill on the table and grab her hand. I pick up the statue and the jacket in the other one. She's silent as I lead her to the back of the parking lot. It's not exactly busy at ten in the evening, and the light barely reaches back here, which is precisely why I parked in this spot.

Hope has looked over her shoulder once, most likely checking to see if her driver has noticed us. If he has, he certainly seems to know better than to interrupt, or perhaps he's as incompetent as the other one. I'll make sure a background check on him is the first thing I do when I return to the office.

Just as we reach the front passenger side door, I turn her and slam her back against the car. I'm so fucking impatient. I crush my lips to hers, needing to taste that vile darkness within her.

She sucks in a breath, surprised, but it's only a matter of seconds before she's biting and sucking at my lips, whimpering into my mouth like the needy little thing she is. I trail my hands over her dress. Fuck, I've missed her curves.

We're partially concealed by another car in front of us, but I honestly don't give a flying fuck right now who sees us. I just need her. I bite her neck, and she moans and gasps, tugging at my hair, demanding more.

"So fucking beautiful," I growl.

"F-four m-minutes," she stutters, and I can't help the smirk as I kiss down her stomach and then drop to my knees in front of her. She looks down at me with a hooded gaze, her vibrant red hair shining even in the dark. She will always shine in the darkness like a fucking beacon.

I push her panties to the side, wasting no time as I lick and savor my favorite type of dessert. Her legs tremble, and I run my hand from her heel all the way up to her hip, unable to restrain myself from touching her. Her skin is so fucking smooth. I devour her pussy, lapping and sucking as I worship her.

I know I shouldn't allow myself to be provoked by the statues, but I can't help enjoying the game she's set up for us. If she wants to play, I'll fucking play. Not necessarily by her rules, though.

"Fuck," she whispers as her hips begin to roll against my face.

"Not bad for a detective, huh?" I growl as I pull my head back and then insert a finger into her tight channel.

She goes to reply but sucks in a breath as I add a second finger. I stare up at her, my needy little vixen riding my hand shamelessly in a parking lot. I love pleasing her and seeing this unfiltered version of her that no one else has witnessed. This is all for, and because of, me.

"You talk too much," she spits.

I chuckle as I pull out my badge. The thought of arresting her and handcuffing her definitely comes to mind. Her eyes widen at the sight of it, even as she continues riding my hand.

"You'll remember who I am," I growl as I bring it up to her cunt.

"What are you—" Her eyes spring wide in surprise as I rub my badge against her pussy, using the cool metal in place of my tongue. I want to watch her come undone.

"Soak my fucking name. Be a good girl and mark me."

"This is—" She's breathless as I intensify the friction, and she gasps, hitting a new high.

"Fucking perfect. Fuck it like you were fucking my face."

I want her scent; want to carry it with me. I want to know she did exactly as I told her to. That she's so corrupt, she's willing to tarnish my name, my career.

That's how obsessed I want her with me, just as fucking much as I'm spiraling out of control for her.

"You fucking hate that I'm a detective, don't you?" I grit, intensifying the strokes against her delicate flesh.

"Yes," she breathes. "I fucking hate you."

My cock twitches painfully, wanting to be inside her. But I'm willing to play this torturous game a little longer. I'll wait for her to come to me, crawling on all fours.

"You think you're so clever, don't you?" I berate, then suck on my finger.

She's watching me, barely able to focus, as she whispers, "Yes."

I slide my wet finger around to her ass, and she stares at me in bewilderment.

"You want me to break you, don't you?" I taunt. I can tell she's close to the edge because of her posture and the way her legs have begun to shake. "You want me to claim every inch of you."

"Yes," she quietly admits.

I press my finger into her asshole, and she moans, her head rolling back as I pump her from behind and rub my badge against her cunt, riding her into oblivion.

She's so fucking starved for it, chasing her own bliss, and I'm the man on his knees feeding all of her body's demands. It's become my number one goal to destroy this woman. To crack open her beautiful mind, figure out how she thinks, and shatter her body into pieces along the way.

I want this.

I want *her.*

"Oh fuck!" she cries as her fingers dig into my hair. One hand drops to my mouth, shoving her fingers in deep, her nails scraping the back of my throat as I suck and bite at them. "Fuck," she squeaks as her body contorts, and she comes.

I swipe up her juices with my badge, and her fingers curl against my tongue. I move her hand from my mouth and then lower my head to suck on her clit. Her body spasms as I coax out more and more aftershocks.

She grips my hair tight as if she's clinging to me in order to remain upright.

"That's my girl," I growl, lazily licking up my reward. She fucking soaked my badge like a good girl. When her breathing calms and I've licked her clean, I smile up at her. She's looking down at me as if she wants to rip me apart.

"There she is," I say as I look into her lust-filled eyes, and hold in my chuckle. My little shortcake doesn't hate me, but she does hate how much she loves this.

"You took six minutes," she complains as she slips from between me and the car, not even waiting for me to get up from my knees. I feel the loss of her body immediately, but right now, this is victory enough for me.

"Fuck. you taste good." I lick my lips.

"Remember the taste because it's the last fucking

time you'll get it," she says, flicking her hair over her shoulder. "I mean it. Don't come looking for me again."

I'm unable to keep from laughing as she storms off. Her gait is stiff as she makes her way to her car.

"Don't come looking for me again."

I can't help wondering if she truly means what she said. Perhaps what she feels building between us terrifies her as much as it should terrify me. But then would she be sending me little presents, demanding my attention?

"Goodnight, Shortcake," I call out after her, and she flips me off right before sliding into the back seat of the car.

I adjust my cock as I stand.

Fuck me. I've well and truly lost my mind.

Then again, I'm not thinking with my head whenever I'm near her.

I'm obsessed with all the ways I can claim her again and again and again.

CHAPTER 25

Braxton

"How the fuck have you not figured this out yet?" my boss screams. The vein in his temple looks like it's about to pop as Lucas and I sit in his office. "Nine bodies, and still no one is in fucking custody? You're bringing me street rats that can be put behind bars for far pettier crimes. Why the fuck is this so hard for you two geniuses to figure it out?!"

We remain quiet. It's always for the best when he's in this type of mood. I don't need to be the one to remind him of his dirty dealings and involvement with very bad people who might, in fact, be prime candidates for this type of shit, but because of their "silent" association, we can't touch them.

"Get the fuck out of my office and figure your shit out. I mean it! Fucking get in there. The press is killing us."

"Yes, sir," Lucas and I say at the same time, then take our leave.

Dickhead.

Every set of eyes in the office suddenly looks down as we step out into the bullpen. I can't even be mad at their curiosity because I'm the same way when someone else gets eaten alive in there. We're not invincible, and our job security isn't guaranteed. One fucking thing I know for sure is I'm not handing in my badge anytime soon.

"What the fuck are we going to do?" Lucas begins to stress. "How the fuck are we struggling so much with this case? It's like all the evidence we need to link the cases just suddenly vanishes."

"Or the killer's so immaculate, they just don't leave anything behind," I remind him.

"But they'll have to make a mistake at some point, right? I mean, they practically flaunt the bodies. They always want them to be found. I don't know left from right at the moment, and I can't fucking sleep. This case is really killing me. What if the chief brings someone else onto it?"

"He won't." And I believe that. No one wants to draw attention to their own misdeeds. But if we don't start getting answers, even his hand might be moved against his own will.

"Maybe I should try to get in deeper or something," Lucas says quietly as he takes a seat at his desk.

"What do you mean? You can't go undercover; they

already know who you are," I say quietly, then add, "You'd survive for far less time than your friends."

This seems to anger him. Lucas is often the stable one of the two of us. He doesn't play his hand too much, and up until a few months ago, I genuinely thought he was lacking in emotion, considering how well he seemed to compartmentalize. Especially considering some of the fucked-up shit we see. But he's starting to crack with this case, and it's not surprising since his friends died because of it.

"I just... I need to solve this case. This person thinks they're invincible."

"People like this killer always do," I remind him as I glance down at my phone. I'm on Instagram, looking at Hope's recent post. Again, I know it's not her who personally uploads to her accounts, but her PR company makes it far too easy for me to track her movements. She's been gone for two days and should be back in three.

"How the fuck do we hang the Grim Reaper?" Lucas asks quietly. I look up at him then. He's exhausted. For the first time, his shirt isn't ironed, and I'm certain it's the same shirt from yesterday. Fuck, we both need to sleep.

"We go back to the beginning," I say, thinking of Hope, "and remind them that they're human. If they bleed, we'll get to the bottom of this."

He lets out a heavy sigh.

"How about you go home and get some rest. We're

not doing ourselves any favors by both being here with this little sleep. I'll take care of the paperwork and let you know if anything new comes across my desk."

He seems reluctant to leave. I can't blame him, as I'd be the same way.

"I just really want to put this fucker behind bars. We need justice," Lucas says, surprising me when he begins to pack his things.

"We'll get them. We always do." I grab his shoulder and nod reassuringly. "Make sure you say Hi to Heidi on the way out."

His cheeks pinken, and I try not to smirk at how awkward he is. But he's right. With the boss breathing down our necks and the number of bodies, we need to start getting answers.

Perhaps I haven't been smoking out my little vixen enough. I want her to expose herself and, in the process, her family. I want to see that beautiful neck on the chopping block and be the executioner above her to bring down the axe. I want her pulse beneath my fingers beating only because I allow it. I'm certain she shares the same sentiment. That makes me smirk.

She won't admit it, but these glass statues she designs are precious to her. I'm certain she started them to spook me. To prove that she can get into my home and express herself in a way that she thinks is unrecognizable. Unfortunately for her, everything she is, touches, and breathes into existence has her dark touch. The moment I saw the first piece, I knew it was hers. Instinct defies what I can see in this world, but I came to depend on it even before I started my career.

So, I'll use her little gifts as a way to coax her out. She thought we were playing a game, and we are, but now it's time I kick it up a notch.

Time is ticking, and soon, I'll have to strike.

When I return to my apartment that evening, I'm not surprised to see a black box on my bed. I grumble my complaint that she got in yet again. I even had extra security added to the building across from me, but that was wiped out, too. Everything within a block radius of me was wiped.

Whoever is behind it is clever. I immediately thought of Will Walker. But because he's friends with Hope's father, I didn't entertain the idea for long. I'm certain Alek Ivanov would've come to hand me my ass by now if he knew.

I pull out the new sculpture and look at the immaculate detail of the man with a slit throat, red bleeding through the wound. I don't even know how someone can be this fucking talented and is able to put in so much detail. I walk over to my crime board and notice the angle of the body in the statue is the exact same as the photo taken by our forensics staff.

She's copying from the crime scene photos that hit my desk; there's no denying it. But how in the fuck is she getting these photos in the first place?

No problem, I'll figure it out, and if Hope Ivanov has an ego and quirky creative flare, which I'm certain she does, I know the one thing that will offend her the most is by sending the statues back.

I drag out the box where I've carefully collected her pieces. I wrap them, ensuring they don't crack or break on the way, and stick a label on the box, ready to send to the rightful owner. She can claim all she likes that she doesn't know who made these or what they are, but her reaction to this will tell me plenty.

Hope might want to spook me with these, but I'm certain there's a part of her that wants to be seen. I've been studying her these past few months, and every hitched breath, small lingering look, and bitter word that comes out of her perfect fucking lips have been for me to figure out.

Now, I'll start using that knowledge against her.

I could hand deliver them myself, but showing up to Alek Ivanov's house without a warrant will probably get me killed.

I'm guilty of being many things, but stupid isn't one of them.

Then again, this might be one of the most reckless things I've done—handing back evidence—but I'm certain she won't be able to help herself from throwing the ball back.

CHAPTER 26

Hope

"Do you think when someone is bad, like really bad, that a good person can accept them the way they are? Like romantically?" I ask my father. He picked me up from the airport, which is nice. It's been a while since he's done that. I'm so used to the drivers coming to collect me that when I see a familiar face, especially my parents, I can't help but smile and feel like a big child again.

It's a relief coming back home, but the older I get, the more I realize I'm not a child anymore. I wonder if this is what it's like for Billie and Ford. They don't live together at the moment but they spend as much time as they possibly can with one another. Is that what it feels like for them? Like coming home to a big hug? I know my parents will always be here, and if anything, my father is probably the most reluctant about me moving out. I've considered getting my own place before, but right now, with my schedule and how much I travel, it just makes sense to stay with my parents.

But lately, I've been thinking more about my privacy. Most likely because my secrets only continue to grow.

My father is studying me in a way that often leaves most people unsettled. Maybe the question was too random, or I exposed myself too much by asking about relationships. "One of my friends from college recently started dating a guy, and she said he's really bad, but she's a good person..."

"Is this Charlotte you're talking about? Your mother doesn't like her."

"Ouch," I mumble, and he chuckles.

I haven't spoken to Charlotte recently, but I don't correct him. My mother's too nice to say that to my face anyway. My father, however, doesn't pull any punches.

"Your mother is good, and I'm bad. Yet here we are," he says simply. And I guess he's right. While I understand that my mother doesn't like to get involved in any of my father's business arrangements, he makes an effort to keep his work away from her whenever possible because he respects her boundaries. They are the most diverse a couple could be, in my opinion.

She is the epitome of what it means to be good and wholesome. She's charitable and kind and is always creating ways to empower women, which couldn't be more different from my father, who is infamous for his skill at killing and his underground auctions.

"But how did you know she was the one? Didn't you have obstacles?" I ask, pressing him for more. My father is a man of few words, and although my mother has often gushed about how my father persuaded her to give him a chance, I feel like they gloss over certain details. My mother simply said it wasn't always easy, and she had to be patient with him. Aunt Anya let it slip that he almost died killing an ex-girlfriend to protect my mother, and my mother was quick to usher me away into another room, trying to laugh it off. I was six at the time. And when I reflect back to my upbringing, I remember how much my mother tried to hide from me.

What if all of that darkness is somehow finding its way to me now? What if I truly do take more after my father than my mother?

"All relationships have obstacles. But if he's a piece of shit, I can deal with him... For Charlotte. Even if your mother doesn't like her," he says.

"You don't have to keep adding that last part, Dad," I say, and I can see the humor dance across his eyes. I try not to laugh as we pull into the estate.

Lately, I've been feeling shitty and conflicted about the lies I keep telling, but I don't think I can pull away from the path, curious about where it will take me. My family has always supported me in every aspect of my life, so hiding these things is starting to make me feel... guilty isn't the right word, but I question how much of a conscience I have. Because I know it's bad, and I know I shouldn't be doing it, but I just can't help myself. And I don't understand why I can't stop. Braxton complicates everything.

I was always quiet and reserved. Just observing everyone around me. I like to take in people's actions and their words to see how truthful they are. People accepted me that way, but Braxton tugs on an entirely different part of me. And it scares me. I know he's bad for me. I know I should stop. But I can't. And in truth, I'm not ready to. How bad is bad? When will I stop? When will I draw the line and actually kill him?

Would my mother be disappointed in me? She uses her talents to express emotion in song and movement. When people hear her sing, it's like floating on clouds. She used to sing me to sleep every night, and some nights my father would lie in bed with me as she did, and we would both fall asleep to her lullabies.

My greatest creations are born of something twisted and grotesque. Where mine make people's lips curl in disgust, just like the person at the café. That's how my true art would be received, and I'm incapable of putting myself out there for it like she can.

My father pulls up at the front of the house to drop me off. He has a business meeting to attend with my aunt, so I lean over to give him a hug and thank him for picking me up before I get out of the car.

I once asked what he thought of my mother's singing, and his answer stuck with me. *"It's like heaven and hell all mixed into one. It can soothe you, but at the same time, it can move you."*

I always dreamed of having a love like theirs. If there's one thing in this life I know I want someday, it's that. But lately, I've been thinking about it a little more, and I feel like I'm in foreign territory.

The butler comes to collect my bags and welcomes me home. "Welcome back, Miss Ivanov. A package came for you. It's on your bed."

"A package?" I ask.

"Yes. It appears to be from a gallery. Don't worry. We've checked to make sure it's safe."

I sigh, not because they opened it but why it's necessary. My father put in place a process to ensure no kind of weapons, like bombs or poisons, would reach the members of our family. See, not entirely normal.

I walk into my room and see a medium-sized box on my bed. I don't recall purchasing anything or being offered any gifts, but things are sent to me from time to time. A box cutter is waiting for me, and before I slice it open, I pluck the white note from atop the box.

These are as beautiful as their creator.

But my shelves are full.

xx

A bad feeling begins to swirl in my stomach as I slice open the box and pull the bubble wrap away. My teeth grind as I look down at the collection of my glass statues.

He sent them back to me?

How fucking dare he send them back to me!

He had the cheek to send them back to me, convinced with the absolute certainty that I created them. Not only that, but he's daring enough to send them to my home. Is this guy for fucking real? Does he not fear me even in the slightest?

Does he not appreciate the time I put into creating these? Granted, initially, they weren't for him. But as of late, I've kept him in mind as I methodically create each and every piece. I fucking sweated for hours to make these, and he thinks they're worth so little that he can just ship them in a box with fucking bubble wrap?!

Fucking bubble wrap?!

I want to grind them into dust. Then, it occurs to me that he might be baiting. I sit at the edge of my bed, biting the edge of my nail. If I were Braxton Hero, what would I be thinking? Why would I be doing this?

A lethal hum rises under my skin.

I hate him so fucking much.

Then, an idea sparks in my mind. It's risky. It could backfire.

But Braxton and I are far from playing a child's game.

I grab my phone and send a message to Hawke to schedule another shooting practice.

I tape up the box, fucking furious.

The sooner I put a bullet in his head, the better.

"Miss Ivanov, your dress for this evening is ready. Where are you going?" our butler asks as I hurry out, carrying the box that's most likely half my fucking weight, with the determination of a woman on a warpath.

"I'll be back soon. I'm just making a quick delivery to a friend. I won't be late," I call out to him.

I can tell he's nervous. Most likely because my agent, Candice, allegedly lost her mind at him once when I was late for an event. I don't intend on getting anyone in trouble today.

Except a certain asshole who needs a taste of his own medicine.

CHAPTER 27

Hope

"Motherfucker thinks he's funny," I grumble as I glance over at the passenger seat where I've placed the box. "He just assumes it's me. Just assumes I'm the one with the twisted and fucked-up mind."

My hands grip the steering wheel tightly. I don't know why this feels like a rejection, but it does, and I can't fucking stand it. Not only does he have the balls to have this delivered to my home, but he also sent every fucking piece back. They can't all be shit!

When I drive by his apartment building, I notice his car isn't where it's usually parked. I could dump it at his door, cameras be damned. I want him to know I returned them. But even better, I decide to go to the next place I think I can find him.

He wants to come to my safe place, then I'll fucking go to his.

The police station is only a ten-minute drive from his apartment—naturally, he wants to be close to work. I'm smiling when I spot his car, barely hitting the brakes as I drive straight into the back of his car.

I brace myself at the impact. My head hits my forearms, as I anticipated, and I breathe out, a jolt of adrenaline rushing through me. Someone screams from the sidewalk, but I ignore them as I get out of my car, open the passenger door, and grab the box. I must look like a fucking mess after traveling all day and then coming straight here, but I don't care.

There's damage to my car, but I'm certain it'll still get me home. A police officer gapes as he rushes out of the precinct doors. "It was an accident," I say sweetly as I carry the box inside and straight to the reception desk.

The woman at the desk is gawking with her mouth open. She looks at me and then at a side door, which I expect Braxton to come out of at any moment.

"I'd like to see Braxton Hero. I'm under the firm impression he's working today since I *accidentally* just rammed my Ferrari into his car. I have a gift for him."

"And an apology?" the woman asks, flabbergasted.

My eyebrows furrow. "No. The box contains statues."

Suddenly, I'm wondering if he works with a bunch of morons because she doesn't seem to be moving.

An officer slowly approaches me. "Ma'am, you've just damaged a police—"

"Leave her." Braxton's voice carries over the room as he appears from somewhere deeper in the precinct, and I smile like it's the happiest moment of my life to see him. "I'll handle this."

The officer seems unconvinced and points to Braxton's car. Braxton looks out the glass doors and his jaw tics.

"Too short for the brake pedal, Shortcake?" he growls.

"No, my heel slipped," I say innocently as I glance over his shoulder and into the area he came from. The same one he took me into months ago.

People are cuffed to chairs as they sit there and wait their turn, and officers walk around talking, eating, or drinking coffee.

He makes a point to bring his hand near his waist, drawing attention to the gun in his holster. He's wearing all black, and the badge I came all over only a week ago hangs around his neck. I feel rather smug with a twisted idea of how it might look as a noose instead. His sleeves are rolled up to showcase the tattoos on his arm, and I can't help but smile as those blue eyes darken with anger.

Oooh, I really got to him this time. Good.

He takes a few steps and reaches for me. People are watching us, but I don't really care. I make a pointed look down to the box in my hands, and when he follows my gaze, it's like he hadn't noticed it before.

"What are you doing?" he hisses.

"I think your package got lost in the mail and somehow ended up at my house," I inform him. "While I appreciate the compliment that you thought I was the one to create them, they're not mine to take, so please take possession of your belongings." His gaze flicks to the box and back to me and then back to the box again like he can't believe what I'm doing. What did he expect to happen when he sent this to me? Did he really think I'd just accept it?

He then looks back at his car. That's just a fucking bonus. *Asshole.*

"You're still denying you made them?" he asks in disbelief.

"I can't possibly be the only gifted person you know." I lean in. "Also, please tell me you understand there's a difference between what I do and what's in this box because it's not the same."

"*You* are the most gifted person I know." I'm taken aback by his words. I didn't actually expect him to admit that. He looks back down to the box again, avoiding my gaze, and I wonder if he's realizing too late what he said. "If they aren't yours, then throw them away. I have no need for this trash," he says.

Trash?

Fucking *trash*?

He thinks my work is trash?

I mask my imploding thoughts, too stunned to reply, which he takes advantage of and continues. "I'll be in touch about the insurance for the car. Have a good day, Shortcake. Don't want to be late for your event this evening." Then he turns back toward the bullpen. I stare after him. For the first time in my life I'm actually shocked into silence. I don't know what to do or say.

What the fuck is this asshole playing at?

My nails curl into the box, and I hold my head high as the receptionist watches me anxiously.

Piece of shit. Asshole. Dickhead.

Wait to see what's coming to you. You fucking deserve every slow torture in the world.

I fume on the inside as I leave with the box. I'm not so furious and stupid as to leave it in the center of a police station. Even though I was here to hand it to a fucking detective. I don't know what the fuck I'm thinking lately, but it's certainly nothing sane.

I set the box back in the passenger seat, start the engine, and throw the car in reverse. His bumper falls off when the vehicles are no longer pinned together, and I smirk, a tiny bit satisfied by the damage.

Piece of shit.

I don't know what I plan to do with the statues now. I expected him to take them back because they're his.

And he will take them back.

* * *

My mood hasn't gotten any better since I smashed the asshole's car. If anything, I want to return and throw gasoline on it. I'm surprised Braxton hasn't yet filed the insurance claim, but I wonder if it's a strategic move. Neither of us want my parents to know about me being anywhere near him or a police station, and had I been smarter, I wouldn't have left behind evidence. But the damage is quite literally already done.

Part of me hopes the asshole keeps this to himself. I try my best to smile for the cameras at yet another event. Thankfully, I didn't have to travel far for this one, and it's more of a social event to raise money for a charity, which my mother has always been an advocate of. So doing things like this always makes me feel good about myself because it reminds me that although I'm not the same as my mother, I can follow her lead and try to do some good with my fortune.

I would have much preferred to stay home tonight. I'm in such a shitty mood already, and now I have to mingle with a fellow artist who is represented by the same agent I am. To say Kylie hates me is an understatement. Every time we're in public together, she plasters on a fake smile and pretends to be my best friend, when in reality, she can't stand to be near me.

She's been rather boisterous about her displeasure with my level of success compared to hers, accusing me of favoritism or somehow buying my way up the ranks, and that's even with her having no understanding of who my family is. It's a pretentious concept among the inner circles, which is why I hate it here. Even if you have talent, everyone assumes someone paid someone to get where they're at.

The success I gained, especially over the last four years, took her much longer to accomplish. She's only become popular within the last year when she hit her stride in her thirties. Part of me doesn't blame her because if I were working that hard for so many years without recognition, I'd probably be bitter as well. But to place the blame on me is a bit fucking stupid if you ask me. This industry has temporary seasons and favorites. Anyone can be spat out at any second.

I walk up to one of her pieces and admire the craftsmanship. She is definitely skilled.

See, I can fucking admit when something great is sitting in front of me, so why the fuck can't a certain asshole appreciate my art?

Gah. I want to rip out my hair since my thoughts have, yet again, returned to him. I'm going so fucking crazy; I might actually kill someone tonight.

"I see you've sold out." I turn to find Kylie standing next to me, her fake smile plastered to her lips.

Fuck me, her timing couldn't be any worse. She'll probably be next on my shit list, right behind a certain asshole who's always on the top of it.

"And you?" I ask, trying to keep the same level of enthusiasm.

"Close." She side-eyes me.

"Good," I reply, not entirely sure what she wants from me. It's never pleasant when we're talking among ourselves, and I don't have the patience for her tonight. I'm already fuming so much on the inside I'm not sure how collected I can remain. But I do what I was taught to do in these situations—I grin and bear it.

She's wearing a black, fitted dress with black heels, and her dark hair is pulled back in a low ponytail that cascades down her back. She goes to say something else, but someone walks over and asks her a question. I couldn't be more grateful for their interruption.

I glance once more at her piece before I circulate through the rest of the room. I'm always more interested to see the upcoming artists and their styles. I enjoy finding the small faults and revisiting my own years of polishing a talent that, to some degree, will never be perfect.

I spot a woman around my age with someone I assume is her mother, admiring one of my pieces. It'd be nice to have my mother here, but I learned a long time ago to keep my worlds separate. Whenever Lena Love walks into a room, people notice. And I don't mind at all when my mother takes the spotlight. In fact, I prefer it. But I know it makes her uncomfortable when it happens at my events because she wants the light to be on me.

People also create a narrative that I could've only come so far because of her influence so I realized it's easier to draw a line between the two things I love most in this world.

"Hope." I turn back to Kylie, who is give me a narrow-eyed once-over. Without her saying a word, I know she's thinking of some bitchy comment. In public, though, she's usually well-behaved, but if she can slip an underhanded comment in, she will. She knows how to hold her composure, but I know when the shift happens inside her. People are predictable if nothing else. "Next week, don't wear that." She looks down at my dress and shakes her head disapprovingly before walking away.

There it is.

I look down at my purple dress. I like it; it's one of my mother's. I do love going through my mother's closet and stealing her dresses. She has exquisite and expensive taste. Jealousy is a bitch, and Kylie is both jealous and a bitch.

Kylie mingles with the crowd, hyping up our joint show next week. Tonight was just a taste of what's to come, and no matter how much I don't want to see her again so soon, I'll have to.

Lucky for her, I'm only obsessed with ruining one person's life right now. And it's not hers.

CHAPTER 28

Braxton

I've been getting questions all day about who she is. The gossip spreads quickly in the office. And everyone wants to know who the little redhead with glasses who smashed into my car is. The rumor's already going around about her being an angry ex, and I don't bother to correct them that what she is to me is far more complex than that.

Despite it costing me a pretty fucking penny to get my car fixed, it amuses me to know I got under her skin that much. And I don't mind using a rental car until my vehicle is repaired.

I knew sending the statues back would be the catalyst to her crumbling and inevitable downfall. Hope is clever and beautiful. And she has the world at her fingertips. She's not a snob but she does care for her craft deeply.

And if I have to exploit that to get to her, then so be it. I've never been above being a petty little fuck.

I decided to pay for my car out of pocket instead of going through insurance because I didn't want any of her family members to discover our association. Though, I remain prepared for one of them to possibly sniff too closely. Especially a certain Ivanov twin whom I've kept close tabs on. Well, as close as one can get to Hawke Ivanov.

Lucas walks in, places his briefcase on his chair, and leans against his desk as I get ready to leave. I have somewhere to be, and I waited for him to come in. I know she was at an event this evening, but it's her afterparty celebrations that I'm interested in.

"What the fuck happened to your car? The boys were telling me about it. Is it true that Hope Ivanov crashed into it?" Lucas questions.

"Apparently so," I say dismissively. "Must've still been pissed off about me cuffing her months ago."

"And you didn't bring her in?" he asks incredulously.

I raise a brow at him. "You know we can't touch them."

"If she hits your car in front of the fucking station, yeah, you can. You have evidence and grounds to—"

"Lucas." I place my hand on his shoulder to stop him. "Do you trust me?"

His eyebrows furrow. "Well, of course. I have your

back. I don't get it. There's more to you two than you've told me, isn't there?"

I shake my head. "I need you to trust me. I'm working just as hard on this case as you are, okay? Let me do this my way. When have I ever failed us before?"

He seems unsure as he stares at the floor. "It just doesn't feel right."

I tighten my grip on his shoulder. "I know. That's why I'm not getting you involved. Just stick to what you're doing now. We're so close, I can almost taste it."

Lucas nods curtly. "Thank you for forcing me to go home. It felt good to actually get some sleep. You're going home to do the same, right? You look like shit."

I laugh. "I know that's a lie. I'm handsome even when tired," I say on my way out.

I kill the headlights about a quarter of a mile from the shooting spot where they practiced last time. They've set up a large light on the car, and Hope hopelessly aims for the target, Hawke shaking his head in disapproval. She's a pretty shitty shot. And part of me knows it's my face she imagines in the center of that target.

From now on, I plan on watching her from a distance. Hope demands attention, if only from me. I know her secret even if she's not willing to admit it. She'll want me to reach out to her. She'll expect it. I'll watch her from the shadows, waiting to see when she fucks up.

Because it's only a matter of time.

CHAPTER 29

Hope

I dropped the box at his apartment last week, and I haven't heard from him since. The package hasn't been sent back, and he hasn't even so much as returned to the café. I thought I'd be fucking elated when he stopped popping up where I was, but instead, I'm seriously pissed off. Is he giving me the silent treatment or something?

Fuck him. Who cares? If anything, it's reminded me to harden my resolve about killing the fucker.

I watched the news last night. There was another murder, and the image of the body had already come through on my burner phone. This time, the man was stabbed multiple times in his home. The police allegedly have not yet been able to identify the culprit, but it's assumed to be the unnamed serial killer.

My eyes lit up when I saw all the red, bleeding holes,

and my hands itched to replicate them in glass. That's what I'll be working on next, and hopefully, it'll help me purge this building rage.

I almost lose track of time in my studio until my agent calls me to let me know she's getting her hair done for tonight's event, and she hopes I'm in the process of getting ready. I lie, of course, then hightail it out of my studio and back home to get ready.

I'm certain my mom will be home at this time. We're not usually home at the same time, and my mother once made a joke that I work the same schedule as my father. It's usually early in the morning when I get home, and I sleep most of the day and then go back out and do it again. I know it's not a healthy habit to be working most of the night, but it just seems to be when I'm the most creative. And I don't want to stop that just yet, especially when it keeps me productive and feeling less stabby.

I search through my mother's closet to find another purple dress. Just because Kylie told me not to wear the same thing again—I'm going to fucking do it. Kylie always wears black; she thinks it's professional, I guess, so she's going to shun away from anything that might bleed some color into her bitter soul. I find a dress that is very close in color to the last one and do my hair in a similar style to how I had it done last week, but this time, I pair it with silver heels.

"You working tonight?" Mom asks as she sits on my bed.

"Hey, Mom." I give her an awkward hug, as the dress is only half zipped up. I was hoping I'd see her before I left, but she wasn't here when I first arrived.

Her gaze scans my room, her expression going soft as she takes in the pale pink feature wall, the small balcony that overlooks the courtyard, and the pictures I have tacked to a board next to my vanity table.

"Yes. It's going to be a long night," I admit as I try to get the dress zipped the rest of the way. She laughs and beckons me over to help me. I have a similar curvaceous shape to my mother. I'm glad she taught me to embrace it at a young age.

"Can I come?" she asks.

I turn to look at her. It's strange that she's asking. I don't usually like my parents coming to my work events because I don't want people to think I got to where I am today just because my mother is famous. After all, that's the furthest thing from the truth. And my father intimidates full-grown men just by looking at them. I've asked nicely that they don't attend, and they're happy to go along with my request as long as I make pieces for them in return. My sculptures are placed all throughout the house, and the moment a new guest walks through the door, my mother shame-lessly brags that her daughter created them. The guests are always polite, even when they didn't ask about them. It's like a slow torture and rite of passage into our home. At least that's what my father and I joke about since it's rarely us bringing someone new to our home.

"Maybe next time?" I say quietly, a small pebble of guilt sinking into my stomach. If Kylie weren't going to be at this event, I probably would let her come. But Kylie already has it out for me; if she finds out who my parents are, it'll just make her dig her heels in even farther.

"Yes, of course," she chirps, as if unfazed by the subtle rejection. I feel bad, and I know she's feeling sentimental about something, or she wouldn't be looking around my room like that. I sit beside her and grab her hand.

"What's wrong?"

"Nothing's wrong," she says, then cups my cheek with a sad smile. "I've just been thinking a lot lately about how quickly you're growing up. Everyone's kids are getting married."

I nudge her shoulder. "Well, not everyone, just Eli and Dutton. And, to be honest, they're probably the bad eggs we should've been worried about, so it's a relief, right?"

She laughs, hand to heart. I love my mom's laugh. I love her voice. I love everything about her. "Don't worry, I'm not getting married anytime soon," I assure her.

"You might as well be married to your job. You're as bad as me and your father." She smiles. "I just want to make sure you're happy. That we haven't pushed you too much. Maybe we should organize a family trip. It's been a while."

I'm shocked, wondering where this has come from, and I press a kiss to her hand. Guilt immediately floods me. Is she feeling disconnected because of the lies I've been piling on? Or is she anticipating me leaving the nest? Is it time for that? Am I ready? Is that what she's picking up on?

My mother chuckles. "I can always tell when you're thinking." She flicks my forehead lightly. "I just really want to make sure you're okay. You seem busier than usual. I hardly see you, and I miss you, that's all."

She brings me in for a hug, and I sigh. It's nice. I've been so busy and preoccupied with my own lies that I didn't even notice how much distance, literally and figuratively, our schedules have put between us.

I feel an unfamiliar sense of courage building inside me as I look around the room with her. Maybe it is time for a change. Maybe I can't always come back to this house. Maybe I need to stop arguing with my father that I'm not a child and show him that I'm an adult.

Something is changing, and I'm not entirely sure I like it. But it feels like something that's due to run its natural course.

Fuck it.

"Would it just be you coming tonight?" I ask. Her eyes brighten, and she smiles with a quick nod.

"Okay. I just don't want Dad terrorizing everyone into purchasing all my pieces again."

She laughs. "Are you sure, sweetie?"

"Yes." I need to stop worrying about what people will think about my parents. Who gives a fuck if they think I bought my way? I know the truth, and it's a beautiful thing to have my family's support when not everyone has the same luxury. But I've also had my reservations because I know this is the only side of me they'll approve of.

"I have a few things to do before I arrive at the event, but I'll see you there?" I ask, ignoring the call from my agent. I know if I don't call her back after the second call, though, she'll find me. She always does... in a creepy, stalker kind of way.

"Yes. What would you like me to wear?" she asks excitedly.

I can't help but smile. I really did luck out having parents who have given me the world. And I feel so guilty that they ended up with a defective child, which is part of the reason why I won't tell them my secrets.

Some lies are nicer to swallow.

"You look good in anything, Mom," I tell her, then kiss her cheek.

I have to go back to my studio to collect some last-minute things before I head to the event. She walks me out and kisses my cheek as I get in the car, and she tells me how excited she is to come. It's nice to know she'll be there. It's been almost two years since I let her come to an event, and for once, maybe I won't be so uncomfortable being a spot of color in an otherwise dull and colorless crowd.

* * *

Kylie is the first person I see when I walk through the doors, and her expression conveys her horror at my dress. Did she really think I was going to take her advice on what to wear? Absolutely fucking not.

She saunters up to me, always enjoying the fact that she's about half a foot taller than me, so she looks down her nose at me. "You look the same as you did at the last event," she sneers and flicks her hair over her shoulder. She has on a black dress—again—but this time, her hair is down. It's not quite as long as mine, but it's long enough that it covers her shoulder blades.

"And you look as beautiful as always," I say sweetly. She hates it when I'm nice to her because she's only nice to me when others are around. I kill her with kindness because it pisses her off.

"Just don't embarrass me; there's someone here who I admire," she warns.

I glance around the room. I went through the list of expected attendees, and most of them are people we've established good working relationships with.

"You? Admire someone?" I say, shocked. "Are they dead? Is that why you always look dressed for a funeral?"

She pins me with a glare, and I try not to laugh. Come on, that was funny. It wouldn't hurt the bitch to crack a smile and pull the pole out of her ass at least once.

"Ha ha. No, she's over there. Oh my God, she's coming this way. Stay calm, and don't ruin this for me."

I follow her gaze and bite my bottom lip. My mother is heading our way, and I can't help but find it ironic that her idol created and birthed someone she despises. I'd like to consider myself a bigger person, but sometimes I relish moments like these. I never thought there'd be a day when I'd weaponize my mother like this, and she doesn't even know.

I really want to see Kylie's face when she realizes who her idol is, but instead, my mother pulls me in for a hug, blocking my view.

"It's so amazing, Hope. You've achieved so much," she gushes, then turns to Kylie. "And you, Kylie. I love your work as well. I might just have to buy a piece to go with Hope's pieces around my house to commemorate today's events," Mom says.

My mother was never hugely into art until I became interested in it. Aunt Anya, however, has always admired anything beautiful. I don't bring her to these events either because she'll stab someone for looking at her the wrong way.

I finally shoot a glance at Kylie and mask my glee. I

actually expect her eyes to pop out of her head as she collects herself and clenches her jaw. She doesn't know that Lena Love's my mother yet, but knowing her idol has multiple pieces of my work in her home must absolutely be fucking up her system right now.

Kylie's quick to insert herself, offering her hand to my mother, not missing a beat of opportunity. She begins telling my mother the inspiration behind the pieces and basically pushes me out of the conversation. Mom glances at me, but I wave off her concern. If this is Kylie's claim to fame, then so be it. I'm petty enough to know I've already fucking won if this is what her championship looks like.

"I'll be back." I dismiss myself just as Kylie hooks her arm around my mother's and proceeds to drag her around the exhibit. I suspect this kind of behavior is worse in my mother's industry—the need and drive to be the best and cutting down others to achieve it at any cost. So, whether Kylie realizes it or not, my mother is great at spotting people like her a mile away.

But if it keeps Kylie away from me for the time being, I'm happy to throw my mother to the wolves as I head to the bar to grab a couple of glasses of champagne for my mother and me. Although I usually use a glass in one hand more like a prop, tonight, I feel like I'll enjoy a glass with my mom. Having her here isn't so bad after all.

It's nice to be in Manhattan. I wonder when my schedule will slow down enough to give me an opportunity to look for a place of my own now that I've decided that that's what I want to do. I want somewhere with a nice sunroom like my studio has. That way, I can have a similar setup if the mood strikes when I'm at home and don't feel like driving to the studio.

"What, no whiskey?" a voice questions from behind me. I'm terrified the flutes in my hands might crack with how tightly I grip them as I turn around and face... Braxton.

I pretend to trip and spill one of the drinks on him. "Oops. I'm so sorry," I say as I place the empty glass down and grab some napkins. I begin patting the wet spot on his shirt. I look up at him through my glasses. "I'm so clumsy."

Dickhead.

Asshole.

Ghost.

Braxton stares down at his shirt. He clicks his tongue, then smirks as he presses my hand, holding the napkins to his chest, and then begins to move it slowly, almost sensually, over the damp fabric.

"Perhaps you can clean up a different mess." His voice is gravelly.

"How crude," I bite back, pulling my hand away.

"So is fucking up someone's car and spilling a drink on them."

I cross my arms over my chest. "It's weird. I didn't know ghosts talked these days."

"Oh, Shortcake. I'm not ghosting anyone. I'm just doing what you asked, or rather demanded, of me—leaving you alone." He grins. "But by your peeved tone, maybe that's not what you really want."

Whatever.

He's wiping down his shirt, completely unfazed, which bothers me even more.

Now? He wants to turn up now? And here, of all places? The asshole has some balls coming to one of my events uninvited... and entirely unwelcome. Though, I can't help but quickly sweep an appreciative gaze over his attire. He's dressed way nicer than usual. I'm used to seeing him in black slacks and a black button-up shirt. Not that he doesn't have black slacks on right now, but in place of the dress shirt is an undershirt with a long trench coat over the top of it. He takes the coat off, shaking his head at the mess, then hands it to an attendant who's hovering nearby.

He must have just arrived. Did he spot me from the door and just head straight for me?

I take a sip of the champagne, the tension palpable between us. So many fucking things I want to say to him, and yet... I just want to rip his fucking clothes off. The thought of going to the coat closet pops into my mind, and I must be out of my fucking head to even consider that with this man.

Braxton's expression is smug like he's won or is right about something.

"What?" I bite. It's then I realize I'm rapidly tapping my foot. I force myself to stop. *Fuck.* I don't want him reading anything from body language.

"You look ravishing as always, Shortcake," he says and steps closer, basically caging me against the bar. He looks down at the glass in my hand and then back at me. "Do you plan to drink that this time?" I don't bother asking him how he knows I don't always drink it.

It's obvious that I've taken two sips since he's stepped into my vicinity, so with a bit of snark in my tone, I say, "I gave up on drinking; seems I do stupid shit when I do."

"Yes, I guess stealing police officers' wallets would make me want to quit drinking, too," he says. "Please don't tell me you were drinking when our cars had that damaging kiss."

"I'd say it was more like mine forcefully shoving up the ass of yours, which couldn't take it."

His smile grows. "I missed that poisonous tongue of yours, Shortcake."

My stomach drops, and I hate that my body is so responsive to him. The hot flush that immediately washes over me, and my body demands to rip apart this man to show him well and truly how much I fucking hate him.

"Are you stalking me again?" I ask at the same time someone says, "Braxton, you came."

I turn to find Kylie, her face glowing as she leans in

and kisses Braxton on the cheek. He side-eyes me as she does it, and I give him no reaction. *Eww.* My mother, unfortunately, saw it. She moves around Kylie and Braxton to stand by my side.

The moment Kylie steps away from Braxton—you could make the argument that he somewhat pushed her away—my mother cuts in, and I'm reminded that my father isn't the only parent to be wary of.

"Hi, I'm Lena Love, Hope's mother. And you are?" she says with a smile that doesn't reach her eyes.

I watch with growing satisfaction as the realization of who her idol really is clicks in Kylie's mind. She must've been talking so much about herself that she never questioned how my mother and I are associated.

Braxton, on the other hand, knows exactly who she is. He offers her his hand, and they shake firmly as she studies him. I always wondered how someone so soft and sweet could handle someone as cruel as my father. But as she holds Braxton's hand, I see the fire behind her eyes. It's moments like these that I know she probably gave my father hell as he pursued her.

"Y-you're related to Hope?" Kylie stammers and it breaks the awkward moment, reminding us that she exists.

"Yes, she is," I confirm, smiling. "Besties." I cross my fingers over one another, being an asshole.

My mother drops Braxton's hand and seems completely oblivious to Kylie's reaction. No, she's fixated on Braxton, uncomfortably so, as if she already knows the things that have happened between us. "Braxton, how do you know my daughter?"

"You know Hope, too?" Kylie asks Braxton, and I can tell she's really trying to keep her shit together right now. By how friendly she is with Braxton, they've either fucked or are fucking. Or she wants that to be a reality. Now I just feel bad.

"I do," he answers, watching Kylie. "Although we're only acquaintances."

"'Acquaintances' is a bit of a stretch," I bite back.

"Shall I tell them the story of how we met?" He raises a brow at me.

I pin him with a glare, and my mother reaches out and squeezes my hand. "If you'll excuse us, I have to speak to my daughter."

She doesn't let me respond as she practically drags me to the bathroom. She checks every stall to make sure no one else is in here.

When she turns and faces me, her eyes wide, I can tell she knows who he is.

How the fuck does she know who he is? How much does she know?

"A detective?" she whisper-shouts.

"That's what he is. Unfortunately, I'm not in charge of choosing people's career paths for them."

She pins me with her stare. Right, sarcasm is not going to get me out of this one. She's seriously pissed.

"Is this why you've been coming home so late? Have you been hiding a certain detective from us? You know you can tell me anything, but you also understand the issues that would come with having someone like him in our family, right?"

I put my hands up in defense. "Whoa, you're suddenly starting to sound like a detective yourself with this interrogation. It's nothing."

"I know when *nothing* is *something* to my own daughter, Hope Ivanov."

Oh fuck. I'm seriously in trouble if she's bringing out the last name.

"Do you think your father didn't tell me about the detective who took a particular interest in you on the night Charlotte stole that wallet? You give me too little credit."

"It's not like that. I swear I didn't know he was going to be here. Obviously, he came here for Kylie."

She doesn't look at all happy with that response, crossing her arms over her chest. It's moments like this that I know exactly who I adopted that stance from. And when my body goes to do it in response to her, I stop myself. My hands clench into fists and then relax. What the fuck am I supposed to tell her?

"Are you telling me you haven't had anything to do with that man since that night?"

I bite the inside of my cheek, conflicted by the lies I've been telling. I mean, technically, she didn't say *what* night. I hate lying to my mother. There's a difference between this and my sick, twisted hobbies, though. Isn't there?

I do understand everything she's telling me, and I've thought about it several times over the last few months since I've been seeing him. Not that anything happened between us right away, but that kiss led to me going home with him and a parking lot rendezvous. And while nothing else has happened since then, I can't deny there is a very strong attraction between us. Yes, I'm pissed off with him and plan to kill him, but I can't exactly tell my mother that.

"Nothing's happening with the detective. He's a total asshole."

"Your father was an asshole too. A very charming one," she bites back.

I try not to smile.

Whatever this living and breathing thing between me and Braxton is, it isn't going anywhere except to the grave with him—soon. But I don't fucking like the idea of there being more between him and Kylie. I wonder how they know each other and why he's here to see her. He's not dressed like he just came from work; he's dressed for a date. And all the digging I've done has indicated that he's very single. Even his apartment shows me that he's single. So why is he here to see Kylie?

"The way he was looking at you..." Mom starts, shaking her head. "You're lucky it was me here tonight instead of your father, or that man would already be dead."

"I don't know if that's because he's an asshole or because he's a man," I reply, unsure as to which way the threat is swinging.

"Both," she says. "And let me just say, your father is the least of that man's worries if he tries to mess with you." A chill runs through me, and I'm certain my mother, in her own way, could and would destroy any person who tried to hurt me.

It's definitely best that I don't tell her how he hurt me in all the ways I like.

"Just stay clear of him. And be careful. You may not want it to go any further, but sometimes, things have a way of unraveling themselves. There's tension between you two. Don't get caught up in it," she warns.

And I swallow hard. If she only knew the mess I've already gotten myself into.

Then again, fucking a detective surely will be the least of her concerns compared with the other damning things I've done.

Another secret.

Another lie.

It terrifies me how quickly they build.

CHAPTER 30

Braxton

She hasn't come back since she took off with her mother, and I've been left standing with Kylie, explaining that I've met Hope before but not going into detail about it because that's none of her business.

This tangible, living thing between me and Hope is ours; it's not for anyone else. Even if her mother can clearly see there's something going on. I wonder how adamantly Hope will deny any form of association with me. I suppose I'll know in due time if someone tries to take me out. I should be more cautious about antagonizing her family. It's only a matter of time before one of them comes for me, but I really don't give a shit. Let them come.

"Wow, okay. Well, as long as there's nothing

happening between you two, that's fine," Kylie says dismissively as if she has any say in the matter.

If she really wanted to dig further, she would only need to ask her brother, Lucas. My partner is partially the reason why I'm here. He's been asking me for months to go on a date with his sister. Kylie is successful and attractive, dedicating herself to her work, and now considering settling down. I'm nowhere near ready for that. The thought of it revolts me, most likely because my thoughts are preoccupied with a certain redheaded sculptor.

For my partner's sake, to get his sister to stop hounding him, two months ago, I agreed to come to this show. I'm a man of my word, so here I am on a date with a woman I've met a handful of times. But like an asshole, it's not her I was excited to see. It became a bonus when I found out Hope was going to be here. I was wondering how the silent treatment might be triggering her. Epically, I'd say, considering the first thing she did was intentionally spill a drink on me. My lips twitch in amusement. What a handful she is.

Kylie's talking about the inspiration behind her work and practically pitching herself as a potential wife candidate. I'm listening politely but watching the direction that Hope and her mother went in as we order at the bar. I can tell there is jealousy there on Kylie's side, and to be honest, I don't blame her. Hope is very successful, and she's done it all by herself, contrary to some people's beliefs.

"I know why she's so successful now; it's because of her mother," Kylie says spitefully in Hope's direction. Great, another bitter person.

"You think?" I ask. She tosses her hair over her shoulder as she nods, as if it's so obvious.

"Yes. Imagine being the daughter of someone so famous and influential," she says, her tone dripping with envy. I wonder how Kylie would react to knowing the power Hope's father holds and why. I wonder if she'd be so loose with her tongue. "It explains so much. Like how she got access to all these shows, how she's able to wear dresses that cost up to six figures and carry bags that most women dream of. All of it basically handed to her."

"So you don't think there's any skill in her craftsmanship? You think she's put in fewer hours than you because her parents are rich?" I clarify.

Kylie's mouth opens and then shuts. "Well, she has *some* talent, but that's not all you need to get a big break." I zone out the rest of what she says. The reality is Kylie hasn't made it as far in her career because she's been too busy watching others, envying them.

Hope and her mother are greeted by a woman I recognize as Candice, Hope's agent. She's ushering them over to a photographer, and I can see the way Hope dies inside. It's interesting to see her up close this way, in the environment she thrives in—or not so much, I suppose. She clearly hates these events, but she smiles as she has her photo taken.

She's perfect. Inside and out.

I wonder if everyone in this room would still think that if they knew what her twisted idea of a muse is. Then again, it's probably why she feels so trapped.

I'm not a good man. I'll exploit those weaknesses to create space for a confession.

Hope's gaze drifts over to me, but she's quick to look away. Me being here is more than enough to rattle her.

As long as I'm still under her skin, then I know everything I'm doing to piss her off is working.

I smirk. Good. Because the wilder she is, the more likely she's going to make a mistake.

CHAPTER 31

Hope

Maybe my mother telling me this thing I have with Braxton is just a fling and nothing else is the kick in the ass I needed. Even if I lied about the true extent of how I know Braxton, my mother isn't stupid, and she'll most likely be watching me a lot closer now.

Sex with Braxton is great, in a volatile way, but if I'm going to kill him, I need to do it soon. It's all starting to get a little too complicated for something that feels so good. I do the bare minimum of mingling and enjoy a drink with my mother before deciding to leave. I put in my time, and now I'm ready to leave, my social battery exhausted.

My mother is buzzing, and she just got off the phone with my father, briefly telling him all about the show and how proud of me she is. It's nice, and I'm really glad I decided to invite her tonight. We've collected our jackets and are making our way down to the car, which is waiting for us at the curb. The driver opens the back door for us, and I'm halfway down the stairs when a single drop of rain falls from the sky to my cheek as a storm rolls in.

"Shortcake." I take another step, ignoring him, and then my mother snags my attention. She's watching us carefully. *Fuck.* If I don't address him at all, she's going to be even more suspicious.

I look over my shoulder as another raindrop falls on my face. I pin him with a glare that silently tells him not to speak to me. Kylie is next to him, and she slides a hand around his elbow, an obvious claim, and some creature within me claws to get out. It's fucking infuriating wanting to make an obvious declaration of possession. But he's not mine to have. Only in death.

Something transpires between Braxton and me in this moment. Something dangerous and unspoken. He's skirting a line in front of my mother, but I don't know if the risks will be enough to hold him back from crossing it.

"Tonight's been a success, wouldn't you say, Hope?" Kylie interrupts before Braxton can say anything. What, is he going to do some childish grand gesture? Chase after me? Tell me that I have the wrong idea about him and Kylie? Fuck off with that. I have two eyes. And he and I were nothing serious anyway. "You somehow always manage to surprise me," she says lightly as she gazes up at Braxton and then turns to my mother. Pretty fucking bold, considering how much she usually pretends to be my best friend. But it gives me satisfaction to know I've gotten so deeply under her skin, even if she's holding the one man who brings me to life, which is precisely why he has to die. I don't like anyone having this type of power over me.

"Yes, full of surprises tonight," I reply with an insincere smile. This jealous, vicious feeling inside me draws out the part of me I try my hardest to hide. The image of cutting her hands from her body to keep her from touching him flashes clear and sharp in my mind. I can't help but feel the sense that I'm being watched. Most likely by my mother.

"Have a good night." I turn and head for the car as the rain starts to get heavier. I want to claw at my chest to free this vile creature. Is this what jealousy feels like? I can't fucking stand it. And I hate the fact that Kylie has never really bothered me up until now. I don't like her touching him, breathing the same air as him, so much as looking in his direction.

I try to shove it down, knowing too well I need to bleed this into my art.

My mother and I slide into the car, and she's quiet. I look out the tinted window and notice a car parked across from us. I squint and adjust my glasses. I'm certain it's Lucas, Braxton's partner. Well, fuck me, isn't it a family affair.

"Are you sure this is okay?" Mom asks quietly.

"What do you mean?" I ask, keeping my tone even. I don't want her to have any suspicions about Braxton and me, but she looks at me as if she understands every cruel and vile thing going through my mind. I hate not being in control of myself or my emotions. I literally have everything I want, so why the fuck do I care about who he does and doesn't see?

Why the fuck am I spiraling?

I don't glance back at them when we leave. If Braxton wanted to go out of his way to piss me off, he's well and truly made a point. I'm severing myself from him until the final blow.

I pull out my phone and text Hawke. I doubt someone like him would have ever felt jealousy. Perhaps only for his brother's undying attention, but for some reason, I want a distraction. I want to go out for an evening to let my hair down in a way that I haven't before.

I know I should move on from Braxton. But the only way I can see this connection between us severing is with his death. Killing him is what I've set out to do from the start, so when did I become so rusty on that pursuit?

CHAPTER 32

Hope

A week later I'm in a private booth at Lucy's. The whole gang is here, and it's been some time since I've seen everyone together. At least this way, I won't have to worry about a certain asshole detective showing up. He wouldn't be daring enough to come into a place Eli Monti owns.

Jewel is sitting on Eli's lap, laughing at something he said, though he doesn't get why it's funny. But he stares at her with such love in his eyes that it makes me want to gag. Dutton is standing behind Posie, who is dancing with Ivy. I plan on joining them soon.

"Another one," I say happily as I pour us all a round of shots.

"Damn, Hope, you're not wanting to remember tonight, are you?" Billie says from her seat next to me.

She takes a shot glass. However, I was never concerned about keeping up.

Ford sits beside her, his arm around the back of her chair as he sucks on a lollipop and scrolls through his phone. He ignores the shot, like always.

For once, Hawke doesn't have a harem with him. He's just joined Dutton on the dance floor, and it looks like he's giving him shit for being stiff as a board and looking no better than security. But there's no fucking way he's letting anyone come near his new wife. Everyone walks a wide circle around them like there's an invisible wall around them.

Billie, Jewel, and I clink our shot glasses together and throw back the alcohol. It burns my throat, and I suck on the lime afterward, feeling buzzed and refreshed.

This week has been a difficult one for me. International travel, stress levels spiking, and my mind drifting to a particular asshole who I'm trying my best to forget. I've also started organizing a plan of attack that Hawke came up with. One that I can manage on my own without his or Ford's help.

But tonight, I want to get fucked up. I'm twenty-two and shouldn't have a care in the world. So, I decided to use this as an excuse to celebrate dropping out of college. Everyone seemed confused by it, but since I don't host many celebrations, they all made time.

"Come on." I grab Billie's and Jewel's hands and drag them into the sea of people on the dance floor. I'm not one to usually enjoy dancing, but tonight, I just don't want to be myself. I want to move in ways that I haven't before. I let Ivy dress me in leather pants and a leather crop top. My hair is down and curled, and I've replaced my glasses with purple-tinted contacts.

I don't give a fuck tonight.

Ivy scoops me up from behind, her hands on me as she accentuates my curves, and we dance. I close my eyes, awkwardly embracing the beat that I'm always certain my hips sway to a second too slowly. But I don't care. I'm sick of caring. I just want to feel alive again.

"Damn, little red, you're really letting yourself go tonight," Hawke notes approvingly. And within the same breath, he literally snarls at a guy who dares glance in our direction.

"Oh, come on, Hawke," Ivy teases. "Stop treating us like children. We can look after ourselves." She raises her hands in the air and dances like a sexual goddess. I've always admired this part of Ivy. How she freely lives in a way that appears she's tapped into a flow that no one else can see.

"It's not you I'm worried about. I wonder if Alek would be your father's best friend if he knew what a bad influence you were on his daughter," Hawke grits back.

All of us girls laugh because it's the most hypocritical thing Hawke could say. A tray is brought to us with more shot glasses, and Ivy makes a point to give one to Hawke first with a pout. "Come now, Hawke. You and I both know what our girl here needs is a little fun. We can't be nothing but work, right?"

She looks pointedly at Dutton, who doesn't reply. Everyone is laughing as we clink glasses and drink the shots. We're all so different, and yet we just work. I know everyone in this group, including Eli and Ford, who are watching from the private booth will have my back no matter what. So why do I feel the need for something more? Why do I give a flying fuck about a connection I can't place a title on with a certain detective who drives me insane? It doesn't make any sense.

"I need to go to the bathroom," I shout over the music, and Ivy skips to my side. "I can pee by myself, you know." I laugh, but she doesn't seem to care.

"Girls should always go to the bathroom together. You never know who—" A man barges past her, shooting her an annoyed look. "Hey, watch where you're going, asshole!"

He sneers, and I wonder if the idiot has any fucking idea whose club he's in because if he did, he wouldn't disrespect her so openly. "Shut up, skank, nobody cares."

"What did you just call me?" Ivy goes to grab him by his hair, but I pull her back and shake my head. Although I'm certain Ivy can tear a man to shreds, just like Billie, Posie, and me, she's not labeled as a killer in our group.

"No. Fuck that guy. Men like that shouldn't even exist. It drives me insane." She curses, infuriated. I keep my gaze trained on the man to make sure he's leaving. I'm certain I've seen him before. I think he was in one of the classes that I guest lectured for a few months ago. Green mohawks are distinctive and hard to forget. If memory serves correctly, Charlotte said he made a pass at her and that he made her really uncomfortable. I can understand why; the guy gives off a menacing aura.

Obviously, none of the men in our group saw what happened because if they did, he'd already be thrown into the closest wall of spikes in a torture chamber that I'm certain Eli has here.

My phone buzzes again. It's been going off all night. I ignore it as I go to the bathroom. The room tilts, and I lean against the wall as I pee. *Fuck*. I'm really drunk.

"What's brought this on lately?" Ivy asks in the stall beside me. I could ask her the same. I feel like she's been spending more time with me than usual when I come back from trips. Maybe it's for the same reason that Hawke is. Now that Billie is preoccupied in her relationship with Ford, Ivy's looking for her next person. All three of us are close, but I can't help but feel like a consolation prize.

"I don't know. I just want to do something different," I admit. Lies have been piling up on each other, and I don't even know who I am anymore. I thought dropping out of college and refining my schedule would help me pursue something else. But it turns out my calendar just fills up with more projects and events.

I'm tired, and my only outlet is something depraved

and twisted. I feel like I'm drowning as I try to hide such a prominent part of me and replace it with something else.

My phone buzzes again. It's the fourth call from my agent. She doesn't usually call this late, but I ignore her again.

I pull up my leather pants and take a breath to try and center myself as I step out to wash my hands. Ivy is touching up her hair and makeup. She looks at me then, placing a hand on her hip.

"What are you running away from, Hope? I don't mind partying with you, girl, but you've been acting differently this last year, more so lately. I just want to make sure you're okay."

Ivy's so beautiful and sure of who she is. She lives as she pleases and dances only to her own tune. She's incredibly talented and doesn't need validation from others. She's living freely.

Her only secret is how good she is at hacking and tracking like her father. And the only reason she doesn't tell her parents is because she's not yet sure if she wants to pursue that into the underworld, so she uses her skills as a freelance IT specialist.

I couldn't imagine her harboring a dark and unattractive part of her.

She dips her head to the side, looking back at me inquisitively.

"What do you see when you look at me?" I ask self-consciously. I'm curious as to how I come across from the outside. I've never much cared before, but suddenly, I do.

She seems surprised by the question but smiles. "A girl who, for the most part, can handle her tequila considering her size."

I laugh, and it dispels the self-consciousness I was feeling before. She continues. "But you're one of the most incredible people I know, and not because we grew up together. I see a woman who shouldn't be fucked with. I think there's a side to you that even you're not ready to expose. And I won't pry until you're ready to tell me about it. But you know, no matter what, that you can tell me."

A small wave of relief passes through me. Ivy, always the socialite, is surprisingly perceptive. But her true value is her ability to be a vault when it comes to secrets. If I give her a job, like cutting out a particular property's security, she does it, no questions asked, and money exchanged. Maybe one day I can tell her, but I'm still scared of how she'll react.

My phone rings again, and I huff, irritated. This time, Braxton's name appears.

Like fuck I'm answering his call.

My agent calls again. "Oh, for fuck's sake," I grumble, and Ivy tries not to laugh. Ivy and Billie always laugh when I become flustered because it's so opposite to my calm and steady nature. I think it's also why Ivy tries to rile me up sometimes.

"It must be important if she's been calling all night. Just answer it," she says, patting me on the back. It's probably something to do with our flight in two days.

I answer the call. "Oh, thank fuck you picked up," Candice says. Okay, so I've never heard her swear. "It's bad, Hope."

"What is?" I ask, my head starting to spin again from the tequila.

She's silent for a moment. "It's about Kylie. She's dead."

CHAPTER 33

Braxton

For the first time in many years, I'm shocked. I stare at the cold, lifeless body of Kylie, who was strangled from behind with what looks like the belt of a dress. She's still propped up, sitting in the chair of her lover's home.

The man who owns the home is in hysterics in the corner as he's being interrogated by a couple of officers who were first on the scene. I wasn't far behind them.

I look at the window that was easily unlatched from the outside and allowed the killer to break in.

I walk over to the man, still reeling from whatever the fuck is happening right now. "I'll take over here," I say, interrupting the police officer who's asking questions. He continues to note things down as I lead the interrogation.

"So, you're telling me you and Kylie were involved romantically?" I really don't care about her having a partner, but I know Lucas never mentioned him. Then again, maybe he was aware of her new beau and didn't think he was good enough for her. The house is run down, in a bad area of town, and there's no security system or cameras. I imagine for someone who cared so much about reputation, Kylie wanted to keep this relationship private.

"Y-yes," he sobs. "I loved her. We were just celebrating her new collection. We'd just been... Oh God," he cries and looks up. "We'd just made love, and I was making her favorite tea in the kitchen. And when I came back—" He chokes on his words.

My eyebrows dip. It's highly possible he killed her himself, but my gut is telling me otherwise. "You didn't hear any struggle?"

He looks over to the old record player. "No. We were listening to her favorite track. Maybe if I checked the latch to the window... Maybe if I did something different, this night..." He begins to ramble, and I excuse myself. The police officers will take him in, and I can interrogate him when he comes back to his senses. If he ever does. The scene is gnarly. Her eyes and mouth are wide open.

My lips draw thin. This doesn't make any sense. The killer has only killed men so far. So, I have to ask again: are we dealing with multiple killers? The problem with this particular murder is how close I am to this victim personally.

Fuck. I think about Lucas. I try to call him again, but he doesn't answer.

Fuck.

"Close her eyes at least," I snap to the person placing markers and taking photos. Fuck, this is so bad.

A commotion begins to stir outside the room, and I know without seeing him that Lucas has arrived. He would've heard it over the radio. I catch him before he walks into the room, blocking his view.

"Let me in! I have to see her!" Lucas yells. I don't know what to say to him. I don't know how to console him or give him answers to a crime that we are far from tying up. This... This will break him.

"Lucas!"

"No!" he shouts and punches me in the jaw. It has enough force behind it, I stumble back, and he falls into the room on his hands and knees. He looks up, and a guttural cry seeps from his soul. I close my eyes, trying my hardest to block it out.

Kylie should have never been involved.

And it again circles back to one family. The Ivanovs.

"Who would do this?!" Lucas screams, and those in the room try their hardest to usher him out. I clench my jaw and roll my shoulders as I lift his dead weight.

"No! No! No!" Lucas is screaming as I drag him out. "They took her! It's because we've taken too long! They're targeting us now!"

I throw him out into the hallway and pin him against

the wall by the collar. "You need to get a grip. Right now."

His eyes widen, and for the first time, I see the steady Lucas I know pull through, but it's quickly covered by tears. This feels like a nail in the coffin, and that things will never be the same between us. We've failed, and it cost him the price of one of the most precious things in his life.

"They *took* her from me," he squeaks. He stares at the floor, his mouth opening and shutting. Fuck, this is bad.

He begins to cry, and I stand there awkwardly as he hides his face in my shirt, his sobs echoing through the hall. Slowly, he slides down the wall, hanging his head between his knees.

I shut my feelings for him out. I can't be emotionally invested in this case, and he's most likely going to be kicked off the case because of it.

One of our colleagues comes out and she offers to assist him in my stead. Phone calls are already being made, and it's only a matter of time before it hits the news.

I walk around the outside of the house, checking out the window that was broken into. There's a small scrape mark where the person obviously went to the effort to chip away at the window seal to unlatch it. I can see inside from my height, and it really isn't much of a jump from the ground to the windowsill.

A boot mark has been half covered up in the dirt.

Whoever is doing this is good about not leaving any evidence besides the body, almost flaunting the fact they can't be caught. I study the footprint. It looks narrow, but without the whole thing, I can't tell if it's a man's or woman's shoe.

"Fuck." This is going to create chaos in the media tomorrow once they realize the latest victim is related to a detective who's been working on the serial killer case. And, once again, a different method of killing. Not to mention, Kylie being killed ruins the consistency of the murderer only targeting men.

My phone buzzes, but I ignore it, scanning the bushes for hints of evidence. I look at the street and surrounding houses, hoping to spot any cameras, but in this part of town, it's unlikely. My phone buzzes again, and this time, I take it from my pocket.

I'm disappointed when it's not Hope returning my call. My eyebrows furrow as I notice it's one of my colleagues calling for a third time. And a bad feeling sinks into my stomach.

"Braxton," he says. "There's another body."

"Where?" I grit.

Two in one night? Are you fucking kidding me?

"A nightclub called Lucy's."

My jaw tics. Lucy's is owned by Eli Monti, the fucking boss of the Italian mafia. It's very rare a body is found at any of their establishments, and I'm certain the moment I arrive it'll be gone.

"Who called it in?" I ask.

"A woman found it and called us, but I don't think she's local."

No, because if she were, she wouldn't have ever dared call the police while at a Monti establishment.

We can't fucking touch them, and yet I don't fucking care.

Someone's getting ballsy about their kills, and they'll have to answer for it.

CHAPTER 34

Braxton

A week later, I attend Kylie's funeral. Lucas hasn't been in the office all week despite his efforts to try to work on the case. I stopped answering his calls, where he would claim to have made breakthroughs that are dead ends we've already marked off.

The media is eating us alive, and I've barely slept. I've done numerous interviews and given many statements. The official statement is that this is unrelated to the other murders. She was a female victim, so this was an entirely different matter. It doesn't make it any easier to provide them with the answers they're demanding, though.

As I suspected, on the same night I snooped around Lucy's club, there was no body to be found. I took the woman's statement, then informed her she'd better leave town. She was stricken, just another person caught in the crossfire. Apparently, the body she saw was a man in his twenties with a green mohawk. She recalled a distinct tattoo on his arm, however.

As Lady Luck would have it, I'd studied Hope Ivanov so thoroughly that a man with a similar description who attended one of her classes came to mind. For most, this detail might've slipped by, but I have a knack for remembering things after seeing them only once.

"What the fuck is she doing here?" Lucas growls from beside me as he glares at Hope, who is just visible in the crowd of mourners. She stands with her agent, Candice, who I know also worked closely with Kylie.

She offers Candice a handkerchief.

"Calm down," I say quietly. "We can't prove anything." She has an alibi, having been with her friend Ivy Walker. I've had to be careful this last week because I know my every move is being watched. My personal interest in Hope aside, I need hard evidence to prove her guilty or I have to wait it out until I lose the sense that my work's being analyzed.

"It's not fucking right," he seethes. And although I have my suspicions, Hope might be involved in some way, if he gets any closer to her or her family, they will take him out.

"I know. Just trust me," I say, placing my hand on his shoulder as we listen to one of Kylie's friends deliver the eulogy. I'd later found out Lucas did know about the man his sister was seeing, and it was as I suspected; he didn't think the guy was good enough for her, which is why he pressed so much for us to go on a date. And we only had that one date. I left Kylie behind that night after Hope left the event.

Now I wonder if anything might've changed if I'd stayed. Most likely not.

I wait for the eulogies to end, and when people begin to quietly speak among themselves, the tension is palpable. I make a point to walk in Hope's direction. In the distance, on the edges of the cemetery, I can see Hawke's car. He's leaning against it, most likely making sure nothing goes awry.

Visiting a detective's sister's funeral is one of the things that might get you on a shit list.

Hope is staring at the grave vacantly, and I wonder yet again what's going on in her brilliant mind. I casually stand beside her, and she doesn't look up at me as she says, "I don't have the energy for games today."

"Didn't have a good enough look last time you saw her when you strangled her to death?" I accuse.

"Excuse me?" she seethes, looking up at me now, that lethal edge to her gaze.

"This little act of yours is starting to wear thin. You can only hide your true nature for so long."

She scoffs, almost crazed with disbelief. "Are you

actually fucking serious right now? You want to accuse me of murder? Here? We might have had our differences, but I had no reason to kill Kylie. You're out of your fucking mind," she grits angrily as she looks back at the grave.

"You didn't look too happy when you saw us together at the event."

"You're so self-absorbed that it's beyond comprehension. Go hit on some widower who might find your personality refreshing," she bites back, turning to leave. But I grab her wrist to stop her escape.

"Remove your hand before I have something done about it," she growls, her glance in Hawke's direction emphasizing the threat.

I smirk. "We both know you're not going to do that here, in front of a mountain of cops. Your cousin wouldn't so easily get out of that one."

Her eyebrows furrow. "You'd be surprised by how protective my cousin gets when a man is touching me without my consent."

I don't lose my lethal smirk. "I know for a fact I'm the only man you consent to touching you. This murder was too close," I warn her.

"Is that a threat?" she asks, pulling free from my hold and stepping into my space. She might only be five foot three, okay five foot five with her heels, but I tower over her. "And here I thought you were clever. Did you ever think that maybe someone is trying to set my family up? All these bodies conveniently appearing that you supposedly think we have some association with. Come on now, surely you're not that desperate. If you are, let me offer a word of warning—pick a tamer family to target. Because mine will fucking eat you alive." Unfiltered hatred laces her tone.

"You're the only one I want taking a bite out of me," I reply.

She shakes her head. "That doesn't work on me anymore. We're done," she says as she walks away.

"You and I will never be done, Shortcake," I say to her retreating form, then scan the area to see who might've seen us talking for so long.

"If my family were to kill, I imagine it's not without reason," she says over her shoulder. "But if it *were* any of my family, you wouldn't find a body. Clean up your own mess."

I watch her as she leaves. She's not wrong about them not leaving bodies behind. They were so quick to clean up the last one, and I purposely didn't mention that I knew about that either. It could've been any one of them.

I look back at Kylie's grave, and a sinking feeling pulls at my stomach.

It just gets deeper and deeper, this murky water I'm drowning in.

I know all of my damnation begins and ends with Hope. I'm in too deep now. I look down at my badge, thinking about all the highs and lows of my career. All the secrets I've exposed and the lies I've covered for.

Hope reacts in all the ways I think she will, but sometimes she surprises me. She's not a sweet little doll, but maybe I'm not as good of a detective as I thought.

What's fucking worse is she never falls for my bluff.

CHAPTER 35

Hope

I avoid Braxton for two weeks after the funeral. Candice has canceled most of my shows and appearances, which, despite the circumstances, I'm grateful for. She's waiting for the media coverage from Kylie's murder to die down. Apparently, more police have been brought into the investigation. At least, that's what the press says anyway.

Every time Braxton's face appears on the TV, I want to throw the remote at it. I don't. Especially if my mother is watching for my reaction. But every time I see him, he looks more tired and gaunt. The fucker is going to wither into nothing before I get to kill him myself.

After the funeral, Hawke warned me away from Braxton. Despite his best efforts at teaching me creative ways to kill someone, even though I still insist on shooting Braxton, he specifically told me now is not the time to get involved with the detective. There's too much buzz around him now. I'm certain Hawke wouldn't hesitate on a kill, no matter who it is. But I know he doesn't think my first kill will go smoothly or without evidence being left behind.

Kylie's boyfriend has been taken into custody. Apparently, evidence is stacking up against him. And due to my upbringing, I wonder if they're facts or if someone is paying money to make the issue go away.

Nothing in this world is what it seems anymore.

The same night Kylie was murdered, the body of the man with the green mohawk who'd bumped into Ivy was found at Lucy's. The body had been removed from the alley so quickly that I doubt anyone saw it, but the question remained among the group as to who did it. It could literally be anyone. And much to Eli's disgust, the cameras in the alley had been tampered with.

It's all a bit of a fucking mess right now. And for the first time in a long time, I feel stifled creatively. Maybe it's because my muse has been relatively silent. The photo of Kylie's body was sent to my burner phone, but I couldn't find the beauty in her death. It was ugly. The worst.

I keep all of this to myself, and I feel like I'm slowly shutting down. I've never felt this looming darkness. Like I don't want to eat or drink. Even if I lock myself in my studio, it feels pointless.

I don't go to the café because I'm adamant about not seeing Braxton Hero. I avoid it at all costs. Suddenly, the games we've playing don't feel so fun. I just hurt, and my hatred for him for somehow imprinting this sickness within me, this longing that's grounded without rationality, only festers.

I have cameras installed out front of my studio, so I know when he shows up. And he comes frequently. When he does, I make sure to stay inside. Some nights, I even sleep in the studio, just so I don't run the risk of him intercepting me. I know I should tell my father or, at the very least, Hawke. But I'm determined to handle this on my own. Every storm has to blow over eventually, and when it does... I'll finally strike.

I go to London for a week and try to clear my head. When I return, my mother happens to be home. We decide to watch a few shows together, and it's nice.

I stopped looking for apartments when the whole Kylie thing happened. It's not that I fear for my life, but right now, the security of being under my father's roof brings me a sense of safety and peace, even if I'm not staying here much.

My mother is biting at the tip of her nail, and I know that usually means she's thinking of something.

"Have you seen that detective recently?" she asks.

I simply shake my head in response.

Only the sound of the TV breaks the silence.

"Does that upset you?" she questions.

I turn to face her. "Why would it? I told you there

was nothing between us." I furrow my brow as I ask, "You really didn't tell Dad?"

She shakes her head. "No. You told me it was nothing serious." I didn't say that word for word, but I don't correct her and assure her once again it was nothing.

I don't like lying to her, but I can't burden her with this trouble I've gotten myself into. Her art is so beautiful, and mine is so ugly. My soul is tarnished in a way I don't think a mother would truly be able to accept.

Braxton hasn't sent back the statues a second time. I was rattled when he returned them to me the first time. If even he didn't want to look at them, why would anyone else? That is a strange sentiment to have, considering he's not even a critic in the industry.

I don't know how and why everything keeps coming back to him. I feel like I'm stuck in quicksand, and I can't get out.

Mom brushes the hair behind my ear as she says, "Hope, you know if you ever have something to tell me, you can open up to me, right? You're my daughter, and I love you unconditionally."

I stare into her eyes. What does she see right now? How does she view me? Can she see every tainted part of me? I shrivel at the thought. Hers is a love I can absolutely not live without.

"I know. I'm just tired, that's all." Another lie slips off my tongue, and I can tell by her wounded expression that she knows it, too. But better for her be hurt by a little white lie than the truth.

I can't sleep, so I get my keys and drive to the studio. I wait in the elevator, wrapping my arms around myself and shivering from the chill of the night. I need to lose myself in creating something in order to push all of these thoughts away.

I step out of the elevator and then come to a complete stop. Braxton is sitting beside the door, his head leaning against it with his eyes closed. He's wrapped up in a long trench coat that looks way too good on him and a beanie.

Nope. Hard pass.

I go to step back into the elevator, but the doors have already slid shut. *Fuck.* I hit the button rapidly, hoping the doors would open.

"Have you been avoiding me, Shortcake?" His voice carries through the small hallway, and when I turn toward him, those striking blue eyes, shadowed with dark circles, challenge me to run.

The answer to his question is absolutely yes. But it's his direct and insufferable challenge that has me second-guessing myself on heading straight into the elevator. This is *my* fucking studio. Not his. I won't back down just because this asshole plans on ruining my fucking life.

I step toward him, scowling. "You look like a squatter at my door. Leave before I call someone to remove you," I say as I scan my key card to open my studio.

Stupid fucking idiot.

All of my anger and problems rise the moment I see him.

The moment he's close enough for me to breathe in his fucking intoxicating cologne.

He's clearly the problem.

I'm pissed and not surprised when the door doesn't close behind me quickly enough, and he follows me in. I turn on the lights and the heater. The beautiful night sky is visible through the skylight.

"I have nothing to say to you," I say matter-of-factly.

"You always seem to have plenty to say." I can hear the hint of humor in his tone, but it's lacking the life it once had. It offers me a slight sense of satisfaction to know that he looks as shitty as I feel.

"What are you most angry about?" he asks.

"Angry about?" I ask in disbelief, swinging around to face him. "Where the fuck does the list begin, asshole? You not only accuse me of making creepy little statues, but you then escalate it to accusing me of murder. Shouldn't I be questioning whether you fucking her was the catalyst to her death?"

He smirks. "Are you insinuating my sex is that good?"

"You're such a pig."

He shrugs, and I know joking about the dead isn't so fun, even for him. "I didn't touch her. I didn't kiss her. And I told her nothing more would come from it once we left the exhibition," he says as if I need his explanation. I don't.

"Okay, and why are you telling me this?" I question. "I clearly don't give a fuck."

"You clearly do, or she wouldn't have ended up dead."

I shake my head. "It would be so easy for you to pin all of this on me, wouldn't it? You'd fucking love it. What a catch that would be for you, pinning all of this shit on an Ivanov."

"It has nothing to do with your family name and everything to do with *you*." He moves closer. "I came here tonight because you've been avoiding me."

"No, I've been keeping my distance, which you should be doing too. Don't you get it? We don't fit. You're torturing yourself if you actually think anything can come of this."

He steps into my space, and my back hits one of the shelves. He hangs an arm over my head and leans into me. I don't back down as I reluctantly look up at him. "Looks like I haven't been the only one thinking about us, Shortcake," he whispers, pressing his forehead to my shoulder and sighing in exhaustion.

I'm so stunned by the action that I don't know what to do. He looks half his size as he leans against me, and I can feel his weariness as if it were an extension of my own.

"What are you doing?" I ask, unwilling to move. It has to be a trick. He's cornering me. He probably has a recording device on him. Maybe now is my chance to kill him? Is it too soon? Too reckless? Too... much?

"I've missed you," he murmurs.

I hate the way my heart flutters and my arms itch to wrap around him.

No. This is not okay. I cannot be this mad at him for over a month, only for it to dissipate into calmness just because he says one sweet thing. It doesn't make any fucking sense.

"Accusing me of murdering people seems like a strange way to show it," I grit.

"I thought you'd be the least bit flattered," he says against my neck, his warm breath sending a shiver through me.

"Most women aren't flattered by the prospect of murder, Braxton. You need to up your game if that's your pickup line."

"But you're not most women, are you, Shortcake?" He raises his head and cups my cheek. I fucking hate the spell he casts on me. I'm scared to fall into this trap again, even though my body is already melting into him. But when I look into his blue eyes, I can see how tired he is. And there's a peace I feel with him despite everything else that's going on in the outside world.

For the first time this month, I feel like I can breathe.

Like, somehow, it's all going to be okay.

"Come back to my place with me," he says, and it almost sounds like a plea.

"I'm all dirty," I reply. I still have bits of clay on me from working earlier in the day. I'd planned to take a shower but decided to spend time with my mother instead, then came back here when I wasn't able to sleep.

"Then I'll clean you up."

"I can't," I whisper as if someone might hear us. As if my mother is waiting around the corner or one of the men in my family is ready to pounce from the shadows. I know no one has access to my cameras because I had Ivy install them, but it doesn't matter. What we're doing is wrong. At least, that's what I keep trying to convince myself.

"You can. Come with me. I've waited for as long as I can."

"Do you want to die? Is that what you want?" I ask incredulously.

Yes, I still plan to kill him. And I glance over at the knife I'd used earlier in the day to open boxes. It'd be so easy for me to reach over and grab it. I can imagine the color of his blood as it bleeds out, but... No, it has to be a gun.

"You know who my family is. They wouldn't approve of you *at all*. My mother almost lost her shit when she asked me if there was something happening between us, and that's saying something because she is the calmest person I know."

"I'm not afraid of your family."

"Well, that's your first mistake." I go to push him away, but he keeps his stance, barricading me in. I can't fight him, even if I had the strength to do so. He gets me in ways that defy logic and rationality, like the ebb and flow of creating something beautiful through my sculpting. And I wonder what this thing between us would create. Would it be beautiful? Hideous? One thing I'm certain of is I don't know how to put an end to it. I know eventually, I'll be placing a gun to his head. But when? Am I intentionally avoiding it now?

"I'm not afraid of your family, Shortcake," He reiterates. "Now, tell your driver to leave and get in my car." I go to speak, but he cuts me off. "That wasn't a request."

My skin begins to tingle, my lips inches from his. I'm taking in his breath and cologne, all the promises of what this man can do to me only one answer away.

I swallow hard and nod.

I know I shouldn't, but I want to.

Right now, I want to live for myself and damn the consequences even though they're due to catch up with us.

Stealing moments with him like this is what I want. It's what my body needs. There's some underlying thing that I'm not entirely sure how to address. It's something equivalent to hatred that goes hand in hand with the dark part of me he draws out so easily. Even when I try to run away from it, it's him who makes me confront it.

Braxton smirks as he pushes off the shelf. "That's my girl."

Braxton waits inside the building as I approach my driver and tell him he can leave because I'll be here longer than usual. Though he's usually too terrified to leave my side half the time after the rumor of what happened to my last driver spread through the staff, he's also used to me being at the studio for long hours, so the order isn't surprising to him.

But he's not my bodyguard, and when I tell him having him here will hinder my work, he seems torn, as if that might be another reason he might get killed, so he leaves. It's not that my father often kills staff, but they know who they work for, which is exactly why they're paid so highly.

Once he leaves, Braxton comes out and throws an arm over my shoulders. He kisses my temple and says, "Good girl," as he leads me to his car.

As much as I want to fight going with him, we're both so tired. It's not just obvious from the gauntness of our expressions; I can feel it. I can *feel* him with an understanding that's not physical.

I look up at him. He's still wearing his beanie, and I admire the small curls that aren't tucked back completely. I wonder if, in a different life, what we might be to one another.

"That's my girl." Those words make my heart flutter more than they should, and I wonder if I want to be his girl. Is that what this conflict within me is? Surely not, because that thought is entirely unwarranted. It wouldn't make any sense since I'm literally readying myself to kill him.

Braxton opens the passenger door for me, and I slide in with a smirk on my face. Obviously, he got his car repaired after I smashed into the back of it. He's lucky I didn't light it on fire. I'd heard Aunt Anya had done that to several of her husband's cars, and the idea appeals to me.

We drive in silence, which is strangely nice, and he grabs my hand and strokes his thumb over mine. There's so much to be said between us, but nothing at all at the same time. I let the warmth of his hand around mine soothe all of my seething hate for him. It feels like whiplash. Was I pissed this month because he didn't give me any attention, or am I so weak in my resolve that I just need to be patted a little to be tamed?

We come to a stop at his apartment building, and he comes around the car to open the door for me. Nervous energy skitters under my skin. Not only is this wrong, but I feel like I'm stepping into something that will become harder for me to walk away from each time I indulge in it. That my time spent with Braxton is damaging me in ways I might not recover from.

He offers his hand to me, but when he notices I'm not moving, he reaches in and pulls me out.

"No one is going to see us here, Shortcake," he assures me, and it surprises me how attuned he is to my inner thoughts. Though, if he were a mind reader, he'd be running the other way.

He leads me into the building, once again holding my hand, and I stare in fascination at where we're joined as if in a daze. Why does the only man I let lead me in any way have to be an enemy to my family?

At the start, I only cared if they found out because they'd take away my fun of killing myself. I didn't like how closely he was sniffing around my family affairs. But lately, there's been a flicker of concern about what they'll do if they find out there's something between us.

I still want to kill him, though, right? I think it'll be the most beautiful thing, more captivating than any glass statue I've created. But the idea of there being no more Braxton, as much as he terrorizes me, feels... strange.

I don't even want to think about the consequences that would follow if my family found out about us. My aunty is as ruthless, possibly even more so, than my father. She would kill him first and ask questions later, not even caring that she would have the whole police force after her.

He unlocks his apartment door with his free hand and pushes it open before pulling me in with him. It's only then that he drops my hand as he locks the door behind us, as if silently reminding me there's nowhere to run.

I know I can leave at any time, but my legs don't want to carry me away from him, only toward him.

But that kind of gravitational pull is terrifying.

"Shortcake."

"I should leave," I tell him, a spurt of panic running through me. What am I really doing here? What are *we* doing?

"No, you shouldn't," he growls.

He fills the space between us, my chest pressing against his stomach as I look up into those crystal-blue eyes. Eyes that see *me*. That demand my attention. That feel like they're giving me all of him when we're locked away from the outside world. But they can't make the complications between us disappear.

I take a shaky breath. He knows who my family is and says he's not scared of them, but what if he had reason to be scared of me? In fact, it's a little offensive that he doesn't feel that way. But the truth of the matter is, even if we felt deeply for one another, wouldn't he turn on me in a heartbeat?

He goes to kiss me, but I find myself resting my hand on his chest and steeling myself for my next question.

"What if I told you that I like to kill people?" I ask as he brushes his nose against mine. I try to avoid the lure of his lips, heavy with anticipation for his response. He'd betray me, wouldn't he? As he would with my family? If I were the worst of the worst, would he still love me?

My heart stops. *Love me?*

"Well, that would complicate things, wouldn't it, Shortcake? But I've also seen you with a gun," he says with mirth.

"I'm serious, Braxton," I chide, pulling back from him as much as it pains me to do so. I thought this was only physical attraction between us. But what if it's something more? *Fuck.* How did I end up thinking any of this? "Is this all a game to you?"

His eyebrows furrow as he slides a hand over my cheek and cups it, his other hand resting on my collarbone. "If it were a game, wouldn't I have caught you already?"

"Who says I wouldn't be the one to catch you?" I bite back.

"Who says you haven't already?"

My heart falters. Is this a lie? Is he tricking me? It's all riddles.

"What I do know, and what I can tell you now, is that I've tried to keep my distance from you for the last month. But every day, every hour, you haunt my thoughts, Shortcake. You have no idea how much you've poisoned me with an insatiable thirst for you. *That* is the truth."

It goes without saying that it's not *all* of the truth. There's only so deep we can connect without revealing our hands or damaging our careers or my family in the process. Even if I'm realizing I'm falling for the enemy, I can't fall so hard as to hand him anything damning about my family.

My family comes first, and it breaks me little by little to know that our ending doesn't change. Even if I care for him. Even if I'm courageous enough to admit it. It'll still end with me holding a gun to his head.

So irrationally, irrevocably, I want to take from him as much as I can while I can.

I lean into him, pushing aside the thoughts that weigh me down. If we can't express ourselves through words, then all we have left is our bodies. He takes me by the waist and pulls me against him. I go willingly because I very much like his hands on me. He drags me with him to the bathroom and then pushes open the door. The moment we're inside, he removes his beanie and coat, placing them on the hook behind the door before his hands come back to me. He fingers the clips on my overalls above my breasts, then unhooks them.

Fuck. Our hands are on one another, desperately trying to undress the other as quickly as possible.

"Fuck, I've missed you, Shortcake," he whispers as he kisses down my neck. I lean into him, mirroring his words but leaving them unspoken.

I kick off my shoes and step out of my overalls. I'm left wearing only a pair of panties and a black t-shirt. We separate for a second as we both try to remove his shirt.

He pulls it over his head, and I step back, admiring every flex of his muscles. He really is beautiful. I could try to sculpt him for a lifetime, and would never capture every detail and sharp ridge of his perfection.

His jeans come off next, and I lick my lips with anticipation. My body is on fire like I can't be with him soon enough. The darkness within me pacing back and forth and needing to be touched. Needing to be *seen*. In the way that only he ever has.

He turns the shower on and steps inside. I remove my shirt and my panties before I follow him. He shuffles back, making room for me, and my red hair falls down my back as the warm water hits my face.

His mouth is on mine in moments, kissing, biting, sucking, and drowning as we gasp for air through the spray. Swirls of brown hit the tiles of the shower floor as the bits of clay come off me. His hands are all over me, washing away the mess, and it breathes desperation into me as I do the same to him.

I need and want him. It's been torture to only dream of him this past month. Twisting between images of kissing him and killing him. Hating him, then fucking him. But deep down, I'm beginning to understand that this hate might be something entirely different. This hate I feel, might, in fact, be love. And that hurts more than anything else could.

His mouth finds my breast, and his tongue teasingly rolls around my nipple before he begins to suck. His hands slide down my back, past my waist and hips, to my ass, where he squeezes before lifting me up.

I wrap my legs around his waist as I look down at him, cupping his cheeks. Those beautiful blue eyes. This sinfully inappropriate man. *Mine.* I want him to be mine. And if I can't have him in this lifetime, then I'll kill him so no one else can have him, and I'll find him in the next.

"Sometimes I think you'll look better dead," I whisper, a confession of my depravities. I don't know why, but I feel like I have to give him more of me because his rejection might be the thing that helps me end this completely.

He shakes his head with an arrogant smirk as he pushes back some of my wet hair. "Then should I be flattered that you keep me alive but offended that you don't create statues of me meeting a tragic death?"

He doesn't get it. Or maybe he's not right in the head, either. But for the first time, I don't deny the statues. If he's so certain it's me, doesn't it mean he accepts at least part of me? Or am I being lulled into a false sense of security?

I lean forward and bite his bottom lip as I lower myself onto his cock pressing between my legs. The moment he's inside me, I moan as I stretch to take his full size, and he presses my back against the wall as he slams home. The wet slaps echo, mixing with the sound of the water, as I ride the pure bliss. His hand wraps around my throat, and I'm reminded just as I threaten his life, he could take mine as well.

A wave of heat pools at my core, pulsing at the idea. Life and death. Danger. Consumption. It's all the same. I don't know why the thought of nearly dying brings me pleasure while having sex, but it does, and he's the only man not to shun my heated desires.

If anything, he's the one who birthed them.

He fucks me hard and long, biting my shoulders and neck, claiming me. And I want them all. I want all the marks he's willing to give. I want him to brand me, to bruise me so irrevocably that I won't be able to forget about this moment for days, even weeks, after. An ease settles over me as a scream rips from my lips, brought on by his forceful thrusts.

I'm broken for any other man.

I'm choosing to tie myself to him because I never want to forget this feeling.

I never want to forget Braxton Hero. Even when I try, I can't get him out of my head. And I haven't been the same since that fateful night four years ago.

CHAPTER 36
Braxton

She turns over in her sleep, and I see my teeth marks imprinted above her breast and on her throat. I trace my finger over them, and she doesn't even stir. She continues to softly snore next to me.

I wonder if that was her admitting to me in the shower about the statues. Is she just fucking with me to cure my addiction to her? Because that's what it's turned into—an addiction. I can't seem to stay away, even though I know I should.

Her mother came to see me the week after I met her at the art show. Everyone in the police station was happy to see her, flattered by the famous singer making a generous donation to the patrolman's fund. But she wasn't there for a social call or a photo op. She warned me that a relationship between myself and her daughter would never work.

That's when it hit me that the women in these families don't need to depend on their men. They're powerful and influential in their own right, as Hope has always been.

I understood her mother's message well and clear. Her donation was her subtly trying to pay me off to stay away from Hope. Instead of heeding her warning, I kindly showed her the door. That was the day before Kylie was murdered, and to say the timing couldn't be more suspicious is an understatement.

It's the wake-up call we both needed. We shouldn't fit. Shouldn't want each other. She's slowly undoing everything I've pieced together in my life for stability and security. Hope Ivanov is no doubt my weakness and undoing.

So when I realized she was avoiding me, I tried to stay away. But I was still there. In the shadows. Watching her from afar, practically pining as I fought with my demons to keep my distance.

I rub a lock of her hair between my fingers.

Hope's so reckless, especially with the statues beneath my bed, but equally, a careless part of me wants to protect her.

And that's my biggest problem.

I always thought she listened to her family. That she was mostly a sweet, innocent girl. She's always been intriguing to me. Someone like Hope Ivanov will never stop learning. She respects her family but is independent of them. She works hard, although she doesn't like being publicly recognized for it. She doesn't need her parents' money, but she lets them spoil her. She's the perfect daughter. The perfect facade for the creature that lurks beneath—the one she's only willing to show me. And I stayed away for four years because I knew my curiosity would lead to nothing but destruction.

My eyes grow heavy as I stroke her cheek, my touch soothing us both after I broke her in various positions. And I never want to let this moment go. I don't want to let *her* go. And I know she's it for me. She has been from the moment she first approached me, hiding behind those glasses like they were a mask. She'd piqued my interest.

I let her slip through my fingers once, but I'm not so sure if I'm capable of doing it again. But I don't know if I'm able to give up everything I've built in order to have her. That's a lie; I know I am. But it doesn't make it any easier to swallow when the truth of the matter is she wouldn't do the same. Her loyalty will always be to her family. Something I've never quite understood. Loyalty to myself is the only thing that has kept me alive for this long.

I listen to her breathing, my fingers trailing down to her throat and lightly squeezing. It would be so easy to solve this problem. To put us both out of our misery. My hand continues drifting down to her chest, and I rest it between her breasts, feeling the low thud of her heart under my palm. She's so vulnerable with me, and for the first time in a long time, I can feel myself falling into a deep sleep, content with the idea of not waking up because sleeping at her side offers that risk. But she's also the only thing that's been able to bring me to a level of relaxation that will allow me to get any rest.

I'm conflicted. Stay awake and alert or fall asleep by her side?

The choice is taken from me as I'm pulled into a deep slumber moments later.

Loud banging and my name being called startles me awake. I grab my gun on my nightstand, but it's not there. At first, when I can't feel her beside me, I think she's gone. Then I see her sitting at the end of my bed, holding the gun and staring at it curiously.

"Someone's at the door," she says with a sly smile, not at all explaining why she's holding my gun and watching me while I sleep. Some might consider it creepy, but I consider it endearing.

She's still naked, and I'm tempted to claim her all over again, my cock twitching at the sight of her perfect tits with bite marks all over them.

"Braxton!" More banging. I know that voice. *Fuck*

me. Her timing couldn't be any worse. I spring out of bed and throw on a pair of loose sweats.

"Did you double book your fuck buddies?" Hope asks, and there's a dangerous glint in her eye as she points the gun in the air and squeezes the trigger. "Oops," she says innocently, and I can't help but laugh. Jealous indeed.

I scoop her up in my arms, even though she tries to fight me, and throw her back onto the bed, then toss the sheet over her. "Do you think I have time to double book myself when you're such a little psycho?" I kiss her lips.

She's trying to hide a smile as she says, "Why? We're not anything to each other."

It's a daring question. "If that's what you want to think, then fine. Now, don't let anyone else see your body, or I'll be the one pulling the trigger."

She aims the gun at my head. "You're not scared of me aiming this at your head now that I've got what I wanted from you?" she taunts.

I smirk over my shoulder. "Not after seeing you at shooting practice. Not a care in the world."

She grumbles something as I walk to the door to more banging and shouting. My smile quickly drops as I mentally prepare myself to see the woman I despise most in this world.

"Mother," I greet, my voice toneless.

Her hair looks like it needs to be brushed, and she's wearing old clothes that are half torn and two sizes too big for her. Her pupils are dilated, and she's skittish as she stumbles back when I appear at the door. She licks her lips, looking confused as to why she's here.

I don't even know how she found my address, but that's the least of my problems now that she's on my doorstep. She never saw me when I checked up on her, and I've been ignoring her calls for the last six weeks, so she must be desperate to have personally tracked me down.

I never wanted her showing up at my door, especially the way she is right now. She was hardly a mother to me when I was a child, and she's less than a stranger to me now.

"What, you don't want to invite your mother inside? It's cold out here." She hugs herself, and I notice she's only wearing a thin sweater. The temperature has dropped significantly in the last few days, and we're no doubt due for snow soon.

"You're good where you are," I growl. She doesn't have the right to barge into my life or encroach on all I've built. She tries to peek over my shoulder, but I block her view.

And she certainly doesn't get to look at my woman. My mother is the type of person who would try to use Hope in some way once she found out about her family's wealth. My mother only ever takes, and I certainly won't have her associated with something that I've found for myself. Something to call my own, even if Hope won't have me. My mother doesn't get to contaminate this any more than I already have.

"What do you need?" I grit, partially closing the door behind me.

"Can't a mother see her son?" she hisses. Actually, hisses like a cat. Fuck me. Only God knows what she's on right now.

"That depends if the mother actually wants to see her son or if she's only here for money or help getting out of trouble."

She throws her hands in the air. "Always thinking the worst of me you are. It's neither."

I stare at her, and she fidgets uncomfortably. Because it's always something with her, it reminds me of why I envy a family like Hope's. How undeniably they have each other's backs, whereas mine would tear me down in a heartbeat if they knew they could get even one cent from doing so.

My mother is many things, a coward, mostly. She and her boyfriends would beat me until I got big enough to defend myself. I never hit her, but when I was thirteen, I fought with her to get her to drop the belt she'd been whipping me with, and she landed on her ass. It had crossed my mind to hit her back. To inflict the same pain that she had on me for all of those years. But I refused to stoop so low. At that moment, I saw her for what she was —a broken, cowardly woman.

I didn't want to be in that life anymore. I didn't want to turn into her.

Hope was the first woman I met who showed me what true power is in a woman. As quiet as she might be, her presence always called to me with confidence and a lethal edge.

"I need something else," she finally blurts.

"What?"

"They arrested Teddy!" she cries out, and crocodile tears spill from her eyes as she tries to explain how he's the victim in the situation. Teddy is her on-again, off-again man who likes to beat her and fuel her addictions. I tried to get her to leave him many times. Even paid for her to go to rehab twice. But I concluded that it's better to cut some things off. If it's poison, it'll eventually infect everything. But I haven't been able to completely cut her off. *Yet*.

"Good. I hope he goes to jail." I smile because I absolutely hate the fucking guy. I'd even considered killing him myself but decided against getting further involved in her life. I can't control my mother or change her path. But this hatred I harbor for her still festers.

Her mouth opens in shock. I don't know what she expected from me. I hate that man. The man she claims to love more than her "useless" son. I've heard it all. How disgusting I am to her. How I'm less compared to the scum she lets beat her daily. And she holds the resolve that that's the absolute truth.

I feel the anger rise in me again, sparking to life that small part of me that was a fourteen-year-old boy thrown onto the streets because he wanted something better for his family. I bury that back down, though, because it has no place here. Not in this life of mine.

"Have a good day, Mother. And don't ever fucking come back here again, begging me to help that man." I go to shut the door, but she throws herself against it.

"Come on, Braxton. One call from you, and it can all go away," she says desperately. "You have that kind of power, don't you?"

"No," I tell her again. Because she only contacts me when she finds it convenient to have a cop in the family.

"Now, leave before I have you arrested." I push her back, and this time, when I go to shut the door, she's too stunned to stop me.

I take a deep breath and look through the peephole to see her still standing there.

My teeth grind. I feel a part of me has been exposed as I focus on the only other presence in the room. Someone who I didn't want to see this side of me, completely in denial about my roots. Hope and I come from different worlds entirely, and though she certainly isn't here for my money, it's the understanding in her gaze that rocks me when I turn back to her. She looks... sympathetic, and it pokes at something ugly inside me.

I don't want her to see my past. I don't want her to see me as weak.

What a hypocrite I am, wanting to see all of her but hiding this shame within me.

"I should leave," Hope says, flicking off the sheets and going to grab her clothes. I step into her path. Her breath is shaky, and she still holds the gun as she stares up at me through her glasses.

She isn't allowed to go anywhere.

CHAPTER 37

Hope

As curious as I might've been about Braxton's past, even going so far as having Ivy dig into it for me, I know I was just a witness to something I shouldn't have seen. He shuts the door on his mother and then turns around to face me. She was at the door begging for his help, but I could tell from the tense set of his shoulders that he couldn't stand her.

I'd read that he'd come from rough beginnings. I don't judge it because Ford and Hawke had a similar background, but I feel like I was privy to something he hasn't fully dealt with. We all have our own demons to face.

"No, you should stay," he says as he stalks toward me. I take a step back, landing on the bed as his imposing size towers over me. He's mad. Not at me, though. But that aggressive thing within him calls to my own, and I hate the fact that I want to exploit it, to have him fuck me into oblivion with that hatred if it'll make him feel better for even a single moment. My body is more than capable of handling it. In fact, it thrives off it. And that's the terrifying part of me. Aren't I a terrible person for getting off on that?

He grabs my ankles and drags me across the bed, so I'm closer to him.

"I should leave. It looks like you have something you need to deal with," I say.

He releases my ankles, and before I can say another word, his pants are gone, and he's on his knees, spreading my legs and lowering his mouth directly between my thighs. A moan slips from my lips as I dig my fingers through his curly hair, focusing solely on the skill of his tongue. It's as if he's a man possessed as his finger slips inside me, and he grips my waist to pin me into place. I know I'm going to have bruises there.

I like it.

I want him to bruise me. I want him to hurt me.

And I want to hurt him in return.

My hand covers his and I whisper, "Harder."

At first, it's his tongue that works harder. And while that's nice, it's not what I want. So I grab his hand at my waist and slide it up my body to my neck. He doesn't need me to tell him what to do from here. He wraps his hand around my throat and squeezes. I can feel a small part of him trying to restrain himself as if he's scared to unleash that coiled anger and pain. But I want him to feed it into me.

His hand tightens around my throat, and when my head tilts back, hitting the mattress, he pulls away completely.

"You want it rough, Shortcake?" he growls. I bite my bottom lip and nod once.

He leans forward and removes my glasses. When he places them on the bedside table, he brings back his cuffs. "How rough?" he asks. "How messy?"

"Rough. Destroy me, Braxton."

The grin he gifts me could have been stolen from the devil's own lips. He wraps my legs around his waist and pulls me even closer until I can feel him at the entrance of my already bruised pussy.

"Rough," he muses.

I keep my legs wrapped around his waist as he palms my breast and then pinches my nipple before sliding his hand back up to my neck. He squeezes my throat at the same time as he takes my nipple into his mouth. He presses just the tip of his cock inside me, sliding in and then back out, rotating it around my entrance, careful not to give it all to me. He's taunting me because he knows I'll go feral once I have all of him.

My hand covers his where it's still around my neck, and he applies more pressure. Then he bites down on my nipple as he thrusts into me. My nipple is on fire, but, fuck, it feels good. When he's fully seated, he releases my nipple. and his tongue darts out to take a lick. All the while, he's still choking me.

His hips start to move, and his hand grips me tighter. *Fuck.* What is he doing to me? And why do I want it and like it so much?

He moves to my other nipple, and without warning he bites that one as well. He fucks me, his hips rocking into mine, and I moan. And that's all the encouragement he needs to start biting me all over. I know when this is done, my upper body is going to be covered, but I don't care. I welcome it.

Because of the release and rush that it provides.

It's like flying high.

He stops biting and releases my throat, but he continues to fuck me.

I arch my back just as I feel the orgasm coming close, but then he pulls out of me and backs up. "What the fuck?" I demand, my eyes bursting open. He drops the handcuffs between us, and I smirk.

"Have you ever been cuffed?" I ask curiously as I move to my knees and crawl over to him, picking them up. I start stroking his cock, enjoying the feel of my juices all over his hard shaft. I want to impale myself on him all over again, that buzzing hum from my pleasure-high not yet subsiding.

"Do you want to cuff me, little devil?" he says. I like the way he calls me that, acknowledging this part of me that I share only with him.

"I want to see you scared," I reply as I step off the bed and drag over a chair from his dining table. "Sit." I motion to it with the handcuffs.

"You will never scare me, Shortcake," he says with a smirk as he stretches to his full height.

"Sit your ass down," I order, and his eyebrows raise, but he does as he's told. When he's seated, I grab the gun.

"I draw a line at you shoving that up my ass."

Now it's my turn to smirk as I close one end of the cuffs around his wrist and the other to the chair. "Then find a creative, safe word that makes me want to stop." I raise a brow at him as I straddle his lap and hover over his cock. Then I point the gun at his temple.

A delicious and intoxicating tension runs between us. "Will fucking you always be like Russian roulette?" he asks, trying to lean forward to kiss me. I pull back, my hand pressing against his shoulder. I like this power. I like the idea of all the times I've imagined his untimely death and how I see red bleeding out of him.

"Fucking me is like nothing you've ever had before," I tell him as I lower myself onto his cock, knocking my own breath away.

"Fuck, Shortcake," he growls. "You're so fucking perfect for me."

I ride his cock, intoxicated by the way he watches me and the power that thrums through me at holding the gun to his head. I could do it now. Who would be the wiser? Sure, there would be evidence of our coupling, but I could call for the body to be removed. I could kill him right now.

I grab his hair, pulling his head back so I can bite his neck. Mark him like he's done to me.

"Use me," he growls. "Fucking milk me." He moans, and it floods wetness to my core.

I never knew sex could be this good. Incomprehensible and make no fucking sense but feel right all at the same time.

I bite his shoulder, drawing blood, and he groans. I press the gun harder against his temple, silently telling him to be quiet.

I want to take everything from him when I've already given him so much of myself. Loving this man will be torture; the lines blurring between hate, desire, wanting to kill him, and wanting him to live for me.

All of these emotions swirl in my stomach as I ride his cock, feeding my own depravity as I take and take, moaning and crying at my own bursts of pleasure. Using and feeding off him.

It's the most beautiful thing I've ever known, and I feel myself lighting up from the inside and, for the first time, not forsaking my inner demon but embracing it.

My eyes shoot open, and I stare into his crystal blues, taking him with me. Taking us to a place neither of us could have ever imagined we'd go four years ago.

"Do you want to shoot me?" he grits.

"Always," I whisper breathlessly.

"It'd be easy. Just pull the trigger."

"Oh fuck," I curse, my pussy flooding at the thought. "This is sick."

"Yes, we're fucked up together," he says as he pants, not able to look away from me. "Take it all. My life is yours, Shortcake."

The orgasm is blinding when it hits, and I scream and shake, the intensity tearing me in two. He groans, and I catch his lips, kissing him as he spills into me. I continue rocking my hips, taking every drop he's willing to give to me as he curses me with unfavorable names. I eat every single one up.

This is twisted and fucked up.

But it's everything right now.

I rub my fingers over his mouth, my eyes darting back and forth over his beautiful face as I contemplate pulling the trigger.

"Take it all. My life is yours, Shortcake."

My heart pounds, terrified of those words. He doesn't know what he's saying, right? He was just in the moment.

He tries to kiss me again, but I pull back and stand.

Fuck.

What have I done?

I cross the room, my mind racing as I consider taking my chance to kill him now. The gun is in my hand, so why the fuck am I walking in the opposite direction to get my clothes?

I catch a glimpse of my reflection. I'm covered in bite marks, and my skin is smeared with blood, and I don't even know if it's his or mine.

I glance back at Braxton, who is now relaxed back in the chair, even though he's still cuffed to it. "So you're just going to run away?"

"It was fun, but I have to go now," I say, sliding on my underwear. I search for my shirt and find it poking out from under the bed.

"You liked that as much as I did," he states.

I reach under the bed to grab my shirt, and that's when I see the box with all of my statues in it. My heart skips a beat at knowing he kept them, and it only riles this wild thing that's trying to free the room.

"I did." I try to sound unaffected as I pull my clothes on. Because, *like,* is an understatement. In that moment, my suspicions became a reality. I don't hate Braxton. I don't like Braxton. I'm *in love* with Braxton. And this type of love is not made to last.

"You know neither of us can run away from this, Shortcake. You're acting like a coward."

I turn, swinging the gun in his direction. That's when I see he's no longer cuffed to the chair.

His expression is smug as he removes the cuff from around his wrist. "Do you really think I don't know how to remove my own cuffs?" he scoffs as he saunters toward me. "Now, let's talk about this like adults." He steps in close enough that the muzzle of the gun presses directly over his heart.

"There's nothing to discuss. If I'm gone for too long, my family will notice."

He chuckles. "How much longer do you plan on hiding?"

"Excuse me?"

"I know all of your secrets, Shortcake. I know who you are as much as I know myself."

"Sounds pretty fucked up, then."

His smile twists. "Oh, it is. *We* are."

Again, he tries to soothe my inner depraved self. But I know it's wrong. Even if he does see me, it doesn't make it right.

His hand slowly curls around the barrel of the gun, and I squeeze the trigger ever so slightly as I imagine blood bursting across the dining table. It'd be magnificent. But, instead, I let him take the gun from me. The moment it's gone, he reaches for me, but I step back.

"T-this was the l-last time, okay?" I stammer, then run for the door.

"Shortcake, we're not done here!" he shouts, but my fingers are already on the doorknob.

"Bye." I yank the door open, glancing back over my shoulder briefly. His blue eyes are locked on me, like a predator's, his jaw clenched as he lowers the gun to his side. Giving him a small wave, I slam the door behind me and call my driver. I run down the stairs as fast as my legs will take me, terrified he might chase after me.

I'm sick. I'm sick, right? There's something wrong with me?

It's not love. It's just a sickness. I've been brainwashed. That has to be it!

As I exit the building, I catch sight of the woman who was at his door almost an hour ago. His mother looks like the picture I saw of her in the files, just a little more run down. Quickly averting my gaze, I stand close to the curb, impatiently waiting for my driver to answer. Maybe I should walk up a few blocks so no one knows I came from Braxton's house. I decide on that as I drop a pin for my driver.

"You were in his apartment," she says desperately from behind me. I glance over my shoulder and step away from her outstretched hand. She looks me over from head to toe.

"Sorry?" I'm already uncomfortable. I don't want to be speaking to her right now. This has nothing to do with me.

"You know my son. You have to tell him to help me." She reaches for me again, but I move out of her range. I take in what she's wearing and wonder how she's not freezing in this frigid weather. She rubs her arms, but I don't think it has anything to do with the chill of the early morning and everything to do with the track marks marring her skin. "I'll give you anything you want, tell you anything you want about him."

Wow, okay. That's weird and desperate.

"Anything," she whispers insistently.

As curious as I might be about Braxton, I want no version of him that she's created a narrative for. It's obvious to me that she has no idea who her son is. It's sad, really.

"I don't think you even know your son," I bite back.

Her mouth drops open. "How dare you speak to me like that. He's poisoned your mind, too, hasn't he? He does that. He—"

"When is your son's birthday?" I ask, cutting her off.

She looks away as if genuinely thinking about it, and I scoff. Braxton is much better without a woman like this in his life. She's a parasite. I stiffen at the harshness of my judgment. I don't know this woman, and yet... I'm being protective on Braxton's behalf.

Fuck. What has he done to me?

I look up at his apartment window and notice him peering down from the second floor, watching us.

"He's bad, that one. Always has been," she whispers. "Only cares for himself. He can't give you what you want."

"You have no idea what I want," I say, irritated.

"Well, you obviously love my son."

It startles me, but only for a moment. I turn to her with a grin. I'm certain it's deranged and wild. I'm letting the mask slip for someone else to see part of my true nature, that for so long I've tried to hide. "I'd actually very much like to kill your son."

Stunned, she stumbles back two steps before her ass hits the pavement. I shouldn't feel powerful for intimidating someone like her, but this part of me feeds off fear.

Is this how my father has felt all of these years?

Maybe it's time I consider having a conversation with my aunt. Am I really that far gone? Am I really unable to hide it anymore?

I turn and head in the direction I gave my driver.

Everything feels like it doesn't make sense anymore, and it's crumbling around me. But I don't think I'm ready for that conversation with Anya. Maybe if I cut out Braxton for good, this part of me won't resurface. Maybe he's the catalyst that's ruined me. But deep down, I know that's a lie because these invasive thoughts and impulses started long before he entered my life.

CHAPTER 38
Braxton

My mother parks herself on the pavement outside my apartment. I'm sure she looks like a beggar to those who walk past. She's desperate, and she's lucky I didn't remove her myself after she accosted Hope. I don't know what they spoke about, but whatever it was, it shook my mother so profoundly that she fell over herself. I couldn't help but smirk at that. *That's my girl.*

Hope is running away. Again. I didn't think she'd stay, but I find it interesting when she reacts in ways I didn't expect her to. Just when I think I've studied her enough to know everything about her, she surprises me. I've come to realize she'll forever be a mystery to me. Her brilliant mind, that is. But not her body. I'm attuned to her needs as much as I am my own.

Letting her have that power over me, to feed off the

control of the situation, was the most beautiful fucking thing I've ever seen. She very well could've blown my brains out. In fact, I know she contemplated it more than once. The killer in her shines through when those thoughts cross her mind, and she fucking got off on it. Loved the idea of killing me while she fucked me.

I wonder if it's me and what we mean to each other that she's scared of. Or if it's her own depravity that drives her to run away. Either way, I know she's right. Her family will eventually find out about us if they haven't already. And if anyone at the precinct finds out, I'm equally fucked. But I refuse to stay away.

Dating Lena Love's daughter would get me applause but connecting her to Alek Ivanov will bring my badge into question.

I get ready for work, dressing in a long-sleeved shirt, beanie, and coat. It's forecast to start snowing soon, so having to bundle up is convenient, considering how much the little she-devil marked me. Shortcake my ass; she's complete sin. But she's my fucking sin.

I might still be unsure how to handle Hope Ivanov, but I've figured out how to manage the only other woman who has ever had an impact on my life. The one who has felt like a noose around my neck.

If I thought my association with Hope would rock my career and threaten everything I've built, then I've sorely underestimated the power my mother still holds over me. Sometimes, not being able to completely cut ties brings unwanted attention and discomfort.

I hate my mother. Even though, deep down, I held a small spark of hope that someday she'd turn into the parent I needed as a child. But that's an idea I've long left behind. Her intercepting Hope makes me comprehend with startling clarity that I have to cut her out of my life completely.

Hope may not accept me, but I know she's the only woman for me. And I don't want something as filthy as my mother or my past reaching out and grabbing for her or me any longer. Some baggage has to finally be discarded.

I wish I didn't feel this way about my mother. My therapist told me I should be grateful to her, to some degree, for bringing me into this world. But I'm not. She never treated me like a son, only a problem. And just like she kicked me out of her life when I was fourteen, I'll now do the same to her.

When I step outside the apartment building, she immediately jumps into my path, blocking me from getting to my car. She drops to her knees. "Please. *Please*," she begs.

I'm sick of being the one to dictate who is good and bad. Teddy deserves to be in prison even if I don't know what crime he's been picked up for this time. I can't protect or save everyone. In fact, I'm the furthest thing from a hero—if you don't count my last name.

"It's not going to happen, Mother." I shove my hands in my coat pockets, speaking my truth. "I hope they kill him in jail. I hope that one day when you're standing at his funeral, it registers what a fucking lowlife he is and everything he's done to cause you harm. I also hope one day you realize how you have no right to come to me for help when the only time you've ever lifted your hand was to beat me instead of help me. You don't get to come here pretending to be a victim because your supplier's been imprisoned. Tell me, is it the fact that Teddy's gone to jail that hurts most, or because you've run out of your stash and don't know who to go to now?"

Her expression morphs from desperate to angry as she stands and lifts her hand. I catch her frail wrist as she attempts to slap me across the face. "You ungrateful piece of shit. How dare you speak so little of me," she snarls.

"It's an offense to hit a police officer," I tell her.

"I am your mother."

"You lost that title a long time ago." I push her hand away and step around her.

"What, you think you're better than me because you have some fancy apartment and live in the city? Fucking useless. You always have been!" she seethes. "Think because you can impress some rich little princess that you've forgotten your roots!"

I turn then and take two steps back toward her. She cowers, her face stricken with fear, and it embodies everything I hate. That she lashes out, but she's so used to men who hit her and beat her as if she's no better than a dog. It makes me feel dirty. I would never hit her or any other woman.

"I suggest you leave. Move away from that trailer park before people start coming for money. If you don't, I might lock you up with him myself." I have no intention of seeing my mother ever again after this, but I know whatever business Teddy is involved with isn't the kind that will go away with him. Especially if he's still dealing like my previous reports indicated.

She seems to think on it for a second before she takes a step back and spits at me. I knew I would never have a relationship with this woman, but this just confirms it. I hate her. Even calling her "mother" is an insult to those who are *real* mothers.

And although I might not know what that type of love feels like, I've met a woman who's shown me just how a woman can step into their own power.

It's a choice.

My mother will never grow or change, and I simply can't accept who she is.

Or I can, but now it's my choice to leave her behind.

I turn and walk to my car.

No father.

No mother.

Up until a few months ago, I had no person to keep me connected to this world. Well, no one who was important enough for me to take their secrets to the grave.

But now there's one.

And she ran away from me as quickly as her feelings for me began to rear their ugly heads.

Maybe I'm unlovable. Though I'm certain she and I share our own form of love.

Obsessive.

Conflicting.

Irreplaceable.

Hope Ivanov will be mine if it's the last fucking thing I do in this world.

CHAPTER 39

Hope

By the third day, the bruises have started to turn yellow. My mother came into my bedroom after I'd showered one morning, and I'd accidentally walked out wrapped only in a towel. When I noticed, I literally was in such a rush to close the bathroom door that I slipped and awkwardly landed on my hip, causing another bruise. But crisis averted.

If she found out I was seeing Braxton, she would've told my father. I really don't want to deal with that situation, especially when I have no idea how I feel about it myself.

Have I been avoiding him again? Yes. Absolutely. I ran so fast out of his apartment, and I've been in a spiral ever since.

Accepting my feelings for Braxton is one thing, but knowing what to do with them is a completely separate matter. Because I can't act on them, can I? There are so many other things I should be focusing on. And yet, he consumes my thoughts night and day. He literally haunts me not only in my waking hours but also when I sleep. I'm pretty sure I'm going crazy. That's the only answer to all of this.

As I get out of the car at midday, preparing myself for a full evening in the studio, I take a sip of my black coffee. I've hardly been able to sleep these past three nights, analyzing all of the different outcomes, but they keep coming to the same end. There can't be a relationship between me and Braxton. Not the type I might want. And I think I want to be with Braxton. The thought of any other woman with him curdles my stomach and brings an immediate rage that overrides clear thinking.

But he's a detective. The last person I can introduce to my family. And I can't imagine any sane man throwing his career away for me. No matter how great I am. He'd have to fall from grace for me, and even then, my family would never trust him. Even if I made them vow not to touch him, they'd find a way to permanently remove him from my life. This will only end in bloodshed. He's not mine to have. So doesn't it make sense for me to be the one to pull the trigger?

I take another sip of my coffee as the elevator stops on the floor for my studio. When the doors open, I can't say I'm entirely surprised to see him waiting for me, but that feeling of unease swirls in the pit of my stomach. It makes it hard to swallow my coffee. I know I've come to the same conclusion for us over and over again, but it doesn't make me any less affected by the outcome because I do want him, even when I pretend I don't.

I grip my bag as I walk closer to the door. He reaches out and takes the bag from my hand, as if it's something he's done many times. These moments of time we steal together are as natural as they come, even though every time, it risks something for both of us.

"No pancakes this week?" he asks. He and I both know why I haven't been to the café lately—because I'm avoiding him.

I push my glasses up my nose and shake my head as I unlock the door. He follows behind me, scanning the room. It's a mess. The counters are covered in clay and pieces that I have discarded. I don't really like to clean up too much because I find the chaotic mess somewhat of a comfort. I have a cleaner come in once a month, though. I just like it when it feels busy, like a room full of treasures. He picks up a piece of clay, inspects it, and then puts it back on the counter as he looks at me. "Are you working?" he asks.

I remove my coat and hang it on the back of the door, revealing my overalls. "Yes." Obviously. That's why I come here. It goes without saying, but he doesn't care if he imposes here, and, surprisingly, he's one of only a few I don't mind being in my space. "Aren't *you* working today?"

The dull topic is a way for us to dance around the questions and answers we really want. The ones hovering over us like a scythe that neither of us dare to touch yet. Because what conclusion has he come to? Does he even like me? What if it's all gone to my head? *Fuck.* What if I'm being conceited? If that's the case, I've definitely spent far too much time around Hawke.

"Day off, actually," he says, which means very little to him since he works even when he's not working. I suppose he and I are similar in that regard. "Do you want me to leave?"

I glance up at him then. He's left my bag beside the door and moved deeper into the studio. It feels as if he swallows the space around him. This space of mine, this sanctuary. It doesn't look so bad on him.

"You can stay," I answer quietly. I mean, he's already here, and there's an ease he brings with him, as much as it unsettles me that we could be caught.

He smirks and drags a stool over to the station where I'm working. It feels strange having him sit next to me, but I'm not entirely against it. In fact, I lean into it a little as I turn my classical music on to play quietly in the background. I usually have it blasting, but this time, I keep it lower so I can focus more on his breathing.

"Is this where you do your glass sculptures as well?" he asks inquisitively.

I smirk, not yet admitting to it openly. I actually work on those in a completely different studio. Somewhere small and quaint that no one knows I bought about a year ago.

He grins as he grabs my coffee and takes a sip. I go to reprimand him for it, then stop myself. I suppose it's no different to when he steals the remains of my pancakes and drinks my coffee at the café.

"How's your skin?" he asks.

"See for yourself," I tell him while my hands are preoccupied with a clump of wet clay. He unclips my overalls and lifts my shirt, revealing my breasts. His fingertips brush against the skin, tracing one of the yellowing bruises. His crystal-blue eyes darken as he stares longingly at the marks he left.

"I liked it," I remind him, quite enjoying his touch. I try to focus on the sculpture in front of me.

"Tell me all about your favorite parts of that night," he whispers into my ear, and it elicits goose bumps along my arms. A steady pulse begins at my core.

"Behave while I'm working," I growl.

He chuckles as he clips my overalls back up and then leans back, watching me. "You must have liked it. You came if I remember correctly," he says.

"It must've been a figment of your imagination. Surely, you're not that good," I sass back.

He laughs, and it relieves all the tension that's settled in my shoulders over the last few days. How can one man make me feel so at ease when he's one of the main reasons I'm in a fluster in the first place?

I lick my lips as I think about when I left his apartment: his mother and the things she said. Perhaps I should be sorry for scaring her like that, but I'm not. I glance in his direction, and he rolls his eyes.

"Ask your question, Shortcake."

It's unnerving how well he knows me after such a short amount of time. Then again, I suppose he's been watching me for months. Someone as clever as Braxton is literally paid to be observant.

"Did you help your mother?"

"No. And I don't intend to." Silence stretches between us and then he expels a long breath. "I've never had a good relationship with her. So I cut her off."

"Oh," is all I can manage to say because the fact that he's telling me this means something, doesn't it?

"No Dad?" I inquire. From the file Ivy curated for me, I noted there's no father named on his birth certificate, but I want to hear it from him. I'm even more curious to see if he lies about it.

"Nope. Lone wolf. I have a sister somewhere, but she disowned me the same as my mother. They only come crawling to me when they need something."

I think about how sad that is. I couldn't imagine not having the supportive and functional family I have despite its shortcomings. I've always known love, felt provided for and cherished. I wonder if Braxton has ever felt loved or if it's something he can't accept. Maybe I really am in over my head to think he could accept me and what I have to offer him.

What *do* I have to offer him?

"Does it... hurt?" I ask, unsure of how much I can pry.

"No. I came to terms with that a long time ago. Besides, I'm not looking at the past anymore," he answers, and when I meet his gaze, he's staring at me. I can't help but wonder if there's more he's not saying. "You know I'm here for a reason, right, Shortcake?"

The sculpture wavers between my fingers, and I quickly correct my hands as I stop working on it. "And why are you here?" I ask carefully, my heart racing as his gaze dips to my lips. I can hear my heart thumping in my ears.

A knock sounds on my door, disrupting both of us. I stand quickly as if I've been caught doing something wrong, a spike of adrenaline fueling me for an entirely different reason now.

Hardly anyone comes here, especially during the day. So I'm confused that someone has access to my studio. I'm surprised when the door opens, and I see my father, whose gaze immediately narrows on Braxton.

"Dad?!" I squeak. A muscle in Braxton's jaw jumps as he holds the same strangled gaze with my father. That's a big fucking mistake.

I step in front of him, then approach my father, wiping my hands on my overalls. I'm not sure what type of cover story I can come up with for having a detective in my workspace, but I'll have to think of something quick-smart.

"Your mother asked me to check on you," Dad says as my aunt pushes past him.

"Pfft. Is that the story we're sticking to?" She rolls her eyes and comes to give me a kiss on the cheek in greeting. She quickly scans the room, a low hum of approval, considering she was the one who bought me this place as a gift for my eighteenth birthday. And then her gaze lands on Braxton.

She eyes him up and down, and I know she knows he's a police officer. Even if he's not dressed like one, she knows when someone isn't one of us. She's very good at managing people, or more so identifying them for who they really are.

"And you are?" she asks suspiciously as my father steps farther into the room and shuts the door behind him. My father's glare shifts to me, and I'm uncomfortable at its fierceness. I've never disappointed my father. Never so much as given him a reason to ground me, let alone not trust me. But it's as if I'm feeling all of that tenfold.

I go to speak, but there's a lump in my throat. I've never felt the wrath of the Ivanov siblings, and I've never had to endure their judgment. That dark little thing within me wants to stand up to them, but who am I but a child in a game they've been playing all their life?

"I'm Braxton," Braxton says as if saving me from my own cowardice. He jumps off the stool and leaves my coffee mug on the counter. "I was just dropping off a coffee for Hope."

"Is it poisoned?" Aunt Anya asks with a thick Russian accent. It means she's angry. My father remains quiet, and it unsettles me the way he watches my every move. Especially when I deliberately step in front of Braxton, too terrified that either of them will act on impulse and ask questions later.

"Poison is not my forte, although I heard it was for one of your sons recently."

"Excuse me?" Anya grits and steps forward. I seem to surprise both of them as I shove myself between them. I have my hand on her shoulder and the other pressing against Braxton as he smirks.

My aunt will definitely kill him, especially because of the mention of her sons.

I give Braxton a disapproving glare. Picking a fight with my aunt is not the way to do this. "Braxton was just leaving. He was following up on that case from when I got arrested."

"Arrested?! You didn't tell me this," Anya seethes at my father. But my father says nothing, just stares into Braxton's soul as he readjusts his gloves, most likely thinking of all the creative ways he's going to kill him.

"You should leave town," Anya is quick to say to

Braxton. "Not that I think you'll get far with broken legs."

"That's enough!" I yell as Braxton goes to reply. "You should leave. Now."

Braxton's gaze shifts to me, staring at me like I'm a stranger. It hurts more than it should, and my stomach sinks as if I've betrayed him, but I'm literally doing all I can to de-escalate the situation so he leaves here alive. Why does he not understand that?

"I'm not scared of your family, Shortcake."

But he should be. Right now, though, the way he looks at me, it's as if he's pitying me. As if I'm more scared of them finding out about us than he is. That makes him, by definition, crazy.

"Go," I mouth. He's reluctant to leave, but I don't need to remind him that this is my family. They may be dangerous, but never to me.

He grinds his jaw and kicks up an insincere smile. I'm certain he does it to piss them off even more. My aunt looks at him like he's filth and doesn't move out of his way. He steps around her, and then my father blocks his path. My father is slightly shorter than Braxton, but he oozes a cold sense of control. My skin prickles with the deadly intention in the air.

"Dad?" I say, grabbing his attention. His gaze grudgingly moves me, and I mouth, *"Please."*

His eyebrows furrow slightly as if confused. Perhaps it's because of the words that go unsaid. I've never begged my father for anything. But I've never had anything I've wanted to protect so badly besides my privacy. And I'm certain that, even if I haven't said it out loud, that my father realizes I love Braxton. Even when I deny it, which I will. I'll stand between them if he tries to hurt Braxton in any way.

That hits me with a terrifying force.

Oh, how far I've fallen.

I'm a disappointment.

My father takes a step to the left so Braxton can pass. When he crosses the threshold, he looks back at me, words unsaid, betrayal, and pain surfacing in his eyes. But what did he expect me to do? What was he about to say?

Anya walks over and slams the door in his face. It's so loud that I grit my teeth instead of flinching as she turns around. "Seems we have a few things to discuss."

My father starts looking around as if he's about to discover something else that I've been hiding. When I look back to my aunty, she's studying me as if she's discovered something new and foreign.

"How long has this been going on for?" she asks, crossing her arms over her chest. "And so help me, God, little one, if you don't give us answers, we *will* kill him."

"That's not what we came here for," Dad growls.

"Oh, come on now, don't be so stiff, Aleksandr. I know you want to know, too," she bites back at him. I can't help but feel like I'm being circled by two sharks as I try to keep myself afloat in a tank full of blood.

"A few months," I confess.

Her eyebrows rise. "My, my. We are good at keeping secrets, aren't we?"

"He's the detective from that night Charlotte stole the wallet," Dad says as he stops at the piece I'm currently working on.

"Yes."

"And he could ruin us. Could be using you," he says, looking up at me. I know that look. It's the one he gives every time he's about to dispose of an immediate danger.

"Please don't kill him. I—" The words cut off at my throat.

"You love him?" my aunt says condescendingly with a roll of her eyes. "Men come and go. There's plenty for you out there. Don't settle. Especially for one who isn't rich."

"I'm not like you, okay?!" I snap. And for the first time, my aunt looks like she might be... hurt isn't the right word. I'm certain my aunt doesn't even bleed. I adjust my glasses, wanting to hide behind them. But the part of me that Braxton has nurtured—that *I've* nurtured—rises up to challenge them. "I'm not like either of you." In many ways. "You can't tell me that it was all smooth sailing between you and River," I say to Aunt Anya. I then look at my father. "Or you and Mom. You've said it yourself that you two come from different worlds, and yet, you make it work."

"This is different, Hope," my aunt argues, and my

father simply stares at me as if seeing a side to me he's never witnessed before. "You're young, impressionable—"

"I am my own woman!" I shout. "And I can't live under the perfect little bubble you expect of me anymore."

She's taken aback, clicking her tongue. "No one has ever put expectations on you, little one, except for yourself. Don't blame others for situations or routines you're not yet brave enough to get out of yourself."

It's like a slap to the face.

"Enough," Dad says. "We'll discuss this at a later time. We came here for something else."

"We're not moving on from this discussion until both of you promise me you won't touch him." I raise my hand at my aunt and add, "Or order anyone else to touch him."

They share a look, and my aunt tsks disapprovingly.

"For now," Dad agrees, but it doesn't give me any confidence in the matter.

Palpable tension fills the air and then shifts into something else. Something deadly as my aunt speaks. "We got a tip. A concerning one, to say the least." She smiles. "You've become messy, Hope Ivanov."

I look at my father in confusion. What the fuck are they talking about? "Tip?"

"Yes, you know that when bad things happen in the city, those things will, in some way or another, end up coming through us, correct?" Anya says, and my father watches me carefully.

"What are you talking about?" I'm so confused. Are they still referring to me and Braxton? That he and I are bad? I already knew that, but I didn't think they knew that. I assumed I was doing a good job at hiding it all, but maybe I was wrong. Maybe I'm doing this all wrong. I should've ended it with him because now I have my family standing here, and my father is looking at me like he hasn't seen me before.

I don't like it.

I love my family; I truly, deeply do. It's one thing in this life that I know God gave me right. And I understand how completely fucked up that sounds to an average person, but who else has an aunty who would literally kill for them? Because I know for sure mine would.

"Hawke has been teaching you how to shoot," Anya says.

I roll my eyes. "He told you?"

"No, of course, he didn't. I worked that one out all on my own. He's been miserable since Ford made his relationship with Billie official, so I've been keeping an eye on him to make sure he doesn't do anything stupid while he's bored."

"Does Mom know?" I ask my father. I don't think me using a gun is worse than dating a detective. She specifically warned me off, but it feels like a mountain of crimes is piling up against me.

He shakes his head. "It's best she doesn't know about this. To protect her."

My hands are clammy, and I wipe them on my overalls. What is he talking about? What's going on that I'm not aware of? And why is it taking so long to get to the point? Is it the glass statues? Do they know about them?

"Are you... mad at me?" I ask my father.

"No," he replies at the same time Anya says, "Disappointed."

I wipe my hands again. I fucking hate how much weight that word holds. They're *disappointed* in me. I'm successful. I tried to be the perfect daughter. I tried to push away all of these murky and ugly impulses. Yes, I may be fucking a detective, but I'm not in a relationship with him. I don't tell him any secrets. Granted, he knows how I like to be fucked, and that's probably a secret in and of itself. But disappointed? It hurts more than it should because, for the last four years, I feel like I've been fighting an upstream battle, and now I'm drowning.

"Can one of you tell me why you're disappointed?" I snap. I'm sick of this game, sick of them trying to pry without giving too much away in case I confess to something more.

My aunty reaches into her purse and pulls out her phone. She swipes at the screen a few times as she walks over to me, her heels clicking on the floor, and then she turns her phone around and shows it to me. It's a man with a green mohawk; he's dead. I try my best not to give her any reaction because I know she's watching my every move. My clever aunty is always assessing everything.

"It's a dead man," I say and meet her eyes.

"I always wondered about you. I assumed you'd end up more like your mother than your father. But it seems, for the first time in my life, I'm actually wrong. And you're a combination of deadly as well as beautiful."

"Hope," Dad says nothing but my name, and everything feels like it's going in slow motion. *Fuck.* They know.

They know.

They know.

They see me! The dark little voice in my head speaks with glee.

"You never wanted to share this with me?" he says.

Everything stops. My heart. The airflow in the room. My existence. Everything I've built on lies comes crashing around me, and a twisted sense of relief and freedom comes with it. My shackles feel like they've finally been removed.

Somehow, someway, they've discovered my dirtiest little secret. It could've been someone worse that caught me, I guess. I turn and walk to my closet, which houses a safe. I bend down and enter the code to unlock it. I grab out a knife, then I turn around and show it to them.

My father once owned this knife, and I stole it from

his collection when I was thirteen but never used it until I was sixteen.

"Amazing, really," my aunty says, clapping her hands excitedly.

"You should have told me," Dad says in warning.

"I didn't know I'd like it so much," I confess. I've kept this secret for so long that when I finally chose to act on it, I wasn't sure if I could ever share it with anyone close to me. Yes, my family are killers. But they usually kill because someone is threatening the family or their businesses. I kill for the absolute adrenaline rush it gives me. I like it. I like it about as much as I like art. Or when Braxton fucks me. The way he fucked me the other night is probably top-tier with how it feels when I take a life.

It might've started with a knife, but I've experimented since then, exploring all the ways a soul can leave the shell of a body.

"It's perfect, really. No one would suspect you." Anya takes the knife from me. "But this?" She waves the knife in front of me. "Holding on to things that could easily get you caught when you have a detective in your space is very fucking stupid. I want you to think better. I want you to never keep anything from any kill. Do you understand me?"

"Yes," I say quietly, still in shock that they know my secret.

"How did you know it was me who killed the guy

with the mohawk?" I ask, still trying to figure it out. Was I betrayed?

Anya clicks her tongue. "Well, having Ivy cover for you and tamper with the videos was an impressive feat; however, she still has much to learn if she's to surpass her father. Will was able to recall the videos. You're lucky it was at Lucy's where Eli could get rid of the body."

Ah. I hadn't expected Ivy to see it. I'd kept it a secret for so long, and she was the first to stumble across my dirty secret. She was shocked but quick to offer a contingency plan, and her involvement definitely helped the aftermath to try and hide it from my family when I begged her not to tell anyone, so she one upped and decided to tamper with the remaining evidence. I didn't think she'd accept this part of me so easily, and I was grateful because I couldn't handle that kind of disgust from one of my best friends.

I don't really know what I was thinking. Sometimes I go into a daze. My targets have always been men who have hurt women, but lately, my reasoning seems miscued. It's felt like an avalanche, and my brain hurts from all the impulses to take more victims I've had to fight off.

"You're the one who's been leaving the bodies around the city for the past nine months, aren't you?" Dad asks.

My mouth opens and then closes. At first, I was

messy. I didn't know how to hide a body. But then I realized I didn't want to. I wanted them to be found. I wanted to be seen, as risky as that was. I wanted my art to be discovered. I nod, except for the two men. I don't know who took them out, but I'm certainly not strong enough to physically overpower them, and it insults me that the media have placed them into my serial killer count.

My father sighs, looking at the ceiling. "I don't know how I didn't notice."

"It isn't your fault that I'm like this."

"*This*?" My aunt quickly grabs both of my shoulders. "No, no. We don't look at this like it is something ugly. You embrace this part of yourself, Hope Ivanov. Do you hear me? This thing inside you?" She places her hand on my heart, and my breath shudders, as if her every word is something I've been waiting to hear my entire life. "This thing inside you is powerful. Deadly. *Beautiful.* We do not forsake the parts of us that come naturally. Have you ever judged us for killing?"

"No," I whisper. Because the truth is, I haven't. "But Mom..."

I wanted to be perfect for her. She tried so hard to keep me away from all of this. She'd be disappointed in me, maybe even hate me, for becoming this sick, twisted little thing.

"Don't worry about your mother," Dad reassures me

as he pulls me in for a hug. I'm surprised at the action but wrap my arms around him, not knowing how badly I needed this... acceptance. "Your mother learned to love me even with my misdeeds. She'll just have to adapt."

"Gah." Anya throws her hands in the air. "There are no misdeeds in this. We take what we want when we want. That is what it is to have Ivanov blood. We just need to sharpen your fangs, little one. And no more leaving around trophies for others to see. If you're proud of your kill, send a photo to me or something if it's praise you need."

I chuckle, but tears well in my eyes. I pull away from my father to adjust my glasses. This is so stupid. So strange that being caught as a killer by my family has relieved me in a way I thought wasn't possible.

"I'm just sad you felt like you couldn't tell us. If I'd known you wanted to kill people, I would've taken you out myself. We could've created a hunting ground or something. Ooh, perhaps we should create auctions like that for the rich. My niece, you're brilliant!" she says, inspiration lighting her eyes as she places the knife in her purse.

"How does it make you feel when you take a life?" Dad asks carefully.

My eyebrows furrow, and I lick my lips. A buzz of energy rushes over me as I recall every kill.

It's beautiful.

Magical.

Life and death.

In the moment I take a life, I feel something besides the adrenaline, besides the acute, heightened senses. I feel like I'm connected to everything and every color. The world becomes my canvas.

"I like it... a lot."

"More than this?" He waves a hand around the room, and I can only nod. Because I feel like without one, I would no longer have the muse to do the other.

They are both part of who I am.

"Something doesn't make sense, though. Your pattern, or the serial killer's. The strangling of one of the victims and the broken neck of another. You're five foot nothing, so how did you pull that off?" Anya asks me.

I click my tongue and look away, furious. Those two kills tarnished my legacy. "They weren't my kills. And it kind of pisses me off they're assumed to be my victims. But it's not like I can correct the police or the media."

Anya laughs. "My, my. What a little ego. We definitely have to work on that because it will be your undoing, and you'll get caught."

"But you'll bail me out, right?" I ask, batting my lashes.

She smiles in return. "I knew you were my favorite niece for a reason."

"I'm your only niece," I remind her as she pulls me in for a hug.

My father huffs, acting annoyed by our camaraderie.

But deep down, I can see the twinkle in his eyes. The approval. The quiet confidence and pride. He might not ever say it out loud, especially in front of my mother, but I feel it. And I feel whole. Finally.

"We won't share this with your mother just yet," he says.

"Do we have to tell her?" I ask, and he pins me with a glare. It would be easier if we didn't. I don't like lying to her, but I don't think she'll be as accepting as they are.

"Your mother loves you. She'll just need time to adjust. It will eat at her, knowing there is something in your life you can't trust her with," he says. "If she can love a monster like me, let me assure you, she will love her only child." I want to cry all over again. My father is a man of few words, but when he does speak, it's with confidence and conviction. "However, the next time you have the urge to kill someone, you will be calling me. Do you understand?"

I nod, trying not to smile.

"And me," Anya adds with a smirk. I'm not sure why I would call either of them; it's something I enjoy doing alone. But their moral support is nice.

"Anything else we should know about?" Dad asks.

I bite my bottom lip. I think about the glass sculptures, but that feels like mine and Braxton's secret. And if I tell them about them, they'll storm his place immediately to get rid of the evidence. But selfishly, I want him to have those.

"Nope," I lie.

My father stares at me skeptically, and I'm certain he knows I'm lying.

"I have to work now," I tell them, trying to usher them out.

"You know, if you came under our employment, you could get paid for killing," my aunt says.

"No. She'll focus on her sculptures," Dad bites back.

Anya shrugs. "Why? Killing pays more."

I try not to laugh, but then I sober when my father turns before closing the door and says, "Hope, stop talking to that detective. I mean it." And then he closes the door behind them.

My heart drops, and all of my fluttery excitement is short-lived as another burden weighs on me.

Braxton.

He's either a liability or the love of my life.

How could someone in his position ever love a monster like me?

But deep down, I hope there's a sliver of a chance that he can embrace and accept me.

Even without my father's warnings, I know that's a pipe dream.

My back hits the door, and I slide down to the floor, running my filthy hands through my hair, as I once again conclude the only ending we'll ever have...is with his death.

So how do I kill the only man I've ever loved?

Maybe the "how" no longer matters. This is all about self-preservation, so the only factor I need to focus on now...is *when*.

CHAPTER 40
Braxton

I sit in my car, waiting and watching as the Ivanov twins leave. Hope doesn't go with them. I want to know why they showed up. I know they're family, but why did both of them come to visit her? I can't help but think it'll always be something sinister with the likes of people like them.

She seemed surprised when they arrived. I'm certain it won't be long before I receive a visit of my own. When Alek spots my car, I decide going back up to see his daughter is not the wisest decision. But I can't help smirking as I put my sunglasses on. It satisfies me to see his gaze narrow on me. If anything, I find it flattering that he sees me as a threat. As he should.

I see him as one as well, but for an entirely different reason than we're on opposite sides of the law. No, I know for certain Alek Ivanov will do anything in his power to keep Hope and me apart. Too bad for him I'm so hooked on his daughter that I can't seem to set myself free. Looks like he'll literally have to pry Hope from my cold, dead hands.

I decide being alone isn't the best thing for me right now, so instead of going home, I head to the precinct.

Heidi greets me as I walk in, and when I enter the bullpen, I see Lucas hunched over his desk. He hasn't slept since Kylie was murdered, and although he was removed from the case, he's still been working on it tirelessly. I've been trying my best to avoid his questions about the investigation as best as I can.

"Braxton!" He perks up when he sees me. "There's something I want you to go over."

I sigh as I sit on the edge of his desk. "You know you shouldn't be working on this," I say under my breath. "If the chief finds out, you're fucked. You need some rest, Lucas." He looks worse than me.

"I know. I know. But I found something," he tells me. "You know how Hope Ivanov came to the funeral?"

I narrow my eyes on his screen as he begins opening files. "So, obviously, they went to art shows together, but I wonder if your involvement was a catalyst for my sister's death.

"What do you mean?"

"Well, think of the two people who were at recent events with her. Hope Ivanov and Candice, her agent," he says rapidly. "The week before she was murdered, my sister had a falling out with both."

My eyebrows dip as he brings up two screens and begins scrolling. He's brought up text messages. He's grasping at straws, and I don't know how to gently tell him that.

"See? Look here. Kylie texted Hope Ivanov and said, *'Now I understand how you climbed the art world so quickly. It's all because of your mother.'* And Hope replied with, *'Who's number is this?'* An hour later, Candice messaged Kylie, saying she might have to let her go because her work hadn't been selling as well, and their contract was due to end. What if they're involved in this together?" His eyes shine with excitement. "Hope obviously told Candice to get rid of her."

Others are looking our way, and I dip my head to quietly speak with him. "Lucas, I know this is hard for you, and I'm not discrediting that there may be some connection, but this is not enough to indicate they were involved with the murder. If anything, wouldn't it be the other way around?"

"I'm telling you, I know she's a part of this. She has to be. It's so obvious," he insists. I pity Lucas. This is not enough evidence. If anything, it's going to get him a temporary dismissal, which he should already be on.

I sigh, knowing what I have to do. He's going off the rails. Hunting for his sister's killer is driving him mad.

"Hope Ivanov had an alibi that night. She was with Ivy Walker," I gently remind him.

"It's all a lie! Of course, they're going to have each other's backs. They're just pompous little bitches who cover for each other!" he yells. I jump to my feet, then grab the collar of his shirt, fisting it. I bite my lip as the words I want to freely say need to be held back. *You don't speak about her that way.*

My gaze alone enforces that as I'm conscious of onlookers. "You need to calm down, Lucas. You need to trust me."

"Trust you?! My sister is dead!" he shouts. "You're covering for her too, aren't you?!" He points at me. "You're in on it! You're all in on it!"

My fingers curl into his shirt to restrain all my violent thoughts. He's absolutely fucking cracked. But is he really that far from the truth? His actions might discredit him, but his words hit home for me.

"You need to be careful with these families," I remind him. "Remember what happened to your friends?" I say even quieter. If he goes further down this road, there will be no coming back. I'm on a tightrope myself, but someone like Lucas has no fucking chance. He's never stuck his neck out. Never spoken or lashed out, and if he does this time, it'll cost him his life.

"What's happening here?!" The chief steps out of his office, and we look around the room as onlookers gawk at us. I release Lucas and take a step back.

Fuck me. Does it already look like I'm choosing her over my own? But everyone in this room knows well enough how quickly people disappear when trying to interfere with these families. I didn't mind playing with them a little at the beginning, but there are deadly consequences in these games. Ones that Lucas will not survive.

"Nothing, sir," I say, giving Lucas a pointed look.

He falls quiet and sits back in his chair, scowling at me.

Fuck. Being here wasn't a good idea either.

Everything is falling apart around me. And I'm not so sure I can control where the pieces will land anymore.

Fuck.

She well and truly has poisoned me from the inside out.

CHAPTER 41

Hope

It's midnight. And after finally finishing my piece, I made my way to the diner for pancakes and coffee. I don't know how long I've sat re-reading the same line in my book over and over again because my mind keeps trying to make sense of today's events.

It's strange how much changed today. A weight that I've been carrying since noticing these curious thoughts and impulsive demands has finally been lifted. The stress had grown over the years, to the point of maddening, as I've kept it to myself. The only sense of release was when I started sharing my glass statues with Braxton. Perhaps, as Anya said, I have an ego. I didn't think I'd get caught, and I liked the idea of playing with him.

I felt invincible but also drawn to show someone—anyone—the real me.

No, not anyone. I wanted Braxton to see me for what I really am.

I'm not even sure how this snowballed so much. I thought I'd never tell a soul, but it quickly became a part of me that so desperately wanted to be seen. Acknowledged. To know how bad I'd truly become.

I thought the first life I took was by accident, but in hindsight, it was the beginning of my darkest desires and impulses. I was twenty, out drinking with a few friends from college. The guy began groping me, and I told him to stop. Even after having five drinks, I knew I didn't want him touching me. But he chose not to hear my voice when I told him no. Instead, he decided my body was his to do whatever he wanted with it. Something dark twisted in my stomach as I considered letting him have his way, just so I could get out of there sooner. He was twice my size, after all. But another part of me beckoned, telling me it would protect me, and other women like me, from men like him.

When he pushed me behind a building and held a pocket knife to my throat, I felt a sense of irony instead of fear. My father taught me from an early age how to disarm someone. Knives were my father's specialty, and I watched him use them. I studied him. He might've not killed in front of me often, but I saw the way he cut the skin off my apples, and I realized that human flesh and other items weren't so different.

Before I knew what I was doing, I'd disarmed the guy

and held the knife to his throat. He immediately put his hands up, feigning surrender as he began to laugh, treating me like a joke. My emotions were high, and adrenaline was rushing through me so fast I couldn't think clearly. But I recalled everything my mother and aunt embodied in me about being a powerful woman. Controlling my own destiny and not allowing any man ever to take what was not meant for him.

His laughing became hysterical, and he took two steps back, bending over with wild amusement as if the shift in power was so hilarious. Maybe he was on drugs. Maybe he was drunk. But it didn't make it okay. And I certainly wasn't to be made fun of when he tried to force himself on me.

By the time he managed to get his laughing under control, his expression had twisted viciously, and he stepped forward to take the knife from me as if I were a child acting out. My hand moved of its own accord so fast that before I could stop it, it sliced across his throat in one swift movement. His eyes grew wide in shock, hands flying to his neck. I guess to stop the bleeding. The thing is, when you cut someone's throat and neck, blood kind of goes everywhere. It splattered across my clothes, and I stepped back, inconvenienced by how messy his life spilled out of him. I pocketed the knife and watched, mesmerized, as he grappled with the realization that there was no coming back from this. That I was his undoing. His Grim Reaper.

He dropped to his knees, one hand stretching out to me, silently begging for mercy. But there was a power and thrill in seeing a man on his knees like that. Being the justice and silencer of vermin who would never touch a woman again. I just stood there, watching him, not making a move to help him.

I found it all very fascinating. The way his blood poured out of his neck and down his white shirt and eventually made its way onto the dirty cement. I wondered if that was the reason why my family was so bad. I wondered if they got the same high.

A pool of blood gathered at my feet, and when he finally dropped his hand from his throat, his body went limp, his eyes still wide in disbelief. What was I supposed to do? It's not like I could save him; he was already dead. There was literally no point in me even trying. But most importantly, *I didn't want to.*

The music from the club was loud, and I could hear people yelling and cheering over it while I stood there looking down at my first kill.

Nothing is ever as satisfying as the first.

That was one of my favorite nights.

It was a year before I did it again. And the fun fact about it is I used the same pocket knife on the next man. After that, I was intrigued by other methods.

I get that I'm all types of fucked-up. I understand that. And I also know how to present myself as a decent person to the rest of the world. They think I'm innocent, and it helps me fly under the radar. If Braxton knew half the stuff I've done, he wouldn't look at me the same way he does now. Or maybe I'm wrong about that. After all, the sex we have is primitive in a way that I know is not normal for most lovers.

The door to the diner opens, and I glance up, my gaze connecting with crystal-blue eyes. He's out of his mind coming here so soon after we were caught by my father and aunt, though I expected to see him here, which is precisely why I came.

This diner has somehow become our place.

He takes his usual seat across from me. I offer him my fork to finish the last pancake, but for the first time ever, he shakes his head, refusing the meal. Though he still picks up my mug of black coffee and takes a sip.

I try not to smirk.

Asshole.

"What are we?" he asks. I suck in a sharp breath. Oh boy, we're really finishing this conversation.

"That's a loaded question." I should close the book and focus on him, but I can't; it's like a shield. Ironic since I can handle myself when killing someone, but when it comes to social connection or matters of the heart, I am very much a coward.

He rubs his face, tired. I don't know what's happened in the twelve hours since I saw him last, but he looks even more exhausted. I suppose it's a good thing he actually survived these twelve hours, considering my family is aware there's something happening between us.

"Why is it a loaded question? You like me, and I know you like the way I fuck you. We both know there's more to this."

My heart begins racing. I want to deny it, want to fight it. I'm still not entirely sure what the right decision is. I want to think with my head, but my heart is screaming at me that this might be my chance. But my chance for what? To be girlfriend and boyfriend and skip down the road in public? There are so many things tied into this. It's a complicated mess.

"So because I like the way you fuck me, we have to label it?" I ask, giving my best impression of a wall, even though I'm still scared he'll see between the cracks. He massages his temple and sighs heavily.

"Fighting until the very end. I don't know why I expected anything less. You know that's not what I meant," he says.

I peek over the top of my book. Those crystal-blue eyes stare at me, making me uncomfortable. What would a future with Braxton look like if we could walk down that path? I know I'd never be able to leave him alone. He would be the first person I would want to see every time I get off the plane after a show. I'd be consumed by our sex. But that's a fairy tale. That's not all we are or could ever be.

"We"—I wave a finger between us— "would never

work. You know that, and I know that. My family would never accept you."

He slams his hands on the table, and everyone looks in our direction. "Stop thinking about what everyone else wants and just focus on us for a second."

I snap the book shut, surprised by his outburst. He's really on edge. A small part of me appreciates being the one who put him into this maddening haze, even though I'm trying to push him away for our own good. *It is for our own good, isn't it?*

"I care about what my family thinks. I understand that's a foreign concept to you, but it matters to me," I say coldly.

His smirk is evil. "Don't try to push me away by digging into old wounds. That won't work on me, Shortcake."

"Seems to work plenty. Look how riled you are right now," I bite back.

"Because you're making me fucking crazy," He seethes. We stare at one another across the table. I want him more than I've wanted anything else, but there are things I can never share with him. Secrets that will jeopardize not only me but my family. Yet he's the one person I want to run to.

"Just let me in," he pleads. My eyebrows dip because I wonder if he truly understands what he's asking for. I doubt there's anything of equal significance that he can offer me.

"The fact that I've let you live this long shows I care, doesn't it?" I say quietly, picking up the coffee and taking a small sip just so I can focus on something else.

"It's not enough. You're buried so deeply under my skin now that I need it all, Shortcake. I need all of you. Not just a taste or a moment. You're mine."

I want to laugh at him and publicly humiliate him so he'll never blurt such absurdities again. But my heart races, pounding hard, as I realize I'm on the edge of having something I never thought was possible.

Why is love the most dangerous thing I've encountered? I want to trust him, but how could I be stupid enough to give my heart and secrets to my family's enemy? Yet, I haven't shot him down.

"I don't know what to do," I say in an even quieter tone. "We're not meant for each other."

"You don't believe that. You know damn well you're the perfect fit for me. I'm the only man who indulges your fantasies, plays your games, and actually survives them. You're the only woman for me. You can't tell me you don't feel the same."

"I think you've lost your mind," I whisper, trying my hardest to flick away his honesty. But what if it's a trick? It doesn't feel like a trick, though. I'm falling further and further into uncharted territory, and I have a choice to remain in my comfort zone or fall— even if it's my undoing.

"Come home with me," he says, standing and tossing some cash on the table.

"No."

"It wasn't a request. Come home with me," he repeats, offering me his hand. "There's something I have to show you."

I'm conflicted. I can either reach out and take his hand or leave without looking back. I want to go with him, and I'm doing everything in my power not to. I don't know who or what to trust anymore. For self-preservation sake, I should walk away. I've done so many reckless things in my life, but I know Braxton Hero is the one thing that will utterly devastate and ruin me.

It's precisely why I take his hand. Because no matter what, I have to see where this will end. Even when I'm certain I already know the outcome—him in a body bag.

He asked me what we were, and I had no answer for him. Because, in truth, I don't know what we are. I'm not sure I'll ever know. I don't want to kill him, but I don't want anyone else to kill him, either. I like the way he looks at me and the way he touches me. Braxton is not a man I ever thought I'd be attracted to in this way. I mean, I want him by my side permanently. I'd never even thought about permanency with someone until he reentered my life.

I make a quick detour to my car to tell the driver to leave. As usual, he's reluctant, but this time, I take a chapter out of my father's book. The most effective ways to motivate someone are by threatening them or bribing them. So I throw a thousand dollars in his lap and tell him to enjoy his evening.

Then I allow Braxton to lead me to his car. It's stupid, really. Every step by his side is leading to the inevitable. But I can't stay away. I don't *want* to stay away. And I want answers just as much as he does.

We sit in silence as he drives us to his apartment. His callused hand holds mine, and I stare down at it, thinking about all the possibilities if we could have a future together. I don't care about his financial situation; I can afford anything I want in this world. But the one thing I need more than I ever realized is to be understood. I need Braxton to see the *real* me, but it's a gamble. It's torture to love this man. My secret is right on the edge of my tongue, even when I've surrounded myself with so many lies.

I want Braxton to know I'm a killer, not just someone who finds inspiration in photos of dead bodies, but who actually craves the high and thrill of sending someone to the land of the dead.

Would he still hold my hand like this, or would he immediately put me behind bars?

When we pull up at his apartment building, Braxton's gaze narrows, and I follow where he's looking. His partner is standing out front, smoking a cigarette. It's almost one in the morning, and visits around this time— unless from a lover—aren't usually a good thing.

"Stay in the car," Braxton grits as he undoes his seat belt.

"Am I a dog?" I reply indignantly. I might've come here willingly, but I won't be told what to do.

"What?"

"Don't tell me where to stay."

"Fucking hell," he mutters as he gets out. If I know one thing about Braxton, it's that he lives for the bite. I'm not sure why he expected me to stay in the car because that's not going to happen. Sometimes, I despise when people think they need to protect me. I'm not helpless.

I don't need protection. It's actually other people who need protection from me.

On top of that, if he so boldly claims he wants more from me, then I will not be a secret in his world. I don't exactly know how it would work, but he needs to prove to me he doesn't expect me to hide in the shadows.

Because fuck all if I'm scared of a cop, especially one like Lucas.

The moment Lucas spots Braxton, he stomps out the cigarette and heads toward him. That is, of course, until Braxton opens the passenger door and offers me his hand to help me out. Lucas is stunned, frozen in place, as Braxton leads me over by the hand, a clear statement made.

"Are— Are you fucking kidding me?" Lucas fumbles for words.

"You shouldn't litter," I say matter-of-factly as I point to the cigarette he left behind on the ground.

"Who the fuck—?"

Braxton stops in front of me, sizing up his partner. "Don't speak to her like that."

Lucas's eyes widen. "Oh my God. You're in love with her."

Braxton doesn't deny nor confirm it. My heart flutters as I realize he's taking a stand. For me. *With* me. Against one of his most loyal colleagues.

"It's late. Why don't you come upstairs so we can quickly discuss this?" Braxton replies. "I know how this looks, but I'll explain."

Lucas's mouth opens and closes, a flurry of rage rolling through him. I almost expect him to deny the offer, but then he splutters, "I-I'm not letting her come between us. There's s-something you should know. I-I think she should leave."

"She's not leaving," Braxton states.

Lucas swallows. "Okay, then let's go upstairs. But I don't think you're going to like what I have to say."

The walk up the stairs is awkward. Braxton places his hand on my lower back, guiding me to the second floor. It's always so quiet in this building, and when I'm acutely aware of his partner glaring at my back, it makes me feel... a little stabby.

"I thought it was going to be just us when you asked me to come over," Lucas growls, irritated. My eyebrows furrow in confusion. Braxton set this up? I go on high alert as Braxton comes to a stop at his door and unlocks it.

Fuck. What if this is an ambush? I offer a tight smile as Braxton pushes me into the room, and his partner follows. A low twist in my stomach stirs as I get the feeling that something is off.

His partner leans into him, and I can just hear as he asks if they can talk in private as he looks over his shoulder at me. Something isn't right. Braxton is watching me carefully, and I'm certain he already knows I'm ready to run out the fucking door. But he's blocking the way. If I leave now, it'll only seem more suspicious. But he organized for Lucas and me to both come here. Did I fall for a trap?

"I'll go to the bathroom and give you a few minutes to speak," I say with a tight smile.

Braxton grabs my elbow and slides his hand down to mine as I walk past him. I look over my shoulder at him, and he mouths, *"Trust me."*

Then, my gaze flicks to Lucas, who is still glaring at me. Trust him, my ass. I'm in a fucking trap.

The moment I'm in the bathroom, I call my father. He answers on the second ring. "I think I've fucked up. Can you come and get me?" I whisper quietly and then hang up. I don't wait for my father's reply; I simply send him my location as I lock the bathroom door behind me and scan the space for a weapon.

Fucking minimalist asshole. At best, I have a pair of trimming scissors. I scoop them up and sit at the edge of the bathtub, and my ears strain to hear what they're saying. I think Lucas is attempting to whisper, but Braxton's apartment echoes. Braxton must know this, but he speaks clearly and precisely. Everything feels off. Why did he invite Lucas here when he had every intention of bringing me here, too? I'm literally trapped in a bathroom with no fucking window or other way of escape.

"You need to get away from her immediately," Lucas whispers. "I thought you were smarter than getting involved with the enemy."

"I know who her family is, and it doesn't bother me," Braxton tells him.

"It should." Lucas lets out a groan, and I can imagine him throwing his hands in the air. "I can't believe you fell under her spell. Sure, she's easy on the eyes—"

"Don't speak about my woman like that," Braxton growls. "Or this conversation will change very quickly. I'm telling you now, you need to back off."

"Have you taken money from her? Is that how you're able to own this apartment building?" Lucas asks in disbelief. My nose scrunches up. Braxton owns this place? And not just his apartment, but the whole building? How did I not know that? Maybe he's sneakier than I initially thought.

Braxton is quiet for a moment, and I wonder if that wasn't common knowledge. "Have you been digging up information on me, Lucas?" he asks, his tone becoming more noticeably clipped.

"No, I just... I knew something about this case was making you act differently, and it didn't make sense."

"You told me you had evidence against her, which is why I invited you here. But if you're wrong, Lucas..."

Fuck. Fuck. Fuck. I'm definitely in a trap.

I look down at my phone. I know my father will be here in a matter of minutes.

My heart breaks as I realize I'm as gullible as Aunt Anya accused me of being. She was right. I was foolish to think he genuinely cared for me more than his job. He's literally set me up.

A wild rage fuels my blood, and an insatiable urge to kill him takes over. I do everything in my power to stay where I am. My gift is being able to take men by surprise, but right now, there's no way I'll be able to overpower two men with a tiny pair of scissors. I text my father.

Me: Don't kill him. His death is mine.

Fuck it. I have no loyalties to this man. My parents were right.

I was right.

This was only ever going to end one way.

"I can prove she's the serial killer," Lucas whispers, and my blood runs cold.

All my lies are about to catch up to me. And I grit my

teeth, ready to fight. For myself. For my freedom. For my heart that's bleeding all over the bathroom tiles of a man I thought I loved.

He tricked me. And as a single tear slides down my cheek, I applaud his gameplay as much as I'm ready to fucking ruin his life.

Braxton Hero will die tonight.

By my hand.

He will be the ultimate prize.

Yet, I'm not fueled by the usual rush and adrenaline. Instead, I want to cry.

Stupid, stupid girl.

CHAPTER 42

Braxton

Hope can most likely hear this entire conversation. A crackle of tension stirs in the air as Lucas sizes me up. Neither of us is sure about the other at the moment. Loyalties, once bound in blood to protect one another and have each other's back, are being tested.

I knew the moment he sent me a message about Hope he was onto something. I wanted to hear it from him first. I don't let my emotions get the best of me; I compartmentalize them, preparing myself for what I know has to be done.

It unnerves me to know he betrayed my trust and researched me, finding out about my living situation and this apartment building I own, especially when it might call into question my ability to afford such a place. I'm the only tenant because I prefer my peace and privacy not to be disturbed.

And right now, Lucas is being very disruptive.

"Okay. Well, you need to arrest her. I was coming to you as your friend first. But since she's trapped in the bathroom, we need to work together on this. You need to trust me. There was something that didn't make sense about all the murders. It felt like evidence kept coming up missing or was messed with.

"I noticed Tyson had taken a photo of a weapon at the crime scene of that murder with the multiple stab wounds months ago. The weapon never made it to the labs. But then I found this sucker," He holds up a fine knife which would've aided in Hope opening the window to kill his sister. Fuck, if she wasn't wearing gloves, it has her fingerprints all over it, which means she might've been startled by the boyfriend coming back into the room.

I thought hiding the boot print was enough but I didn't see that in the bushes.

Messy. It's all become so messy.

"I know you said we couldn't trust anyone else, and I think someone really has been covering this serial killer's ass." He's driven by the need to put someone, *anyone*, away for his sister's death.

"The weapon had clay on it. And the footprint outside of Kylie's lover's house..." His voice trembles. "It might've been half covered up, but they're certain it's the same size as Hope Ivanov's. Braxton, *she's* the killer."

His words hit me like a truck. I've been following her for months now. I know Hope better than anyone. I should've known he'd be desperate enough to dig further and further to the point of no return.

"I wanted to tell you first before we took it to the station to arrest her. She's been using you, Braxton."

My jaw grinds as I look down at the evidence he's presenting me. "How many people have you told about this?" I ask as I look over to my crime board near the dining table. I've had the case cracked for months, and memorized since the bodies began to appear.

"I came here first. We've finally got her," he says, his eyes clearing. "I can finally put this to rest for my sister."

Remorse sours my stomach as I nod at my partner. "You really did figure it out, didn't you? Except you're missing one piece."

"What do you mean?" he asks, glancing at his evidence and then me.

I strip away my humanity, as I've had to do many times before. I pull my badge over my head, looking down at it sentimentally.

I knew it would come to this. I fought it for as long as I could. Because up until now, Lucas had served a purpose. He was a pawn on the board, but then he tried to become more.

"Braxton?" he asks, looking at my badge, confused.

With rapid speed, I twist behind him and wrap the cord of my badge around his throat. He drops the evidence, his fingers clutching at the cord and trying to work their way under it.

"I understand. I'll reunite you with your sister," I whisper into his ear as I tighten my grip.

It saddens me to have to do this. I liked working alongside Lucas, but the deeper he dug, the harder it became for me to play the pieces.

"Brax—" He chokes, trying to fight me. His senses had dulled over the last few weeks as he tiredly worked on this case, and I put all my efforts into covering the tracks of my messy little devil.

"This is how one of your friends died, by the way. Send my condolences. It was nothing personal," I confess to him. I hadn't wanted to kill them, but they'd become an immediate obstacle. If the families knew we were sniffing around them, it would have drawn attention to me and how closely I was watching Hope. I couldn't have anything interfering with my obsession. I'm sure it pisses Hope off to have two other murders added to her "serial killer" reputation, but it was also the easiest way to throw off the scent of the killer being a singular woman. I was even the one who interfered with her boot print outside his sister's murder scene. "Oh, and Tyson works for me." I'd be sure to reprimand him for being careless.

Lucas's body begins to go limp, and I turn my face to the ceiling, sending up a little prayer for him. It's not that

I like doing this, but it's a necessary measure. I can see the media headlines already. *Detective Hangs Himself After Sister is Murdered.*

I have every intention of staging his death in his home. It's unfortunate, really. I'll have to reset everything with a new partner. But it's how I've survived so long.

"Farewell, friend," I say as the final gasps of air echo through the room. I didn't want it to end this way.

But I have something more precious to protect.

More precious than myself.

His body goes slack, and I let out a shaky breath as a trickle of emotions begin to come back.

The bathroom door opens as I'm lowering my partner's body to the ground, and Hope stares at me wide-eyed, a pair of scissors and a phone clutched to her chest. Her mouth opens and closes in complete shock.

When I stand to my full height, I growl, "You're in big trouble, Shortcake."

This all became a disaster because of her jealous little fit over Kylie touching me that night. Had that not happened, he might've never dug deep enough to connect the evidence I'd been hiding.

As I take a step toward her, a gunshot goes off, exploding the door handle to pieces. My head immediately whips to the door as I pull out my own gun. Someone kicks the door in, and I feel the bullet hit me before my own shot goes off. And at the last minute, as I recognize the face, I shift the course of my aim, barely enough to just clip him in the shoulder.

And then I'm falling with the acute realization that something really fucking hurts.

I guess every man comes to the day when he's reminded that he, too, will bleed.

CHAPTER 43

Hope

Everything stops. My heart. My life. My understanding of life and death. Suddenly, it's not as beautiful as I once thought, as Braxton hits the floor.

"Stop!" I scream, the sound so shrill that it bounces through the apartment, and I dive for him. The man I love, the man I was certain had betrayed me, but instead, he killed a person he trusted to protect me and my wrongdoings.

I cover his body with my own as he lands beside his dead partner. My father and my aunty are standing at the door, their guns raised. My father's hand goes to his arm where he's been hit, and I'm certain my aunt almost accidentally shoots me as I dive for him. She takes her finger off the trigger as I scoop him up into my arms, sobbing.

Oh God. I did this. *I* did this. How do I undo this?

"Braxton," I squeak as I bring his hand to my chest. He's bleeding in the stomach. It's bad. So bad.

"Shortcake," he gasps. "Tell your family to lower their weapons." He tries to smile at the scissors I'm holding, but I angle his head to only look at me.

"You're not leaving me," I say quickly. "You don't get out of this so easily."

He tries to chuckle but gurgles in pain instead. Red. There's so much red.

My aunt and father are speaking to one another furiously, but I ignore them. I can only focus on Braxton as if I'm his anchor to keep him here—alive. I feel like it's my own life force.

Anya moves closer, pointing her gun at Braxton's head. "He's a problem."

I slap her hand away, quickly scoop the gun that's loosely held in Braxton's fingers, and point it at her.

"You ungrateful—"

My father pulls her back. "Anya," he says as if pointing out something that she hadn't yet seen. She looks at me and Braxton again, the killer fading from her gaze as she blinks once and then twice.

I wonder how they view me now. I probably look like a feral animal, backed into a corner, fighting fiercely to protect my mate who's fucking bleeding out all over the floor.

"You're not a good shot, Shortcake. Lower the gun," Braxton whispers.

I snap at him. Why is he making jokes right now? This isn't funny. He's turning paler by the second.

"I only ever did that, so you didn't think I was capable of killing, you fucking idiot," I say on a sob.

"She loves him," Anya states.

"So fucking what if I do? I'm sure I could find faults with your matchmaking. Just please help me. *Please*," I beg my father, a twist of uncertainty rolling in my stomach as his blood drips onto the floor. I don't think I've ever seen my father bleed. "Please, Dad. Please."

Anya clicks her tongue but makes a phone call. My father reluctantly lowers his gun and kneels beside me.

"Did he kill his partner for you?" Dad asks. I'm certain he did. Why else would he go to such extreme measures?

"Can't we ask these questions later, please? I can't lose him."

I lift Braxton's shirt up and try to look at the bullet wound. I have to stop the bleeding, but I'm not really sure how. I've helped my mother patch up my father before, but she does most of the work.

"Fuck," Dad grits as he stands and goes to the kitchen to grab a bottle of whiskey and some tea towels.

My aunt throws her hands in the air. "Come on, we're not the type who can patch things up. We kill people, not fix them."

"Anya, help me," Dad grits.

"I've called the twins and the doctor. The twins will be here shortly to clean up this mess," she bites back.

"Stage it." Braxton is barely able to get the words out as he hisses in pain. I take the alcohol towels from my father's hands and start to clean his wound. My father can't touch other people. It physically repulses him, and I'm sure Aunt Anya won't be any help, so it's up to me. "In his home like a hanging," Braxton finishes. I pour the whiskey straight over the wound before pressing the towels over it to soak up the blood. This won't do. It's only temporary.

"Hmm," Aunt Anya says with a smirk. "Clever. The doctor is five minutes away from your house, Aleksandr."

My father and I both whip our heads in her direction. She smirks. "I think it's about time you had a family discussion."

I shudder as I think of my mother finding out about everything all at once, and I can tell my father is furious, too. But instead of reprimanding Aunt Anya, he grits his teeth and looks like he's about to puke as he turns a shade paler. My heart flutters as I watch my father, who can't stand touching anyone but my mother and me, gather the man I love under his shoulder and begin to lift him. My father physically recoils, but he pushes through, and tears spring to my eyes as I realize how much he would do for me, even at the sacrifice of himself.

Braxton is barely conscious, and my stomach flutters

with a dread I've never known. *Please don't take him. Please don't take him.*

"Make yourself useful," Dad spits at Anya, and she clicks her tongue, moving to Braxton's other side.

"What the fuck?" Hawke asks when he meets us on the stairs. Ford's eyebrows furrow as he tries to understand the situation. River, Anya's husband, is already in motion.

"I thought we were killing this fucker!" Hawke shouts in shock.

"It's a family affair," Anya says cryptically as she and River share a kiss as they walk past one another. Anya is a capable woman who can help carry his body down the stairs, and she speaks so quickly, instructing the others to move, that I can barely keep up. The only thing I'm focused on is Braxton.

"Stay with me," I beg as his blood drips down the stairs.

"Fucking stairs. This is what you get when you date peasants who can't afford elevators," Aunt Anya curses.

"Anya," Dad scolds.

"Don't you, *Anya* me. He's getting blood all over my favorite jewels."

Braxton is barely coherent, his head flopping back and forth. We carry him to my father's car. I lay Braxton's head on my lap in the back seat, still trying to apply the pressure.

My father is zipping through the streets at a speed my

mother wouldn't approve of. My aunt is trying to clean herself up and looks over her shoulder.

"Does he know about your little secret?" she asks.

I swallow. Hard. "I think so."

"And he killed his partner for you?"

"I don't know if it was for me. I don't get what happened at all. All I heard was that they should arrest me and that his friend had evidence."

"Is that the only evidence?" Dad asks.

"Yes." We all look to Braxton as his breaths come in shallow pants. "I've covered the ressssst."

His head becomes heavier in my hands, and tears stream down my face. "Drive faster!" I scream.

"Don't go. Don't do this. Please don't do this to me. I'm sorry." I press kisses to his forehead. "I didn't mean to. I thought you were going to take me in. I'm sorry I didn't trust you." I kiss and kiss and kiss him, hoping it's enough to keep the Grim Reaper away.

I can feel my aunt and father looking at me, but my aunt no longer interrogates me. But I hear her quietly say, "It brings back memories, doesn't it?"

I look away from Braxton for only a moment to catch my father's gaze in the rearview mirror, watching us. I'd heard my father had almost died once protecting my mother. I wonder if my aunt and father are reliving that memory now.

I silently beg him, the man whom I've known to be capable of so many things, to help me save Braxton. To save this man I stupidly love and will do anything to protect. For him to somehow fix all my problems like he always has. But when he looks away, that's when it hits me that sometimes, not even my parents are capable of impossible things. Life and death can't always be controlled.

CHAPTER 44

Hope

The evening is a blur. My mother is confused as we pull Braxton's bleeding body from the car, and a wild storm rages in her gaze but is quickly taken over by the need to help. We arrive at the same time as the doctor, and although they try to take him into the spare room, I'm adamant he's taken into mine.

I hold his hand the entire time the doctor works on him. Phone calls are made, and my mother's voice becomes increasingly louder as she demands answers from my father. Some questions he answers, others he tells her she'll have to ask me.

I don't care about any of that right now. I just focus on Braxton, praying he makes it through the night. Grateful for my family, who are so quick to clean up this mess I made. If I hadn't lost faith in him, if I hadn't freaked out and called my father, none of this would have happened. It's all my fault.

There's so much blood on my bed, on my white carpet. But I don't care. I don't care about any of those things.

I'm exhausted, and at some point, I must fall asleep. When I wake up, it's because my mother puts two glasses of water down on my bedside table. Braxton is hooked up to an IV drip, and I rub my tired eyes, shocked I was even able to doze off.

I immediately look at Braxton, who still isn't awake. "The doctor said he should pull through and just needs some rest," Mom says. I know she was supposed to leave in the early hours for a flight, but looking at the time on my alarm clock, it appears she has chosen to stay. "You need some rest, too."

"I'll rest when he wakes up," I say adamantly, taking a sip of the water she offered.

She nods once, and I can sense my father looming at the door.

"We have much to discuss, it would appear," she says as she goes to pull over a chair. My father, however, is quick to do it for her, and she tries her hardest not to smile. He's in trouble because of me. But I know the argument won't last long; it never does between my parents. She takes a seat, and my father stands behind her, his hands resting on her shoulders.

The doc patched my father's arm up while he was

here, and we're both certain that at the last moment, Braxton adjusted his aim.

"How much do you know?" I ask quietly. My mother looks up at my father, but he says nothing. He might've told her everything or nothing at all. But it's not up to him to tell her my secret and shame.

I swallow hard as I look at Braxton thoughtfully, rubbing my thumb over his hand and asking him to give me support. No... strength.

I can't even look at my mother. What will she think of me? How will this change us? *What if she disowns me?*

"Hope," Dad says, grabbing my attention. "It's time."

My eyebrows furrow, and I know he's right, but confessing to this amount of sin isn't easy, even if he and my aunt accept me. Hell, even if Braxton accepts me. It's my mother who I look up to most, so being anything but the perfect daughter to her is crushing.

I take another sip of water to moisten my dry mouth, then clear my throat. But the thing about lies is they seem easy at the start, but when they become too deep, too bold, they begin to take a form of their own. Into something ugly, even if they were told for self-preservation. I became conflicted by these lies, thinking I was doing it to protect her and others' opinions of me, but deep down, I was scared to face it myself.

"I kill people for art," I confess quietly. She takes in a sharp breath, and my father's fingers dig into her shoulders as if grounding her. "It started when I was twenty, and I've been doing it ever since. Lately, it's been increasing, and it inspires my glass sculptures." She looks confused. "Everything started piling up recently. I felt like I couldn't breathe with so much happening. I thought quitting college would help, but it didn't. What I do is an outlet for me. I know it's not right. I only target men who have hurt women, not that it justifies it."

"Did someone try to hurt you?" she asks carefully.

That question catches me off guard. Is that the first question she has to ask through all of this? But I'm being honest now. "The first man I killed."

"Good," Dad says with a curt nod.

My mother stares at Braxton, but I'm quick to assure her. "Not him. Never him." Although, I suppose, in many ways, he does hurt me, but I like that type of pain. "I actually met Braxton when I was eighteen. We only spent one night together back then." My father looks like he's about to murder him all over again. "I didn't know at the time he was a cop. The night I was arrested was the first time I'd seen him since. I know it doesn't make sense. I still don't know what to make of it all. But I know I love him. I know I can't stay away from him. And I'm certain tonight I learned that he's been covering for me this whole time and making sure no one catches me."

She lets out a shaky breath. I can't read her rolling emotions or expressions. Suddenly, she looks at me. "And Kylie? Who killed her?"

I swallow hard and look at my hands wrapped around Braxton's. I clear my throat. "I was jealous."

"Jealous? You killed her because you were jealous?" she asks incredulously.

"Yes." My voice quavers. I'm not proud of it. It's the reason why I couldn't sculpt the image of her body. I wouldn't confess to having remorse because I don't, not for any of my victims, and it's already done. But I didn't feel elated by it like I had my other victims.

I turn to my father, who's trying to hide a smirk, and it twists a sick confusion in me as to whether I should be proud or ashamed.

"Why didn't you tell me any of this?" Mom asks desperately. "Do you trust me so little?" I look at her, and I'm wounded by her stricken expression.

"I just—" My voice cracks as I hold her hand, my other still on Braxton, unwilling to break our connection. "I didn't want you to hate me. I didn't want you to know how fucked up your only child is. I didn't want to be a disappointment when you've always been so proud of me. I didn't want to be your shame."

"*Hope.*" Tears stream down her face, and she cups my cheeks. "I would never be ashamed of you." She pulls me in for a hug, and I'm so shaken by everything that's happened these last twenty-four hours that I begin to cry, not knowing how badly I needed this from her. She kisses my head.

"I will always love you. You are our daughter. It'll

take me some time to get my head around this, but I would never forsake you. I was able to love your father not in spite of this side of him but because of it. I just don't agree with killing people because of jealousy. Your Aunt Anya might feel differently, though."

I choke on a laugh and wipe away tears as I gaze up at her. She cups my face again. "Just don't keep these things a secret. We're a family. We look out for one another, no matter what. But if you don't tell us these things, we can't protect you."

"I think our little one is very capable of protecting herself now, sweetheart," Dad says, pulling her back slightly. It's like my mother sees me in a different light now. I'm not their baby girl anymore. I think they'll always see me like that in some ways, but I feel like, for the first time in my entire life, they truly see the woman I've become. No matter how messy or dangerous I might be.

She lets out a slow breath and shakes her head. "And people ask why I drink so much." She tries to laugh it off, and an uncomfortable laugh bubbles from me as well. I remove my glasses and wipe my eyes.

"We need to put a few boundaries in place, though, so you don't get caught," Dad says, and my mother whistles, holding her hand in the air.

"Can we just take this one day at a time? I still need to process this." She pats my hand. "I love you, but it's a lot to take in. I still remember you taking your first steps."

"And I remember you ignoring all of the boys," Dad grumbles in complaint as he side-eyes Braxton. I smirk, gazing back at him as well. I wonder what he's dreaming of, if anything at all. Most likely, he's catching up on the sleep he lost while tangling himself in my games.

But there are still things he and I need to discuss. We're not in the clear yet, and I'm still not entirely sure my father or aunt will leave him unscathed.

The storm hasn't yet passed.

CHAPTER 45

Braxton

My body is heavy, and my mind is hazy. I feel like I've been stuck in a dream despite not recalling any of it. A woman is rapidly speaking in the distance, and I note a Russian accent. I groan as my eyes flutter open, and she goes quiet.

"We should just shoot him now," Anya Ivanov grumbles from the doorway.

"Braxton?" Hope's voice breaks, and my searching gaze lands on her. "Oh, thank fuck," she says on an exhale as her hand squeezes mine. My eyebrows furrow as I look down at our joined hands, and everything slowly starts creeping back to me.

"Where am I?" I ask groggily.

"Well, it's good to know, at the very least, you haven't been sneaking into my daughter's bedroom," Alek Ivanov says, coming to a stop at the end of my bed.

"Dad," Hope chastises, but I can't help but smirk.

"We prefer public spaces," I taunt, and gain so much satisfaction from the vein in his temple that looks like it will rupture at any second.

"Braxton," Hope reprimands.

"Can we kill him now? Like actually kill him?" Anya growls. "The little shit got blood on all my favorite things."

I slowly try to sit up in the bed, grimacing, and Hope's hands are all over me, trying to help, but it's definitely more of a nuisance, which checks out for this little pain in my ass.

"Shortcake," I say with a small smile. She didn't give up on me. She didn't leave me to die. "You can let go now," I say and give her a knowing look. "I'm not going anywhere."

"Not with broken legs," Anya snaps, and I can't help but smile at her. If I'm being honest, I actually like her. She says all the things I've forced myself not to say publicly in order to keep my image.

"Why did you kill your partner?" Anya asks. "And you owe me, by the way. My sons were quick to stage the hanging and clean up your apartment, making it look like only a ghost lives there. Which can quickly be arranged."

"Your aunt is actually quite funny," I say to Hope, and she rolls her eyes.

"Flattery won't get you far in this family," Anya bites out.

"Who said I was complimenting you?" I reply, pinning her with a glare. Her gaze narrows, but I swear I see the corner of her lips tilt slightly.

I then look at Hope and exhale. "I knew it was you. I knew from the moment I found you in that park and started following you." I can't help but grin as I think back to the night I met her again, drunk in the park, with a lack of stamina that's misleading as to how much she can provide in the bedroom. "You are the perfect killer, really. But you became sloppy."

"So why did you continue to see me?" she asks.

"Because despite everything, when I looked at you, I didn't feel like I was lost in this world. I was intrigued by how your mind worked and how far I might be able to push you." A soft smile touches her lips, and it's precisely for that that I was willing to give everything up for her. "Did you really think I would let someone take you away from me?"

"Fucking hell," Anya mutters. "Now we have a detective in our family."

"I'm everything you're against," Hope reminds me as if she's giving me an out. As if she wants me to push her away. But she's stuck with me.

I can't help but laugh. Hope Ivanov is everything I'm against? It couldn't be further from the truth.

"No, you aren't. You're the brilliant mind that will captivate me until the end. You and I aren't that different, Shortcake. We do what we have to for self-preservation."

"I kill people." She finally confesses it to me for the first time. "And I enjoy it," she adds with a half-smile.

Beautiful.

Lethal.

Unhinged.

She couldn't be more perfect.

"Yeah, you need better training," Anya says, rolling her eyes.

Her father is watching me carefully. I know his approval means a lot to her, but someone like Alek Ivanov is not easily swayed. In fact, I might have to try my entire life to win him over.

"Something doesn't make sense to me," he says, still trying to intimidate me. I'm already half dead, so I don't know why he thinks glaring at me will have me shriveling into my blankets. "We pay an exorbitant amount of money to keep our business under wraps in that station. So how did you end up with all the evidence?"

I smile, surprised he hasn't already figured it out. It makes me feel good to know I've had one up on him this entire time.

"You didn't think the name you were sending all that money to was the real person, did you?" I ask carefully.

His eyebrows dip. "I've reached out to your chief multiple times. Personally."

I can't help the arrogant smile that forms on my lips.

"The chief who works for me." His eyes narrow. "You didn't think I'd come all this way without corrupting the system and creating a business that works for me, did you? You don't think you're the only family paying us handsomely to make things go away, do you?" The chief was the first person I bought out and answers to me.

"Little shit," Anya says, sounding impressed.

"So why haven't you made this serial killer business go away yet?" Alek asks. Hope is staring at me like I grew a third head.

"Oh, you thought you were the only bad influence out of the two of us?" I reply.

I learned from a young age how to study people and decipher their patterns; it made it easy to manipulate and exploit them. It started with self-preservation, but then it became something more. I've made a fortune from it, more money than I know what to do with because of it.

"I was enjoying our game too much," I tell Hope as I rub my thumb over her hand. "I wasn't ready to catch you yet."

"Young love is getting stupider by the day." Anya scoffs, rolling her eyes and throwing her hands up in the air.

Hope's eyebrows furrow as if she's seeing me for the first time. "You always knew," she whispers in disbelief.

"I always saw you," I reply, and the tension in her body releases with a heavy sigh. I was right—Hope had always only ever wanted to be seen and embraced for this part of her nature. I just never thought my curiosity would lead to an obsession I would never be able to come back from. It's specifically because of that part of her that I love her.

"I love you, Hope Ivanov. For all your ugly, deranged, twisted, and conflicting lies."

"I love you too," she squeaks, and her father looks like he's going to fucking kill me. I can't help but smirk as Hope leans over and kisses me. I deepen the kiss. Fuck the audience. Fuck the games. Fuck her family. This is my woman, and I will never be told how to act around her, even if to make others feel comfortable.

"Let's go, Alek. We have no need to be around horny youngsters," Anya says, and I can tell she's dragging her brother out of the room, but I'm too preoccupied by my trophy.

Hope moans into my mouth, and I eat it, the realization hitting me that I might've not had a chance to taste her again. Not in this life, anyway. I lean into her and wince as sharp pain explodes in my stomach.

"Fuck, that hurts," I growl.

"Crybaby," she teases, but I can tell she's concerned.

There's one thing that's been on my mind this whole time, though. "You pretended to be bad with a gun?"

"No, I *am* bad with a gun," she admits. "But I wanted you to see that; to throw you off so I could catch you off guard with one. I'm curious about murdering in other ways." I suppose that makes sense because she was never consistent in her method of killing, only her targets.

"Why did you have the photos sent from the precinct instead of taking them yourself? How did you even do that?" I question.

She bites her bottom lip, and I'm certain she doesn't want to reveal all of her secrets, but then she answers, "I didn't want evidence on my phone. And, besides, this way, you couldn't prove it was me, and I figured it would rattle you more to know you had a leak in your security."

Security that I paid handsomely to filter what went out, on top of their cybersecurity. "Who did that for you?" Whoever it is, they're impressive. Not many people could bypass the security.

She averts her gaze, and this time, I know she won't tell me because it's not just her secret.

She takes a shaky breath. "Why did you continue to see me if it was just a game at the start?" It's not often I see my beautiful girl lacking in confidence. Where she might fool others into thinking she's shy, she actually isn't. Socially awkward, yes, but never lacking in confidence. So, if she feels this in any way because of me, I will correct it.

I pinch a lock of her red hair that doesn't look like it's been washed in days—it's got what looks like clay and blood in it—I rub it between my fingers and then tuck it behind her ears.

"Even evil needs to be loved," I say with a smirk.

Her expression twists in shock, disbelief, and humor. "Are you saying I'm evil?" she whispers.

"The worst," I reply. "But what does that say about me because I love you?"

"That you're an idiot," she replies quickly.

"Then we're idiots together. But I prefer if we settle for just being crazy about one another. No more killing women if they touch me, though, okay?" I say as I try to bring her in for another kiss.

She leans back and stares at me. "You fucking loved it when I killed her."

I try to hide the smile. "You're such a jealous little thing."

"Don't make me jealous, then," she bites back.

"Then don't give me a reason to look away from you."

"Braxton!" she snaps, and I laugh as I pull her in to join me on the bed.

"I was kidding, Shortcake. When I close my eyes, it's only you I see. It's torture fucking you, hating you, wanting to be with you. It's torture to love you. You're my personal hell, and I don't want to be anywhere else. Know that I have my own ways, too. If a man looks at you with lust or desire, I'll have him imprisoned and disposed of. You'll never hear or see from him again."

She bites her bottom lip.

"You like that, do you?" I ask with a smile as I crush my lips to hers again, taking and consuming the only bundle of evil I'm willing to gamble my life with and for.

CHAPTER 46

Braxton

I stay in their house for a few nights. The first night after waking, the doctor left me some pills to help with the pain and another for sleep, and I contently fell asleep staring at Hope after I told her I loved her. I don't care that she's a little fucked up in the head. In fact, it's precisely *why* I love her.

I think I fell for her that night in the park when I saw her again, and she sat there giving us attitude. It was clearly the alcohol speaking, considering the facatextde she hides behind in her everyday interactions. But I knew the moment I saw her spitefully looking up at me through those thick glasses that I could stare into those blue eyes all day, every day, with the added bonus of her scathing tongue.

When I wake up on the third day, my side is fucking

killing me, and she's nowhere to be seen. Managing to sit up, I look around for a shirt but can't find one. The whole room smells of her. I walk to her closet and pull it open, and what I see inside makes me smile. There's an array of beautiful dresses and overalls, but it's the glass statue that she's been hiding from me that has snagged my attention.

I pick it up, turning it over in my hand. It's me, and it's so detailed that it's terrifying. Red sprays from the back of my head from a bullet wound to the forehead. It's the highest form of flattery from her.

Closing the closet, I inspect her room. It's simple and clean, and other than a few of her sculptures, it doesn't look like it's been updated since she was a teenager.

When I open the bedroom door, I hear someone speaking softly and head toward the sound. I stop at the end of the hall and find her mother in the kitchen. She isn't cooking; she's leaning against the kitchen counter, talking to someone on the phone. She takes a sip from her mug, and that's when she spots me. She hangs up and waves me in. The last time I saw her, which was at the art show, she didn't look too impressed with me, so it's a refreshing surprise to be greeted with a small smile as I approach her.

"You seem to be healing up quickly," she says as she pulls out a bottle of water for me. I thank her for it.

"Thank you for your hospitality." I'm unsure of

what else to say. *How much does she know? What can I discuss with her?* This is the woman Hope idolizes, and as much as I love terrorizing her father, I need to impress her mother. It's a foreign concept to me—trying to gain anyone's approval. Especially a mother's. Admittedly, I don't even know what a real mother is, but I'm willing to learn for Hope's sake.

"Hope is a good girl," Lena says with a bright smile. "But she's a lot like her father and her aunt. She has a darker side not many people will embrace. I was afraid of your relationship going further, for the simple fact you would endanger her and potentially judge her for it. She isn't perfect, but she is perfect in my eyes, so if you do anything to betray her, it won't just be my husband coming after you," she warns.

I'm a little taken aback because she delivers the warning with a perfect smile on her lips. "With all due respect, Ms. Love, I love your daughter *because* of her faults. Which is why I'm also the best person to protect her."

I wonder if Lena's protective mama bear routine has more to do with the fact that Hope has never brought a man home. I know this because I dug up as much as I could about her. "My husband says you can make all this serial killer business go away."

"I can pin it on anyone at any time," I tell her because I can. It can all be swept under the rug within minutes.

But that's up to Hope and if she's ready for it. There's a part of her that has an ego, one that wants to be seen and fawned over in a way that she can watch from the shadows. It's not like her real life as a sculptor, where people demand her to take credit in the spotlight. This she can admire from afar.

Lena bites her bottom lip, and I figure that's who Hope gets the habit from. "Please just look after my girl," she whispers and then pulls me in for a hug.

Pain immediately flares in my gut, but I make sure not to wince or flinch. At first, I don't know what to do. I don't think my mother ever hugged me. I'm sure there were times I wanted her to when I watched other families with envy. But I'd never received this kind of love.

I wrap an arm around her, and a tiny, fragmented part of me from when I was a boy returns. It was a part of me that I released when I let my own mother go. And it's suddenly clear why Hope cares what her mother thinks —because her mother is loving and good. Kind and fair. In that moment, I decide I want to do right by Lena Love as well.

She pulls away with a smile, and an unsettling feeling stirs in my stomach. Is this what it might've felt like to have a loving mother?

And I can't help but wonder if I had, would I have turned out any different? Probably. But I wouldn't have wanted any path that didn't lead me to Hope.

"Welcome to the family then, I guess," she says with a

small smile. "Though, I hope you know what you've signed up for. Everyone is a little unhinged around here." She laughs as she leads me down the hallway again. The house is beautiful, and it's filled with so many of Hope's sculptures. I wonder if her mother will ever proudly display the morbid, grotesque ones. If not, I'll make sure to display each one of them proudly in my home.

We come to a room with two large wooden doors, and I hear Hope's laugh flutter through the open one. I immediately look over Lena's shoulder as she leads us into the room, and I see Hope is playing chess with her father.

"You're awake," Hope squeals and immediately jumps out of her chair. "How do you feel?"

"Like I've been shot," I deadpan, glancing at Alek, who tugs his gloves on.

"I had arrangements made with your chief. I told him you're feeling unwell," Alek says, then pulls my phone from his pocket and hands it to me. "I suggest you stay sick for the next week."

"You went through my phone?" I accuse.

"Yes," he replies without hesitation or remorse. "And I'd appreciate if you didn't stalk my daughter's Instagram so often."

"Dad!" Hope chides.

"Just because you're in a relationship, it doesn't mean you should get distracted from your career," he warns.

Lena pulls him by his hand. "Come on, dear, we're

going to have another private discussion about how our little girl is all grown up." She leads him out of the room, and at first, I don't think he's going to leave until she whispers something in his ear that immediately has his attention.

"Eww," Hope says as they close the door. "What did you and my mother talk about?" she asks, wrapping her arms around me and looking up at me through her glasses.

I don't go into detail about my revelation about my mother and my slight envy that Hope has always had parents like this to support her. What I do say is, "Your parents would do anything to protect you."

She smiles. "Hence why you got shot in the stomach."

I smirk, my cock twitching at the thought of taking her in her father's office. I'm certain it'll piss him off.

"I'll take as many bullets as I have to. I do have a serious question for you, however," I say as I lift her. She squawks in protest but wraps her legs around my waist, and I ignore the searing pain as I step over to her father's desk. "Do you want all of this serial killer business to go away?"

Her eyebrows furrow. "I can't just switch it off. If that's what you're asking of me, then—"

"No." I quickly cut her off. "I meant with the media. I can make it all go away. Or do you want it to remain unsolved?"

Her mouth opens and then closes as if she's not sure how to answer as I place her on the desk and begin kissing down her neck.

She giggles. "We're in my dad's office."

"Answer the question, Shortcake, or you'll be punished until you do," I warn, reaching under her dress and pushing her panties to the side, then inserting two fingers inside her. She hisses, her gaze going hooded as she tries to speak but can't. "Tell me what you want me to do."

"I'm not ready for it to go away yet," she says breathlessly as she leans back and watches me with amazement as I pump my fingers into her pussy. My little she-devil is full of ego. I fucking love it. Love how she gets off on her own scandal, all the while pretending to be sweet and innocent.

"I have another question for you," I say as I undo my belt and free my cock that's itching to claim her all over again. I never thought I'd see her again, never again experience what her pussy feels like. *My* pussy. *My* woman. *My* claim.

"Aren't you awfully chatty today," she sasses, then gasps as I shove my cock into her pussy, impaling her. I wrap my hand around her throat, squeezing just enough to restrict her air, and her cunt envelops my cock. Fuck, she feels good. Like home. *My* home.

"I want you to tell me you're my woman and that the only way you're getting out of this, *us*" —I slam into her again to make a point, and she moans— "is by one of us dying."

I pound into her, claiming and bruising her from the inside. "That sounds like marital vows," she whispers, her eyes rolling into the back of her head as I thrust into her. My hand grips her throat harder. It'd be so easy to break her, and it's so tempting to chain her up and keep her to myself.

"Call it what you want." *Thrust*. "And I'll do whatever you need." *Thrust*. "Matching tattoos." *Thrust*. "Rings." *Thrust*. "Everything I have is yours. But you will always be mine." I bite her jaw, and she hisses as her fingers dig into my wound. I keel over, my vision dancing with light.

I'm still inside of her as she smirks and says, "Of course, dear. But don't ever forget who's truly in control here." Her nails drag from my wound up to my lips. I can taste my own blood before she leans in and kisses me, my cock twitching with excitement at how feral this woman makes me.

"But, yes, I'm yours for as long as you can make me come," she whispers sweetly against my lips.

I bite her bottom lip and pick up my pace as I pound into her, going completely savage for this woman who is definitely my undoing. "Fuck, I love every part of you."

I know that to be the truth. I also know that Hope Ivanov will be my ending. And it sounds like a lifetime of thrills and games to be played. She couldn't be more twisted or perfect.

"I'm going to break you," I growl as I slam into her, knocking items off the desk. Her legs are quivering as she reaches her high, and her nails dig into my back.

"Give it your best shot, Detective Hero."

Also by T.L. Smith

Black (Black #1)

Red (Black #2)

White (Black #3)

Green (Black #4)

Kandiland

Pure Punishment (Standalone)

Antagonize Me (Standalone)

Degrade (Flawed #1)

Twisted (Flawed #2)

Distrust (Smirnov Bratva #1) FREE

Disbelief (Smirnov Bratva #2)

Defiance (Smirnov Bratva #3)

Dismissed (Smirnov Bratva #4)

Lovesick (Standalone)

Lotus (Standalone)

Savage Collision (A Savage Love Duet book 1)

Savage Reckoning (A Savage Love Duet book 2)

Buried in Lies

Distorted Love (Dark Intentions Duet 1)

<u>Moments of Madness</u>

<u>Moments of Mayhem</u>

<u>When He Read To Me</u>

<u>Lethal Vows</u>

<u>Virtuous Vows</u>

<u>Cunning Vows</u>

<u>Deranged Vows</u>

<u>Misguided Vows</u>

Connect with T.L Smith by tlsmithauthor.com

Also by Kia Carrington Russell

Insidious Obsession

Fractured Obsession

Mine for the Night, New York Nights Book 1

Us for the Night, New York Nights Book 2

Stranded for the Night, New York Nights Book 3

Token Huntress, Token Huntress Book 1

Token Vampire, Token Huntress Book 2

Token Wolf, Token Huntress Book 3

Token Phantom, Token Huntress Book 4

Token Darkness, Token Huntress Book 5

Token Kingdom, Token Huntress Book 6

The Shadow Minds Journal

Lethal Vows

Virtuous Vows

Cunning Vows

Deranged Vows

Misguided Vows

T.L. Smith

USA Today Best Selling Author T.L. Smith loves to write her characters with flaws so beautiful and dark you can't turn away. Her books have been translated into several languages. If you don't catch up with her in her home state of Queensland, Australia you can usually find her travelling the world, either sitting on a beach in Bali or exploring Alcatraz in San Francisco or walking the streets of New York.

Connect with me tlsmithauthor.com

Kia Carrington-Russell

Australian Author, Kia Carrington-Russell is known for her recognizable style of kick a$$ heroines, fast-paced action, enemies to lovers and romance that dances from light to dark in multiple genres including Fantasy, Dark and Contemporary Romance.

Obsessed with all things coffee, food and travel, Kia is always seeking out her next adventure internationally. Now back in her home country of Australia, she takes her Cavoodle, Sia along morning walks on beautiful coastline beaches, building worlds in the sea breezes and contemplating which deliciously haunting story to write next.

www.ingramcontent.com/pod-product-compliance
Lightning Source LLC
Chambersburg PA
CBHW051000180726
48291CB00006B/1919